PRAISE FOR *SUPER IN THE CITY*

"One should not simply read *Super in the City;* one should gobble it up like candy. This is particularly intelligent candy, mind you—but don't let that stop you from indulging in a big old sack of fun."

—Elizabeth Gilbert, bestselling author of *Eat, Pray, Love*

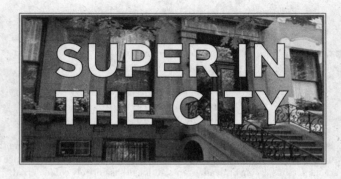

SUPER IN THE CITY

DAPHNE UVILLER

BANTAM BOOKS

SUPER IN THE CITY
A Bantam Book / February 2009

Published by
Bantam Dell
A Division of Random House, Inc.
New York, New York

Book design by Steve Kennedy

Library of Congress Cataloging-in-Publication Data
Uviller, Daphne.
Super in the city / Daphne Uviller.
    p.   cm.
ISBN 978-0-385-34269-8 (trade pbk.)
1. Young women—Fiction. 2. Janitors—Fiction. 3. Apartment houses—Fiction.
4. Landlord and tenant—Fiction. 5. Greenwich Village (New York, N.Y.)—
Fiction. I Title.
PS3621.V55S87 2009
813'.6—dc22
2008032631

Printed in the United States of America
Published simultaneously in Canada

www.bantamdell.com

BVG   10 9 8 7 6 5 4 3 2 1

For Sacha

SUPER IN THE CITY

Ta-pocketa-pocketa-pocketa-pocketa . . .
JAMES THURBER'S
THE SECRET LIFE OF WALTER MITTY

ONE

THE NIGHT I WENT TO THE ST. REGIS HOTEL AND ACCIDEN-
tally crashed the birthday party of the Princess of Spain was
the same night I was crowned superintendent of 287 West 12th
Street. Both events took me completely by surprise and both
led me to Gregory the exterminator, who wound up saving me
in ways I didn't even know I needed to be saved. (I don't mean
saved in a Jesus way. This is not a Jesus-saving kind of story.)

To be honest, I was not even aware that Spain still had a
princess until I was standing under the chandeliers in the hotel's Cavendish Room with my mouth stuffed full of her free
tapas. I thought modern royalty was the purview of the
British—Charles, Harry, William, tragically dead Di—something to keep the international tabloid business afloat. And I
certainly didn't know I was at a birthday party. My black silk
Ann Taylor sheath with cracked rhinestone brooches on the
shoulder straps, a fifteen-dollar score at Housing Works Thrift
Shop, was not meant to be employed in a way that would in-
fringe upon a personally meaningful event: birthday parties,

like wedding receptions, were off-limits under a set of hastily conceived crashing criteria. Tag and I had agreed upon this moral distinction a year ago, beneath the Akoustolith tiles outside the Oyster Bar in Grand Central Station, right after we were unpleasantly outed at the sixtieth birthday party for the CEO of a door-hinge distribution company.

Tanya Granger, known as Tag to distinguish her from a nursery school classmate named Tanya Tokowsky, had called me an hour earlier to announce that she was hungry.

"I've got frozen pizza and orange juice," I told her, proud of my stocked fridge.

"Julia Child would have been thrilled. No, we're going to the St. Regis for *croquetas* and *calamares*," Tag informed me. "King of Spain. An anniversary of some kind of truce. Or a trade agreement. Something."

Tag's days were bookended by strong coffee and even stronger alcohol, and not always in the order you'd expect. We'd begun crashing out of financial necessity—finding free food and drink in New York City was a crucial means of survival—but the entertainment value of our pursuit had rapidly become apparent. And Tag had been in dire need of entertaining around the time we'd started freeloading. Usually rational to a fault, she had impulsively married a Swedish businessman and divorced him six months later, all before the age of twenty-four. "Never accept a marriage proposal made immediately upon surviving the sinking of a Thai ferryboat," she'd warn me sternly, as if this was a peril that regularly presented itself.

Since her narrow escape from wedlock, she had approached fun very seriously, as seriously as she did her work on behalf of the Museum of Natural History, which required her to slit open the bellies of sharks in places like Madagascar and Borneo. Whether she had a Fallkniven F2 fisherman's knife in her hand or a dirty martini, Tag was all business, and she took charge of the ground rules.

In the bowels of Grand Central, decked out and slurping cheap chili in the food court, we agreed that proms were acceptable crash targets. Even though at twenty-seven we were hardly past our prime, we were just old enough to instill some Mrs. Robinson excitement among the restless male members of the Teaneck/Mamaroneck/New Rochelle senior class, who would otherwise be slamming into each other to the beat of "Rock Lobster." They knew we were interlopers and they welcomed fresh blood. The chaperones kept mum because our enthusiasm on the dance floor—we hit proms for the eighties music—lured the future of America into chaperonable view. Occasionally, one of the boys would look up from texting a girl on the other side of the room and approach us, probably on a dare from his friends. I would tell him I'd just served time in a federal penitentiary—self-defense, I assured him, glancing modestly at the floor—and that this was my first night of freedom. I considered it a service I was providing, making his prom night memorable for something other than a white limo and some contraband flasks.

Corporate Christmas parties were also permissible. Company shindigs were, for Tag, all about the top-shelf liquor. For me, they were glorious opportunities to gossip with people I didn't know, which made it less like gossip and more like . . . honing my empathy skills. Selena from accounts, while complaining about her new boss, Andrea, would let slip some details about her affair with her old boss, Susan—yes, that's *Susan*—who was married to *her* former boss, Robert. It was like being inside a soap opera for a few hours, and I usually couldn't resist helping myself to a cameo role. I'd pretend I was a therapist specializing in workplace conflict—Why didn't they know me? Oh, I was a friend of Tom's—and they'd listen intently to my suggestions, which I secretly thought were pretty inspired. Tag suggested more than once that this might actually be some kind of crime, but again, I preferred to think of my advice as a gift, or at least as payment for the free mini quiches we were scarfing in lieu of dinner.

Diplomatic functions, like the one we *thought* we were currently at: we attended those for the superb international hors d'oeuvres. We also went with open minds, receptive to the possibility of meeting people who might happen to own yachts and castles. We were not gold diggers, but rather, equal opportunity seekers: Tag wanted to give wealthy foreign dignitaries a chance to fund her next research project, while I remained open to finding true love and life-guiding inspiration at any income level. Soul, I generously acknowledged, was capable of flourishing in bodies other than those of starving writers and musicians.

These ambassador bashes were my favorites because I got to play Extreme Make-Believe, which was even more gratifying than commiserating with Selena the accountant or Sam the senior headed for SUNY Binghamton. Call it acting, call it lying, but don't knock it until you've raved to a sheik about the heather-filled fields that line your father's property in northern Scotland.

"I'm so thrilled that Papa was the younger brother," I might confide over a plate of caviar, "because although there's less, you know, *money*, he has fewer responsibilities. More time to herd sheep and go on quail hunts. No harm, no foul!" The sheik might or might not get the pun. (Bonus points if he did.)

Finally, I always had my own personal agenda at these parties. Aside from maybe canoeing the globe solo, there was almost nothing I wouldn't try to stop myself from thinking about Hayden Briggs for even a few hours. Crashing a party at the St. Regis didn't register high on the list of antidotes, but here I was, yet again hoping for a life-altering experience to wipe that sanity-skewering redhead from my memory.

Tonight, as Tag and I cased the crowd from the safety of the coat check room, I took in all the dark hair, dark eyes, and caramel skin and immediately began constructing a story about my brother's chain of pubs in Iceland. Because of my unmistakably non-exotic features, I could never invent a brother who owns a Middle Eastern refinery or even a measly olive grove. I'm five-foot-eight—an inch too tall for a lot of guys' tastes—and I reek of second-generation American robust good health. In the old country, I'd probably have great bone structure, but here, among the fortified cereals and protein boosts, my model potential is safely squirreled away beneath a layer of comfortable padding. I long for Jennifer Aniston's upper arms, but am secretly quite pleased with my legs, which would look spectacular in the high heels I can never bring myself to endure wearing. I have a thick mass of honey brown hair that would look similarly stunning if I could bother to blow it out. Instead, I keep it just short of nest status with a collection of bent, chipped, fifty-cent Goody barrettes. I have what Tag calls "ish" eyes—big and round (I would kill for a hint of an almond shape), but of indefinable color: greenish, grayish, blueish.

Now, I opened my ish eyes as wide as I could, threw a giant smile at the stocky scion manning the door, and made a beeline for the buffet. To crash successfully, you must move confidently.

Tag and I grabbed plates and went to work. As I reluctantly passed over the shrimp—their farming requires the destruction of mangrove trees, which are natural filters for coastal waters; ergo, shrimp farming equals death (bibliography: three-Amstel-Light lecture, Tag, 11th Street Bar, circa 2004)—a male specimen to my right asked me something in a voice so bedroom-savvy I felt the polish slide off my toenails.

I looked up. Square jaw—my weakness. Cheekbones that could have cut diamonds, another weakness. A huge flop of, yes, black hair. An Achilles'-heel trifecta.

Alas, I understood not a word out of his beautiful mouth. He smiled at me and pointed, his eyebrows raised in polite inquiry. No doubt it was the same look he gave to fellow NATO members when discussing nuclear proliferation. I could travel the world with him, starting out as his lover/assistant, and learning the ropes. Within a few years, I'd be indispensable to the entire organization. One day, I'd wield the gavel as Secretary General.

Ah. He couldn't reach the shrimp. As I forked one, then two, then—raising an inquiringly seductive eyebrow back at him—a third, I began wondering how long it would take to regain a grip on my high school Spanish, and whether there was a quickie Berlitz course in Spanish-for-flirts. As I deposited the last shrimp onto his plate, Ferdinand (why not?) gave me a questioning look regarding my shellfish abstention. Foreseeing the difficulties of miming "mangrove," I just smiled as coyly as I could while balancing a Coke in one hand and a plate of mini sardine cakes in the other. He gave me a little elbow in the side and grinned in lieu of conversation. Our kids will be gorgeous and bilingual, I thought.

Tag appeared at my side, heartlessly derailing my burgeoning courtship. "Zephyr, did they slip you one of these at the door?" She shoved a picture frame in my face. I glared at her, but she was sipping sangria and frowning at her party favor. I cast Ferdinand a helpless look. He puckered his lips, blew me a little kiss, then slipped away into the crowd. *Ciao*, my beloved! I mentally called after him. I mean, *Adios*!

"Did they?" Tag repeated, unaware that she had in all likelihood reduced me to permanent spinsterhood. The frame she was studying displayed a collage of photos of a pale and slightly bulgy-eyed beauty. There were shots of her as a grinning infant, as a pre-adolescent waving from a balcony above a herd of charging bulls, and one of her as a teenager, holding a scepter.

"Miss Spain! The party is for Miss Spain 2006," I concluded reasonably. I spotted a waiter and mentally dug around for the phrase "Do you have any more of those red and green meat things?"

"Well, if it is, they've done a lousy job. We should be able to tell right away who the celebrant is, what the occasion is, and how we're supposed to feel by being in the same room as her." Tag frowned. "I can't tell who Miss Spain is, can you?"

Tag had recently dumped the vice president of a branding company (I had eventually come to understand that his job didn't involve cattle). Evidently, he wasn't completely out of her system. She tugged at her party-crashing uniform—her wedding dress, hacked off at the thighs and dyed a Rockettes-at-Christmas red—and looked at me impatiently.

I scanned the room, but none of the women was sporting a tiara or cradling a bouquet of roses. A number of them, though, looked like Tag, which meant that the pulchritude percentage in the room was abnormally high.

It was a testament to my self-confidence that I considered Tag one of my closest friends (the label "best" friend, we had decided, was too sixth grade), because she was drop-dead gorgeous, and to stand next to her was to make yourself virtually invisible to most men (save for my loyal Ferdinand). With her full-moon brown eyes, lashes out to Jersey, lanky body with curves in only the right places, and Claudia Schiffer–like stature, all topped off by a fountain of inky black curls, Tag made even the straightest woman go tongue-tied. But when you threw in her genuine obliviousness to her beauty, proven by the fact that instead of earning a fortune on runways, she studied sharks' intestinal tapeworms and did a little dance every time she lit upon a new species, then she was someone around whom you often found your mouth actually hanging open, as if your upper and lower teeth were magnetically repelling each other.

"No idea which one she is," I said, spraying a mouthful of crumbs down my dress. As I was brushing them off, though, I got a clue. Like a punch in the gut, a brass band struck up behind us, causing Tag to spray out a mouthful of sangria.

A *cobla* promenaded in, with a red-and-yellow-striped flag waving prominently above their brass instruments, and took their place pretty much beside us, which isn't the kind of thing you hope to have happen when you're crashing a party. I assumed a half smile and tried to sway to the music, but traditional Catalonian tunes aren't particularly conducive to swaying. I glanced over at Tag and saw that she, too, had pasted on the same slightly constipated smile of a bride being photographed for the hundredth time.

We had begun inching away from the band as inconspicuously as we could when they abruptly swung into a universally recognizable tune. A side door flew open and out strode a middle-aged man with a handlebar mustache and an honest-to-God, real-life crown on his head. On his arm, wearing a floor-length ivory satin dress and, ah, there it was, a tiara, was a dead ringer for Penelope Cruz—if she were fifteen with a thyroid problem. Señorita Cruz smiled and waved (without looking the least bit constipated), while everyone around us began clapping and yelling *"Felíz cumpleaños!"*

I still hadn't hit upon the Spanish for "meat things," but I remembered "happy birthday" at about the same moment that Tag did. She tugged at my dress, but the princess had spotted us—not a hard thing, since she was on a direct course into our embrace—and was frowning. She leaned over and whispered into her father's ear, who locked us in his crosshairs and scowled, too. The family resemblance was remarkable.

We started to inch backward, which seemed to propel the pair faster toward us. Tag bumped into a gaggle of wrinkled *abuelas*, who started waving their arms around, their black shawls flapping like angry bats' wings, and my precious accumulation of quiches, cakes, and crackers slid onto the feet of Ferdinand. The music slowed to a confused stop, and a couple hundred brown eyes stared at us. The infanta began yelling. She was not as attractive up close, with spit flying from between her thick lips. When we didn't respond, her father—the king—joined in, but louder.

This may sound surprising, but being yelled at by a king is not unlike being yelled at by the school principal. I suppose if I had been a prisoner in a dungeon and my life was on the line, I might have felt differently, but the only thing imprisoning me at the moment were my L'eggs control-top pantyhose. However, as any Teaneck High senior could attest, it is awful to be yelled at by the principal in front of everybody. Especially in front of the boys.

A man who could have been Ferdinand's shorter brother broke through the crowd and planted himself in front of us, demanding in an angry, velvety lilt, "Who invited you? Are you friends of the prin*cess*?" He put the accent on the second syllable.

My right eyelid started to twitch, but Tag, who has talked her way past customs officers while carrying a thousand undocumented specimens in her luggage, answered immediately and with righteous indignation.

"The prin*cess*?! We are not here for the prin*cess*." You would have thought from Tag's disdain that Her Highness was a stripper recently demoted to whore. "We are supposed to be at a reception for Friends of OPEC." She glared back at the man, who seemed flustered by the about-face.

"Why," Tag continued, "were we not told this upon our arrival?"

The king said something to Ferdinand's brother, who shrugged his shoulders. The princess tugged on her father's sleeve and whined something. I had been wildly counting little squiggles in the paisley carpet (twenty-three so far). When I ventured to glance up, I met the gaze of my shoulda-woulda-coulda-been husband and found that Ferdinand was laughing at us. Twenty-four, twenty-five, twenty-six . . .

The king started to yell again, but Tag, bless her fearless self, yelled back.

"You've wasted enough of our time this evening. I hope your daughter has a lovely little birthday party. Next time, you might want to consider having a bloody *guest* list!" The last thing a crasher wants is a guest list (as for a *bloody* guest list, that was the British branding boyfriend still clutching a portion of Tag's brain), but it was a ballsy bluff.

Sensing my paralysis, Tag put her hand forcefully between my shoulders and pushed me to the doorway. We feigned calm as we marched out of the room and down the hall. As we approached the elevators, though, we heard angry voices behind us, so we headed straight for the fire stairwell and crashed through the door. Whereupon Tag leapt in front of me and flew down the stairs at breakneck speed, screeching, "Zephyr, you fuckwad, run, goddamn it, RUN!"

I was still holding an hors d'oeuvre plate smeared with tomato sauce. I didn't want to be charged with trespassing *and* theft all in one night, so I carefully set it on the landing and made after my satin-clad friend as fast as I could. Which is not that fast, when you consider that my name means "breeze."

Every few days, I did a waffle-burning plod of about three miles, but that paltry regimen had hardly prepared me for escaping capture by angry Iberian royalty on two-inch heels, in a five-star hotel.

As I flung my way down the cement flights, clinging to the rail and growing dizzier with each step, I pictured myself recounting the evening's story to my parents, whose primary purpose in producing my brother, Gideon, and me was, as far as I could tell, so they'd be guaranteed entertainment for the rest of their days. That, and, when we were small, to have someone hand up the plates from the bottom rack of the dishwasher.

I'd roll out of bed around nine the next morning, pad up the two flights to apartment 4A, knock as a punctilio while letting myself in, plop down at the lox-laden table, and ask, "Hey, Mom, St. Regis security didn't call here last night, did they?" Or maybe, "Hey, Dad, it turns out the King of Spain wears the same cologne Uncle Hy used to wear."

And my father would fold up the *Week in Review,* slap the table, and lean forward, bellowing, "Do tell!" My mom would chuck the *Book Review* and bustle into the kitchen, saying, "Wait, wait, don't start, I want a full cup of coffee for this."

First, though, I had to ensure that hotel security did not actually become acquainted with my parents or their telephone number.

Tag and I race-walked across the lobby and emerged, panting, onto Fifth Avenue—surely the streets were safe, like international waters?—and into the magnolia-scented spring evening.

"Oh my God!" Tag shrieked, her hand on her side, trying to catch her breath.

I could only wheeze and push sweaty, renegade tendrils off my cheeks.

"What is the point," Tag gasped, "of having a party in another country if you can recognize everyone there? Did they just fly in everyone she usually hangs out with?"

Leave it to Tag to find the princess at fault.

"I mean, we could have been, you know . . ."

"Senators' daughters," I ventured between breaths.

"Or soap opera actresses!"

"Or borough presidents."

"Yeah! Or venture capitalists looking to invest heavily in . . . in . . . what does Spain make?"

"Yellow rice?"

"Yellow rice!" Tag put her hands on her hips defiantly. She looked so convinced that she was a venture capitalist wanting to invest in Spanish rice that I started laughing, which left me so out of breath that I had to sit down on a planter. Tag seemed to remember that she was not a wealthy speculator and sat down beside me.

"You have to pay more attention at these things, Zeph," she said sternly. "Not get all googly-eyed over the first bag of tricks to give you visions of villas."

I glared at her. "Me? You were supposed to do due diligence! I would have been fine at home with my pizza."

"Of course you would've." She licked her finger and rubbed at a sangria stain on her dress. "If it weren't for me, you'd never go north of Fourteenth Street."

"This from the woman who's allergic to the Upper East Side," I announced to no one in particular. Tag had spent her childhood shuttling between a mother who boasted that she'd married Tag's father for the alimony, and a father who was now on his third wife (second trophy). Tag had concluded that their behavior was the result of their neighborhood. Reminding her that people behaved badly on the West Side, and even downtown, did nothing to dissuade her from her theory.

We were quiet for a moment.

"Friends of OPEC?" I finally said. "FOOPEC?"

Tag shrugged, but she started to smile.

"So what now? It's only nine-thirty." Though we both knew we'd be in our beds within the hour, we went through the motions as a nod to our youth and to New York's reputation for being the center of the universe.

"Movie?" I said, glancing toward the marquee of the Paris Theatre two blocks away.

"Kind of late to start a movie."

"Drink?"

"I don't wanna spend the money."

"Jazz at Smoke?"

"Since when do you like jazz?" Tag asked suspiciously.

Since spotting the buzz-cut bass player who'd moved into the apartment between my parents' and mine two months earlier.

I shrugged. "Just trying to think of something new."

But Tag was starting to squint in a way that meant she really wanted to go home and get up early and go into her lab to look at her beautiful tapeworms under a microscope. And I was thinking of the three Netflix DVDs waiting in their inviting red-and-white envelopes at home, an orgy of chick flicks, with Julia Roberts, Sandra Bullock, and Jennifer Aniston receiving equal representation. Plus a fresh bag of Newman's Own Ginger-O's. A yawn escaped me.

Ten minutes later, we were waving to each other across the Columbus Circle subway tracks, as Tag waited for an uptown train and I headed downtown. I paced back and forth to the beat of the steel drum player, who was pinging out the grooviest version of "Hava Nagila" I'd ever heard. The guy was grinning and sweating while two Latino guys alternately danced and sucked face in front of him and a tourist family—towheaded, wide-eyed, clutching *Lion King* programs—took pictures of the whole scene, no doubt deriving better entertainment value from their MetroCards than they had from their orchestra seats.

Plugging my ears as the express roared past, I grew giddy from a familiar first-world high, a euphoria that suffused my body like an electric current: I had been born into circumstances that allowed me clean running water, heat, and toilets that flushed, where no tanks rolled down Fifth Avenue and I could find tofu in a variety of configurations twenty-four hours a day. I adored my friends, I loved my parents, and I usually didn't mind my brother. I lived in a city, if not a country, where two men could make out in public with impunity. There was no one to keep me from heading out of the subway station, going to the airport, and, if my bank account permitted, hopping a plane to China. Or Atlanta. Or Spain. I pushed aside guilt, figuring *someone* had to actually experience the freedom to which so much of this subjugated, avian-flu-fearing, war-stricken world aspired. If no one lived it, then what was the point of anyone having dreams?

And I was living It.

Right?

I was pretty sure I was living It.

I boarded my train and tried to hold on to my high.

TWO

I squeezed into a seat across from a sleeping family with teenagers for parents—poof went my life-is-grand high—and reflexively scanned the subway car for Him. Just as quickly, I tried to convince myself that I was studying the bilingual ad exhorting HIV testing.

Oh, the lust of my life, the thorn in my side. The light in my heart, the pain in my ass. Hayden Briggs, that son-of-a-bitch—no, that troubled, sexy psychopath—was the main reason I could not declare myself a well-balanced, completely healthy woman. (Almost, but not quite.) Hayden and I had been broken up for a year already—okay, two years—and I was over him, I really was, but I was still obsessed with him. There *is* a difference, which not enough books, psychiatric diagnoses manuals included, make a point of articulating.

I had moved on, dated other guys, considered what each would look like at the far end of a petal-strewn aisle, but I still dreamed about Hayden at least once a week, and I looked everywhere for that distinctive thatch of red hair falling lazily over one mischievous eye. On the street, at the Food Emporium, in Hudson River Park, through the windows of cabs stopped at red lights. In elevators and cafés, at crashed parties, in the background of murder scenes on the evening news.

I'd met Hayden at the Odeon, that Deco mainstay of West Broadway, where Tag and I had crashed the afterparty for the New York Press Club awards. Hayden was a reporter for the *New York Post* and his homicide beat was one of the main reasons I'd been attracted to him. He'd call me while I waited alone at Café Loup to tell me he was standing in the blood of three murdered men in the South Bronx. It was titillating enough to distract me from the fact that he was also standing me up.

He'd show up three hours later at my apartment, sweaty, with a tired smile, holding a six-pack and flowers, and tell me all he wanted was to climb into bed with me.

"On you, I mean," he'd amend, pursing his lips. And I was so turned on by his lithe, freckled body and his grown-up career—all the other guys I'd dated were production assistants who bossily halted pedestrian traffic or grad students slogging through classes in pursuit of a lofty, low-paying degree—that I let him stand me up over and over again.

When Tag was too busy describing new species to listen to the blow-by-blow accounts of my Hayden addiction, I turned to three other fellow survivors of the Sterling School, which had been a pit of institutionalized snobbery save for them, my angels of snarkiness and sensitivity. I didn't want to bother Abigail, who was grading exams and packing for Stanford to pursue aforementioned low-paying, lofty career. Lucy, perkiness incarnate, was a social worker who might be too easy on me. When I needed tough love, I interrupted Mercedes, who was merely boning up for the Philharmonic's fall season.

"You're a booty call," she bluntly concluded one night over the phone, plucking her viola impatiently.

"Am not!" I growled at her. It was ten-thirty and I had just returned home from another evening of eating sushi in the company of *National Geographic*. Hayden had great taste in restaurants, even if I was rarely at them with him. The door buzzed.

"Ooh, gotta go, he's here!" I hung up on her and checked myself in the mirror. I had on a perfectly worn, soft, clingy gray T-shirt that made my stomach look flat and my boobs round, and boxer shorts that suggested a trail of past lovers. My hair was down and wild and the whole look was calculated to look sexy-sleepy-messy, not like I'd been eating tekka maki solo. It was calculated to get us into bed, the place where our putative relationship flourished. I rubbed my cheeks, licked my lips, and flung open the door.

"Mmm," he said, letting his eyes run over me. "God, it's good to see you after a hard day." Which prompted visions of firing up the camping stove in the middle of the Sudanese jungle, following a day covering guerrilla warfare. Hayden would report and I would take awe-inspiring photos for *National Geographic*. At night we'd make love in our moldy tent and, sometime after that, we'd hold hands at the Pulitzer awards ceremony before our joint acceptance speech. We were going to have a great life together.

If I could just ignore the two beers he swigged while he was inside me. He placed an empty on the headboard and reached for another from under the bed. "Want one?" he asked.

I shook my head in a way that I hoped wouldn't be taken as judgmental, even though I was pretty sure this wasn't normal.

"You don't drink?"

My non-drinking was frequently an issue with boyfriends

precisely because there was no issue. No ascetic streak, no hidden pieties, no alcoholism in the family, and none in me—though sometimes I was tempted to darkly hint that I was "recovering" because it seemed a lot more interesting than admitting I'd never developed a taste for spirits. Getting buzzed was fun, getting bombed was fun, and I had no problem with people who wanted to do both those things—I would have liked to join them more often, but I just couldn't get enough liquor down before surrendering to Pepsi.

"Eh," I told Hayden, hoping to avoid the conversation.

"Are you an alcoholic?" he asked eagerly.

"I'd rather not discuss it," I said quietly, trying to suggest that I was a founding member of AA.

"Is it a problem for you to be around this?" He held up a Red Stripe nervously.

"No," I reassured him. "I'm pretty strong." He looked relieved and popped open a third bottle.

I made the mistake of running this behavior by the Sterling Girls.

"You mean, he drinks after sex, like a cigarette?" Tag asked.

"No . . . during," I said, realizing I should never have brought it up.

"That's disgusting," proclaimed Mercedes.

"Now, wait, don't *judge* her," Lucy reprimanded, her social worker's license burning a hole through every single interaction in her life.

"I'm judging *him*," Mercedes told her flatly.

But then Hayden would surprise me and actually show up for a date on time and we would stare into each other's eyes over candlelight. I'd ask him about his career and his past and I'd throb all over with the novelty of having a truly adult relationship.

And he really was a grown-up: I was a fetus when he was

going through puberty. I had hoped to hide our age span from my parents indefinitely. Actually, I had hoped to hide Hayden from them indefinitely. His past may or may not have included a brief marriage, and he had a mysterious rift with a brother back in California that kept him at arm's length from his whole family. I, on the other hand, lived downstairs from my parents and couldn't have kept a hangnail a secret from them if my life depended on it.

Only months after the relationship finally, finally ended for the final, *final* time was I able to admit to myself that our dates had been elaborate products of my own imagination. I asked Hayden lots of questions and he murmured vague assents, never taking his hand off of mine, never looking away from me, and I had mistaken this performance for deep conversation. He was a writer, a reporter, maybe even a divorcé; ergo, he was a veteran communicator with a soul annealed by all those atrocities he'd witnessed, a still water that ran deep. In fact, he was probably the stupidest guy I've ever dated, and I had projected an entire relationship onto the blankest of blank slates.

Finally, after he went AWOL for ten days—with nary a booty call—and I was furious, bonkers with rejection, and all the more horny for being so manifestly mistreated, I called it quits. I met him for margaritas (easy on the tequila) at Teddy's one hot July night and told him exactly what an asshole he was, which unexpectedly thrilled me. I wasn't in the habit of telling people off and I certainly never cursed at anyone. If people wronged me, I analyzed it with the Sterling Girls, stewed in silence, and waited for the sting to fade.

"You treat me so badly," I told him loudly, hoping my anger was irresistibly sexy. "You treat me the way people get treated on *Maury Povich*. Now I know what women everywhere are going through. Thank you for helping me understand my fellow sisters!" I pointed a finger at him. "I don't intend to be

treated like this ever again!" I was enamored with my own elo-
quence. "I thank you, I really do, for giving me an experience
that helps me understand the stuff of self-help books, but I'm
done with this shit."

He just watched me, chin in hand, smiling his lazy bedroom smile, and I knew I must look good going nuts. It was a
huge turn-on, making a scene like that. He slid his tongue over
the length of my accusing finger and later we slept together
and that was it.

Almost.

I managed not to see or hear from Hayden for about five
weeks. I Googled him every couple of hours and would start to
tingle if I even saw anyone reading the *Post,* but I kept my
sticky little fingers away from his phone number. And just as I
was getting a grip, having invited Rick, a web designer, upstairs after a peaceful first date, Hayden called me. It was
eleven at night.

"Can you come over?" he asked in his gravelly voice, which
sounded sad, though I may have just wanted it to. I might have
resisted except for the fact that I had never, in our four and a
half months of simu-dating, seen his apartment.

"Your place is so much homier. I feel really good here," he'd
say when I tried to steer us toward his place.

So I told Rick that my sister needed me right away.

"I thought you said you only had a brother—in Colorado."
Rick squinted at me in confusion. It gave me hives to think I'd
hurt someone's feelings, which is why I went on so many bad
second dates. But Hayden made me act in new ways. In mean
ways.

"It's my cousin—sometimes I call her my sister. I'm sorry." I
pushed Rick out the door, grabbed a toothbrush and some condoms, and headed for the subway.

It was late, but I detested cabs: they got stuck in traffic, were gut-wrenchingly expensive, and it seemed like pure folly to accept a ride from a stranger just because his car was yellow and had a medallion. But as I frantically paced the subway platform, waiting for a train that was moseying uptown on a late-night schedule, I feared my beef with the Taxi & Limousine Commission would cost me my last chance with Hayden.

I arrived at his building nearly forty-five minutes later, terrified that he might have changed his mind. My fear should have spotlighted the worm-eaten foundations on which our affair was built, but my blinders were firmly back in place. I don't know what I expected—a dark little walk-up filled with smoke and the smell of cabbage, a pudgy Russian landlady in a housedress, eyeing my ascent disapprovingly? Was that how I thought a beat reporter should live? His neat white box of a high-rise apartment in a doorman building was a disappointment. It revealed no more of him than I already knew.

"No photographs," I observed pointedly, giving myself a tour after he opened the door. He had tried to kiss me hello, but I was going to make him beg for it—if I could just keep my shaky legs (purposely on display in last season's floral Gap skirt and painfully high slingbacks on loan from Mercedes) from collapsing out of sheer desire.

"It looks like a Crate and Barrel showroom," I snorted.

"It does," he admitted with a hint of self-pity. "I didn't have the time or know-how." He grabbed my hand and held it tightly between both of his. "Zephyr?" he said plaintively.

Four and a half months of whatever we'd been doing, and he had managed never to utter my name, not on the phone, not to my face. I'd tried not to think about it too much. At that moment, insanely, all the "Hey you"s seemed worth it just to finally hear him say my name. I let him pull me behind a rice-paper screen and onto his bed.

Because there was no beer involved, because he had finally

let me see his apartment, because he had said my name, I made myself believe Hayden had changed. We were at his place. He couldn't slip out the door before sunrise and I sure as hell wasn't going anywhere until morning, so for the first time we spent the entire night together.

I surrendered to bliss. I lay on his khaki sheets listening to the garbage trucks make their pickups and studying his sleeping face, something I'd never had the chance to do before. I told his unconscious self that I loved him. I imagined a wedding in shorts and hiking boots atop a craggy Mayan ruin, exchanging vows in the mist on a quick break from a dangerous assignment. I imagined advising panicked women in volatile relationships, telling them how many great marriages had rocky beginnings. Just look at Hayden and me! But it took effort to tune out my mother's frequently repeated axiom about relationships: the beginning, at least, should be heavy on the happy. Otherwise you don't have a whole lot to work with when the going inevitably gets tough.

I didn't sleep much that night because I couldn't stop prowling around his apartment. I trolled through his medicine cabinet, his linen closet, his refrigerator, his utensil drawers. I flipped through his magazines and peeked behind his shower curtain to examine his soap scum. My brain was growling for more information about him, but he may as well have lived in a hotel suite for all I could glean.

In the morning, Hayden did everything right. He made me eggs and toast and coffee and went back to staring into my eyes, only now he couldn't stop saying my name.

"Zephyr, Zephyr, Zephyr . . ."

What?! I wanted to yell. What? Are we back on? Are we getting married? Will you start showing up for dates? Will you tell me whether you want kids? Whether you like ice cream?

But I just popped the yolk of my over-easy and smiled enigmatically at him.

I was exhausted from my night of snooping, which made it easier for me to leave: what I really wanted was to chain myself to his kitchen table until he outlined our commitment to each other. Instead, I purposely left my earrings next to the bed. That way he'd have to see me again.

"Seriously?" Mercedes said later that night as the Sterling Girls sprawled around Lucy's mother's Riverside Drive living room, picking at cold pad thai and waiting for *ER* to begin. I could barely keep my eyes open, but there was no way I'd have stayed home. It was Abigail's last week in town before she was to become the youngest tenure-track professor of dead and obscure languages at Stanford, and she was terrified of venturing more than a hundred miles west of the Hudson River.

Even Lucy was having a hard time defending my reunion with Hayden.

"I don't think it's healthy," she began tentatively. Tiny, blond, frequently exclamation-pointy, Lucy worked at a free clinic in Bed-Stuy. To our continued amazement, her clients loved her. It seemed like she should be the one heading for the froufy West Coast, while dark, grounded, alarmingly practical Abigail—who once made a potential boyfriend read *The Feminine Mystique* before she would date him—would look perfectly at home in a basement office dissuading meth addicts from suicide.

"Oh, it's not," I assured her.

"It's the job thing, right?" said Abigail, pulling thoughtfully at her Jew-fro curls. "You're thinking that he's got to be really committed to his job to have gotten where he is. And to be that committed, he must be passionate about it. Work passion is sexy, no question."

"Plus," Tag conceded, "he's not anyone we know. I mean, he's not a friend of a friend. He's in the real world, not in our precious little circle."

Mercedes glared at both of them.

"I'm not saying I approve," Tag added hastily. "Not at all. Zeph's gonna get screwed, no question. It's just a matter of time."

"Thanks," I grumbled, closing my eyes just as the green letters "ER" began pulsing across the screen.

Despite the vote of no confidence, the Sterling Girls, otherwise known as the SGs, were there for me when the inevitable happened. A week after my reunion with Hayden, I found a bulky little envelope taped to the front door with just my first name written on the flap. I knew what it was before I opened it, but I still allowed myself a moment's thrill over the fact that he had actually handwritten my name. It was so intimate.

My earrings were tucked inside a sheet of white of paper with a typed message:

i'm sorry i can't do this
its me not you
i have things to work out
your great   you know that right?
and god your hot
i'll miss you, i'll miss your blue eyes
thank you

We held an emergency convention at my apartment that night. I couldn't stop pacing and shrieking, "Fucker!" at random intervals. Tag and Mercedes were mixing up a sickly sweet gin concoction that I'd be able to swallow in large quantities. Lucy was shaking her head over and over again.

Abigail was already in Palo Alto, so we put her on speakerphone. "It looks like *archy and mehitabel.*" she laughed. I had faxed her Hayden's infuriating attempt at a breakup note.

"Who?" Mercedes yelled from the kitchen.

"The book with the poetry-writing cockroach who couldn't hold down the shift key to type capital letters. Mr. Petrone's class. Tenth grade," Lucy confirmed.

"That's perfect," Tag laughed, her face lighting up at the prospect of an invertebrate metaphor. "He *is* a cockroach, a literate cockroach."

"Not even!" I yelled. "He can't spell or use apostrophes or complete sentences or ANYTHING! It's the most juvenile, simple-minded piece of crap I've ever seen! And he's supposed to be a *journalist*!"

"Shh, shhh," soothed Lucy.

"And he thinks her eyes are blue," Abigail cackled.

"They *are* blue," Lucy said toward the phone.

"They're green," Abigail said firmly.

"People!" I shrieked hoarsely.

"What are you gonna do?" Mercedes carried in a pitcher of something purple and made me sit down in front of the coffee table.

"Nothing," Tag answered for me, alarmed by the question. "It's over. He's a shit. It's *over.*" She glared at me, as if she could burn this conviction into me with her eyes.

"Oh, it's over," I assured them, swigging a glass of the violet-hued drink. "Do you realize he orchestrated that little reunion just so he could dump me?!"

"Yeah, we picked up on that," Abigail said dryly.

"Did he spend the last two months harping on the fact that *I* had dumped *him*?"

"At least you know he was thinking about you," Tag smirked.

"I want to humiliate him. I want to crack that cool cover and blow his brains out!" I shrieked.

"Humiliating and killing are two different things," Lucy pointed out gently.

We rejected a number of plans that were technically illegal, and finally settled on using Hayden's own idiocy against him. I made about fifty copies of his moronic letter, intending to send them to everyone I knew. I mailed a few, but it was far from satisfying, since none of the recipients *knew* Hayden. Even the SGs had never met him.

So I added my own note to the bottom of the letter: "This is the handiwork of Hayden Briggs, beat reporter. Perhaps you people should consider raising your standards. Or your copy editors' salaries." It had all the hallmarks of a madwoman's missive, but I made twenty copies and mailed one to every editor and senior writer on the *Post* masthead. Tag, who had once dissuaded actual pirates from robbing her research vessel in the South Pacific, was brave enough to post a copy in the elevator of his building.

We waited.

What was I expecting him to do? Call and beg me to stop? Tell me he had behaved like an ass, and that, by the way, he was sorry for writing a sub-par breakup letter and not caring enough to run it through Grammar Wizard? Apologize for not being who I wanted him to be?

I never heard from him. Which may have been why, two years later, I was still searching for him on every subway car in New York.

THREE

I GOT OUT AT FOURTEENTH STREET AND HEADED DOWN Seventh Avenue, observing for the millionth time how hideous the cab-clogged thoroughfare was compared to my own charmer of a block, just a few steps away. Seventh Avenue was an acne-like cluster of arriviste chain retailers—McDonald's, Duane Reade, Radio Shack, Subway—punctuated by a struggling hair salon, a struggling smoothie shop, and the lovely, funky ship-like building of St. Vincent's Hospital. But turning onto my cobblestoned stretch of Twelfth Street was like stepping into an English garden: old and quaint and aesthetically pleasing, and all the more lovable for its flaws and hidden histories. The two elegant Federal homes at the eastern end of the block might have looked identical to an outsider, but I knew they were occupied alternately by old-timers who'd dug in during the sixties, and the young bankers who'd recently bought in, and that a fragile peace was maintained only by a shared desire to preserve property values.

There were two tiny Italian restaurants, the too-noisy one

that served perfect lamb ragú, and the too-oily one whose mama-and-son owners cheerfully greeted me every day in Italian. Across the street, interrupting the line of brownstones and postage-stamp front gardens, was a century-old boarding-house for young women. They still came from points west, were served two meals a day, and were not permitted to bring male visitors upstairs. In the summer, girls studying at the Joffrey found rooms there, and for two months the block was overrun by packs of giggling, Starbucks-sucking, splayed-foot ballerinas who moved in a blur of tights and torn denim shorts.

My own building was unlike most of the others. Two four-story Greek Revivals that had been joined together by a renegade Vanderbilt now housed me, my parents, our super, and five tenants in four rented apartments. My parents had bought the place during the early seventies for a pittance, back when the Village was still considered a bohemian dump. My brother and I had learned to ride our bikes on the cracked sidewalk, and our double-wide interior staircase had been the cold-weather hangout for all our friends from P.S. 41 (the creaky banisters were sturdier than they appeared). When strangers dared to sit on our stoop, we pretended we were ghosts and wailed at them over the intercom until they left.

Just before I reached Twelfth Street, I waved hello to the deaf woman perched on a milk crate outside the Duane Reade. She was knitting up a storm, making her handout cup look like an afterthought. I sometimes brought her coffee and squatted beside her to chat by way of pen and paper. After a full year of waving and writing, I still didn't know her name, but because she wore her hair in a hundred tiny twists, I thought of her as Braids.

Braids and I knew a surprising amount about each other. I knew she was waiting for her boyfriend, also deaf, to finish his stint in prison so they could try to move upstate and sell her knitting and start a better life. She knew I had lived in Greenwich Village my entire life, that I had gone to the same public school my dad had attended, and that I still lived in the same building I'd grown up in. I knew she'd quit taking her meds and preferred to be on the street than in the shelter. She knew I'd tried medical school for a year, then quit. I knew she had a daughter back in Haiti who had inherited her manic depression. She knew I'd packed a moving truck to go to law school, and then unpacked it before I ever turned the key in the ignition. I didn't know where she went when she wasn't in front of the drugstore and she didn't know which building on Twelfth Street I lived in. In a life of phone call and e-mail obligations, of constant social upkeep—coffee, drinks, dinner, brunch, lunch—my no-expectation acquaintance with Braids was a unique pleasure.

Tonight, though, instead of waving back, Braids frantically gestured down the street, her eyes wide. I hurried to the corner and saw two police cars, an ambulance, and three fire trucks, their red turret lights turning the block into a silent disco. My curiosity flash-froze to panic when I saw that the hub of activity was immediately outside number 287. Adrenaline flooded my veins and I took off as fast as my Nine Wests would allow. I imagined my father on a stretcher, my mother slung over the shoulder of a fireman, my apartment filled with smoke, water, and broken glass.

Ever since September 11, I'd had a "go" bag ready, packed with a checkbook, credit card, notebook and pen, some photo albums, a bank statement, underwear, extra contact lenses, my passport, and some yellowing iodine pills my mother had wrapped up in a little baggie and pressed upon my brother Gideon and me. I wondered if I could get to the bag before my childhood home burned to the ground. I was crying by the time I reached the front door. But even as tears flowed, I couldn't help thinking how convenient it was that I didn't wear makeup, because that meant there was no eyeliner running down my face; at least if I ended up being comforted by a husky fireman, I'd still look decent. We'd have a great story to tell the kids so long as it didn't involve the untimely death or disfigurement of their grandparents. I'd explain to them that it was their father's heroics that had inspired me to start a non-profit devoted to restoring the lives of fire victims in New York.

Just as I grasped the curlicued iron railing, the door at the top of the stoop swung open. Out burst a tangle of cops escorting James, our super, who was in handcuffs. James had always spoken with the diction of an Eton alum and had been unfailingly courteous for the ten years he'd been caring for the seven apartments in our building. He took out trash, repaired leaky faucets, and cheerfully produced spare keys at all hours of the night. At that moment, however, he was cursing a blue streak in a distinctly outerborough accent.

"You pickin' ME up first?" he bellowed at the cop leading him out by the elbow. "You better fuckin' pick up Richie Pantone, too. He said those was Christmas gifts from Fuel Masters' fuckin' CEO." He spat out each letter as if at a bingo hall filled with deaf people. "That muthafucka's gonna eat my balls for breakfast!" He added for emphasis, "Mutha FUCKA!"

Aside from the perp walk being staged on my steps, I think I was most shocked by the instant dissolution of James's pristine grammar before my very ears. As the procession pushed past, James, apparently no stranger to personality disorders, called out in familiar clipped tones, "Zephyr, love, this is a case of mistaken identity. No worries, love, no worries. Your uncle James will be back in a jif. You look smashing in that dress, smashing! Ow, watch yuh fuckin' . . ." James's head caught the top of the car door as an officer pushed him into the backseat.

Mrs. Hannaham, who lived in the garden apartment and

dressed, day and night, head to toe, in Tom Wolfe whites, came out and stood next to me. Tonight, she was wearing a white rabbit-fur bolero jacket over white, sequin-studded vinyl pants. Just as the dejected EMTs and firemen were climbing back into their rigs—no heart attacks, no conflagrations—Cliff, the brooding musician who might make me forget I ever met Ferdinand (though not Hayden), came loping up the street, pushing his bass. The three of us silently watched the procession roll away. In a moment of self-consciousness, I forgot about James and wondered if anybody passing by thought we were a family. That Cliff and I were siblings and Mrs. Hannaham was our mother? Or we were married and she was my mother-in-law? Or maybe they were having a May–December relationship and I was her angry daughter, protecting her worldly assets from this gold digger—

"Zephy! Is he gone? I couldn't stand to watch while they took him away!" My mother came flying down the steps, still dressed in sweaty workout clothes at 10 P.M.

My father, six-foot-six and constitutionally incapable of absorbing bad news, came lumbering after her, shouting to me, "Zephyr, light of my life!" I have never had the heart to tell him that this is a line credited to Humbert Humbert, literature's most famous pedophile. My father is as innocent as a grown man can be while still actually being a prosecutor.

He enveloped me in a bear hug. "What kind of fun were you up to tonight? It's beautiful out! We had the windows open—do you smell those magnolias? You've got to come listen to the most gorgeous Mozart quartets, on WQXR—ba, ba, ba, baaaaa, bababa, BA, BA—!"

"OLLIE!" my mother shouted.

"What?"

"Other things!" She pointed down the block at the receding police cars.

My father paused, his conductor's arm high in the air, and squinted at the scene before us. "It's a bit of a shock," he conceded.

"What the hell happened?" I asked, beginning to understand that these events were not a product of my imagination.

"Kickbacks," my mom said, shaking her head dramatically. "I feel so betrayed. He was like family."

I thought that was stretching it a bit. But I wondered whether my parents would have to declare bankruptcy. Would we lose the building? I gripped the iron railing, and imagined myself turning to Braids for guidance.

My dad put his hand on the back of my neck, sensing my panic.

"Zeph, he only stole from the oil company. He didn't do anything to us."

"But his voice," I said incredulously, "did you hear his voice?"

My dad frowned. "That was disturbing."

"Disturbing?" I shrieked. "He was leading a double life! Can't we prosecute him for lying to us? For not being who he says he is?" The sound of the caring Brit—who'd once worked until 4 A.M. helping me mop up after my dishwasher staged a sit-in—flinging epithets at cops in Brooklynese was still ringing sharply in my ears.

"No one is who he says he is," Cliff piped up. We all turned to look at him, leaning on his bass at the bottom of the steps. He shrugged.

"Well," my dad announced in a voice that indicated he'd like to move on to pleasanter topics, "I never entirely trusted James anyway. Too short." He beamed at gangly Cliff, who managed to return a polite wince of a smile.

"Mrs. Zuckerman—" Mrs. Hannaham began, adjusting the strand of white paper clips she frequently wove through her wiry, black hair.

"Mrs. Hannaham, please, please call me Bella. I've told you umpteen times." My mother doesn't actually want Mrs. Hannaham to call her Bella. She wants to *be* someone who wants Mrs. Hannaham to call her Bella.

"Mrs. Zuckerman, you know my sink frequently clogs and without my darling Compton around to help me—" We all waited a moment while she sniffed theatrically. Compton had been dead for twenty-five years and had been sleeping with his secretary for the twenty-five before that. "I really must live in a building with a super. I must! Now, listen to me."

My mother took a step back. She preferred that people listen to her.

"I have a nephew who's handy with pipes and tools and such," Mrs. Hannaham continued, "and he could come be the super. It's important to have someone. The building can't function without one."

"We know that, Mrs. Hannaham," my mother said impatiently.

"Well?" Mrs. Hannaham demanded. "What if something happens tonight? What if some hoodlums come by and break my window? I will not pay the full month's rent."

The mix of sympathy and irritation I saw in my parents' expressions mirrored my own. She's a lonely old widow, I could see them reminding themselves. She lives off her cheating husband's pension (albeit a generous one) and tells anyone who will listen that she cloaks herself in white as a gesture of solidarity with the disenfranchised widows in India. Never mind that she wouldn't even put pennies in my Unicef box on Halloween when I was a kid.

"You have our number," my mother told her, not bothering to disguise her exasperation. "You have Zephyr's number. If someone throws a rock through your window tonight, call her, okay?"

And who the hell was *I* supposed to call if someone threw a rock at Mrs. Hannaham's window? I was thinking it might not be a bad idea to get her nephew's phone number right now. I imagined us sweeping up glass together and falling in love after I tended to a gash in his hand (he'd be impressed at my fortitude in the face of a crisis). Nephew Hannaham and I would open a mom-and-pop glazing business together—maybe catering to the specialized window needs of landmarked buildings—and I'd have to defend the class difference to my family. I could imagine my parents *saying* they didn't care what we did for a living so long as he was good to me, and me not believing them and accusing them of limo liberal hypocrisy. I looked over at them apologetically and wished I didn't have to give them such a hard time.

"Zeph?" asked my mother. "What do you think?"

"Of Mrs. Hannaham's nephew? I'm sure he's great!" I said enthusiastically.

"I've got his résumé inside," said Mrs. Hannaham.

"Plumbers have résumés?" asked Cliff. What a snob. But I wasn't ready to let go of the fantasy of becoming a cabaret chanteuse in an underground club, my eyes half closed, crooning into a mike while my lover's fingers flew over his bass. On the other hand, what was that he'd said about no one being what they seemed? Maybe he wasn't really a musician. Maybe that wasn't really a bass in there. A human body could definitely fit in his case. It was an ingenious cover for a hit man—

"No, Zeph, what do you think about Mrs. Hannaham—or anyone else—calling you if there's a problem?"

I looked at her sharply, sensing an unpleasant maternal proposition forming. "What do you mean, what do I think?"

"I mean," my mother said, the enthusiasm in her voice building, "since you're not as busy as you might be these days, maybe you could help us out by filling in a bit for James from time to time."

"Zephy's going to be the super!" proclaimed my father.

Surely they were kidding. When I was a child, I imagined that when you dropped a letter into a mailbox on the street corner, it went whizzing along a nifty network of underground tubes and popped up at your local post office, to be hand-delivered by the mailman. The fact that you could clearly see a gap between the bottom of the mailbox and the pavement did not compel me to revise my theory. The physical world was not my friend.

I had never hung a poster or painting by myself because I was afraid the wall would fall down if I drilled into it. I spent valuable time worrying about all the excrement wending its way through the pipes of Manhattan. I maintained a low-level anxiety that it would all back up, and one day Armageddon would come in the form of a massive poop deluge.

My distant relationship with form and function had not prevented me from briefly considering a career as a doctor, but I was certain it would preclude me from becoming a super. And while I had accepted and even embraced my humble fashion sense, I was not prepared, no matter how low my standards, to don a tool belt.

But I looked back and forth between my mother—the certainty of the brilliance of her new idea streaked across her face like the salt residue from her workout—and my enthusiastic father—unmistakable delight at the convergence of need and fulfillment dancing in his eyes—and something grabbed my full attention.

They were not kidding.

*   *   *

SOMEONE WHO TEMPTS HER PARENTS INTO THINKING THEY'RE going to have a doctor or lawyer in the family had better start combing her feathers to become an Indian chief.

My abridged stint at Johns Hopkins med school was maybe a 3.0 on the Richter scale of personal disasters. I learned that I could stand the sight of blood and that I was good at, if not especially fond of, rote memorization. Lymphocyte, neutrophil, monocyte, eosinophil, megakaryocyte, Sneezy, Grumpy, Sleepy, Hungry. For a whole year, my mother got to tell people I was at Johns Hopkins, and my father had a direct source of information to fuel his personal concoction of science and spirituality: "Tell me more about the sodium-potassium pump. I don't believe in God, by God, but I believe in the sodium-potassium pump!"

In my dreams, I toiled for Doctors Without Borders, traveled to Malawi, and single-handedly saved thousands of distended-bellied children. Or I was at a political rally when shots were fired at the candidate, and I'd paw my way to the front, shouting, "I'm a doctor!" and save the guy's life. I imagined winning the Nobel Prize for hitting on an AIDS vaccine and making it as widely available as aspirin. Zephyr Salk. I had my acceptance speech mostly worked out.

Before I had informed my parents of my intention to forgo the privilege of adding "M.D." after my name, I e-mailed the Sterling Girls. I sought their advice despite the fact that they were all oppressively accomplished and had no firsthand experience of what I was going through. I sometimes liked to torture myself by imagining how the five of us could be introduced as a group. "This is Abigail, the academic. Lucy, the social worker. Mercedes, the musician. Tag, the parasitologist. And this is Zephyr. Um . . . uh . . . she likes coffee." Even in appearance, I didn't stand out: Tag and Mercedes were long, lean, and striking; Abigail and Lucy were dark and light versions of tiny and cute; I was not quite as tall as the tall ones, not quite as cute as the short ones, and did not qualify as lean, striking, dark, or light.

It's not that I couldn't make a move without the girls. I just preferred not to. We kept one another from being stupid and doing stupid things, and we reassured one another after the stupid things were done anyway. But this time, they told me to just suck it up and get it over with as quickly as possible, like pulling off a Band-Aid.

I gathered my courage, sat my parents down at their sun-dappled kitchen counter on a chilly March morning, and assailed them with my reasons for leaving med school.

First, after four years of school, four years of residency, and who knows how many fellowships, it would be too long before I could have children. That was for Dad, who was born to dandle a grandbaby.

Second, I couldn't bear to accrue so much long-term debt. That was for Mom, the founder and CEO of MWP, which was originally called Money . . . Women . . . Profit. She had created a seminar franchise that taught corporations how to speak to their female employees about finance, which, apparently, improved everyone's bottom line. But after one woman filed a suit against her employers for hiring a consultant with what she considered an offensive name, MWP was officially born and its lengthier predecessor was shredded, deleted, rerecorded. When all else failed between us, I could talk to Mom in numbers.

The real reason I ditched Baltimore? It wasn't because medicine was not exciting. I mean, it wasn't. Luka Kovac was not berating me in the ER while he intubated a crash victim and demanded a milligram of epi. And Dr. Carter, that trust-fund hottie, was nowhere to be found. Instead, Professor Baumbach was sending us off to learn the modified Duke's staging system for colon cancer. I could have tolerated all of it, persevered, and become a decent physician. But as I paged through *Harrison's* all I could think about was every other door I was shutting.

I would never design parks. Never defend a wronged soul in a courtroom. Never end homelessness. Never create video games. Never win an Oscar for cinematography. Never direct a Broadway play. Never be the drummer in a girl band.

In college, I would often fall prey to homework paralysis: if I were to start working on one paper, it meant there were three others I wasn't attending to. To pick a profession was to let go of twenty others.

I had never yet let down Bella and Ollie Zuckerman. That was my brother's job. Gideon had been born with a mutant Ashkenazi gene: he didn't care about disappointing our parents. He was working in a film-editing lab in Colorado, which is to say he was ski-bumming. The "lab" was a friend's basement in Steamboat Springs and the film was about a snowboarder. He was in his third year of "editing" and showed no signs of returning east or of pursuing a graduate degree. (Even *he* hadn't had the cojones to turn his back on a B.A.)

My folks took the news pretty well. I think what did it, what most definitely contributed to their not falling over dead, was the cowardly, impulsive coda to my monologue that went something like this: "So I'm applying to law school!"

As a deflection method, it was brilliant. Even if my mother had wanted to say boo, my father was instantly over the moon—and once he's in orbit, no one can bring him back. He's the guy who put Tommy "The Manhole" Sanchez away for life in a case that began with a traffic ticket and ultimately busted up a fifty-million-dollar-a-year cocaine ring that served snorters from Bogotá to Brooklyn. My dad loves the law. He cherishes it. He venerates it. To have one of his kids follow in his footsteps, so long as we didn't go the corporate route, was for him to die a happy man.

"Let's see how you do on the LSAT," said my mother.

"You could work in my bureau next summer!" said my father.

Applying to graduate school is a gratifying mini career unto itself. First, there is the fresh breath of prioritizing: your vocabulary must be expanded, your reading comprehension practiced, the logic puzzles mastered. ("Construct a family portrait in an oval album with these restrictions: Aunt Minnie can't be next to Gladys or Grandma Eudora. Teddy can't be next to Rita, but must be next to Minnie." How this is a reliable indicator of whether you can ably carry out justice remains a great mystery, especially to convicts.)

Once the test is over, you vegetate guiltlessly for a few days. And once the scores come, well, you've got the whole application process and its attendant fantasy life to enjoy. Will you be moving to California? The Southwest? Uptown? If you go to St. Louis and your future husband is at Michigan, how will you ever meet him?

So I went to Così Café every day and sat beside the screenwriters who were afraid of Doma Café, and the New School discussion groups who couldn't afford French Roast, and the salesmen who wished they were at an IHOP. I studied my Kaplan books under the approving/understanding/smarmy gazes of grannies/NYU professors/current law students. Then I wrote pointedly meaningful essays. I began crashing parties with Tag and I briefly dated a fat film student named Jake.

I got into seven of the eight schools I applied to. Didn't that mean something? Didn't that mean my value as a brainful human being was quantifiable? On my parents' dime—they agreed to support and house me for that "transition" year—I flew to Palo Alto and got some quality time with Abigail. We had late-night, college-worthy conversations over steaming mugs of chai, all in the name of checking out Stanford Law. I felt directed and purposeful and industrious, but I still had time to go to Liquid Strength class with Tag, watch *Friends* reruns on Mercedes's rent-controlled couch while she practiced Brahms's Symphony No. 4 in E Minor in the other room, and catch the Hitchcock festival at the Quad Cinema with Lucy.

No sooner had I sent in my deposit to the University of Pennsylvania—my passion for a good cheesesteak figuring heavily in my decision—than I began to regret my choice. It's not that I wished I had said yes to Stanford or Columbia or Northwestern or any of the other places I'd gotten into. I just wished I could have said yes to all of them and gone to all of them while also training to become a member of the Olympic luge team and a vet.

But still, I had the contented summer you can only enjoy when you have a solid plan lined up for the fall. One of the loveliest sentences a person can utter is, "I'm starting law school." In late August, I enlisted my friends to help move furniture up from the basement and into a U-Haul. With a close eye on the packed truck, we sat on the stoop in shorts and tank tops, drenched in sweat, inhaling pizza. It felt like college again, except that this time I was the only one moving. I was going off to a place rife with future scholars and judges and activists who would actually be able to help those distended-bellied kids and could feasibly go to The Hague to prosecute the people responsible for the atrocities in Darfur.

I attributed my shortness of breath to hoisting one too many boxes of CDs.

An hour later, my dad slid into the driver's seat and turned to me, beaming. I tried to return his smile, but my stomach began to roil and my mouth felt gummy.

"Darling daught—?"

I opened the door and threw up on the sidewalk, just missing the feet of a traffic cop ticketing her way up the block.

* · * · *

So I COULD SEE HOW MY PARENTS MIGHT BE ENTHUSIASTIC about the prospect of me fixing boilers, sweeping the sidewalk, and plunging toilets.

I, on the other hand, felt my gizzards asphyxiating. Bella and Ollie Zuckerman were eyeing me with missionary zeal while I could only think of my five-year college reunion, which I was planning to attend in two months. As visions of me wielding industrial cleansers danced in my parents' heads, I imagined the conversations I would have on campus.

"... and after Teach for America, I founded a charter school in South Central. It's been soooo crazy, but soooo great. So, Zephyr, what have you been up to?"

"I'm the super of my parents' building in Manhattan."

"I thought you were in med school?"

"I dropped out."

Silence.

"Well, no, that sounds really cool. You gotta do what's right for you."

Or: "... I started out in the mail room and it totally sucked, I mean *totally* sucked, but one day, I just said, fuck it, and I slipped my script into Grazer's mail and his assistant actually read it and they optioned it! But now I have this rewrite I got hired for and it's a total mess and I'm completely freaked out. You were so smart to go to med school. I don't know what the hell I'm doing."

"Well, actually, um ..."

But more than a blow to my pride, my parents' plan for me to earn my keep—not an unreasonable demand, even I could see that—meant learning things I'd never wanted to learn when there were so many other things I really did want to learn. It meant tenants depending on me, which, if asked on a personality questionnaire how I'd feel about that, I would have said it was fine. But what if, I thought desperately, what if one of my friends needed me in a hurry and I was all tied up with super stuff? I tried to think of any emergency a Sterling Girl might have that would require my immediate assistance (and thus prove the inefficiency of installing me as super). There was none.

Thinking about becoming the super of 287 West 12th was accompanied by the clang, squeak, and whump of closing doors.

And the idea of Hayden, ace reporter, chief schmuck, finding out that I was mopping halls . . .

I chewed hard on my lip and traced the curlicues of the iron banister with my thumb. I snuck a glance at Cliff, who was ever so slightly nodding to a beat only he could hear. If he couldn't stay focused on this turning point in my life, was he really going to be emotionally available to our kids?

"It would just be until you figure out what you're doing," my mother said, her voice hitting the high register that bespoke her grave doubts about when that long-awaited clarity might arrive.

Mrs. Hannaham put her hands on her hips. I had an urge to kick her.

"Zephy, it'll be fun," my dad said gently. "You're good at this kind of thing." I looked at him incredulously. "I mean, you're organized and you're neat." If he tells me I'm very special, I thought, I'm going to take to my bed with a jar of Marshmallow Fluff.

"And you're good with people and very responsible with money," he continued. "It's just, what, all of us here, plus Roxana and the Caldwells, right? Everyone's like family."

Was that a subtle way of telling me I shouldn't reproduce with Cliff?

"And whoever moves into James's place," Mrs. Hannaham added.

Who *would* move into James's place? I hadn't thought of that. The apartment was a sweet little one-bedroom, the mirror of my place, across the landing on the second floor. If I was super, I bet I would have a lot of say over who moved in. He would have to be single. Taller than Hayden. And have an exciting career. More exciting than Hayden's. Was that illegally discriminatory? Would I, too, be led away by my wrists like James was? Where would my case be tried? Too many people knew my father in New York. None of his colleagues would touch me. Ha!

"It's not going to take much of your time," my mother said doubtfully. "An oil delivery here, a little sweeping there. Maybe call in an electrician once in a while. I don't think James ever had much work."

"Not much . . . ? You let him have a whole apartment rent-free! It has to be a big job to be worth that." I scowled at her.

She took a different tack. "Of course you don't *have* to do this." Translation: of course I had to do this. "But we need someone we can trust. James just left here in cuffs with an apparent psychiatric disorder, Zephy! This is a small operation that runs on the honor system. You'd be taking a great load off our minds."

So that was the story they were going with. Bulletproof. I was not my brother, after all. And my entertainment value—I hadn't even had a chance to regale them with the St. Regis escapade—was clearly no longer enough to satisfy their standards in the legacy department.

I plopped down on the stoop and rubbed at a blister that was starting to sprout over my big toe. A noisy, stilettoed, bridge-and-tunnel crowd teetered up the block in low-slung jeans serving up healthy rolls of waist. Imported muffin tops. I had always wanted to congratulate the woman who first refused to let anorexic models stake a claim on those jeans, the pioneer who let her belly flop over the top and declared, "Ladies, follow my lead!"

And then I thought, Yes. Let me be like her. Let me be like the woman who would not buy the classic cut. I will not be embarrassed by this odd hiccup in my life. Yes. I am twenty-seven and I have a B.A. worth a hundred grand and I dropped out of medical school and I biffed on law school and my friends are all prematurely successful in their worthwhile, absorbing careers, and I am frightening my parents and maybe even myself with my aimlessness.

But I would go a different route. I would be the person who cheerfully went with the flow, who didn't just make lemonade out of lemons, but who invented a new kind of lemonade and not only won the ribbon for her nectar at the county fair, but licensed it to the U.S. government so that it became the only drink NASA would stock aboard their shuttles. I would create a beverage worthy of a moon landing.

FOUR

Mᴇʀᴄᴇᴅᴇꜱ ᴡᴀꜱ ʟᴀᴜɢʜɪɴɢ ᴀᴛ ᴍᴇ. ꜱʜᴇ ᴡᴀꜱ ᴅʀɪɴᴋɪɴɢ ᴍʏ Chock Full o'Nuts, eating my frozen waffles, and laughing at me for not knowing the difference between a Phillips head and a flathead.

"Haven't you ever had to open, like, I don't know, anything? *Ever?*" We were in my kitchen the morning after James's arrest, surveying the contents of a grimy tool kit my dad had dug up and earnestly presented to me as a first-day-on-the-job-I-never-wanted gift. I told him that even secular humanists were entitled to observe Sunday as a day of rest. He laughed and went back upstairs to the lox spread that was rightfully mine.

I stuck my tongue out at Mercedes.

"You know not to lick electrical sockets with that bad boy, yes?"

"Who the hell is Phillip?" I crabbed, taking a waffle off her plate and sinking down on the step stool. My plan to be a good sport about my life's new path was temporarily on hold. Mrs.

Hannaham had called at seven-fifteen that morning to tell me she smelled something. I had always considered myself a morning person, but I now understood that I was a morning person only when the morning's activities consisted of lying in bed reading.

"What kind of smell, Mrs. Hannaham?" I had croaked, squinting at the Mickey Mouse clock I'd kept alive since the fourth grade.

"Gas, I think. I definitely smell smoke."

"They're pretty different. Could you tell me more?"

"You mean you don't smell it? James could always smell what I smelled."

So that was how it was going to be.

"Oh, *that* smell," I said, yawning.

"What did you say? I can't hear you."

I pulled the comforter down from my face.

"I said, 'Oh, that smell.' I smell it now. Like gas or smoke?"

"Yes!" she replied triumphantly.

"I'll go to the basement right now and check it out."

"The basement? It's not coming from the basement."

I sighed, wondering whether we'd have to play twenty questions every time she concocted a problem.

"Right. I'll come to your apartment?" I asked with dread.

"My apartment! You will not enter my apartment. There's no need to enter my apartment unless it's an emergency."

I declined to point out the love affair between smoke and emergencies. I waited for my next clue.

"You might," she said, as if the thought had just dawned on her, "want to pay a visit to Miss Roxana."

Where Mrs. Hannaham was a meddling, grudge-bearing scarecrow of a widow who had probably been involuntarily celibate for the majority of her life, Roxana Boureau was a lithe, von Furstenberg–clad natural blond widow whose outrageous but genuine French accent oozed sex. Unlike Mrs. H. and her precious Compton, Roxana never mentioned Monsieur Boureau and, also unlike Mrs. H., she mostly minded her own business. She worked out of her apartment, buying and selling on eBay, though what she sold, nobody knew. I asked her once and she answered, with an elegantly dismissive wave that I could only dream of perfecting, "Oh, you know, zees and zat." She never complained and always kept a sprig of fresh flowers hanging outside her door, which eternally endeared her to my mother. She looked like she was in her late thirties, but, seeing as she was born knowing how to turn a steady diet of Brie and Cabernet into a skin renewal system, she was probably a decade older.

Mrs. Hannaham, not particularly generous of spirit to begin with, wasn't inclined to make any exceptions for her fellow widow. I had heard her occasional barbed remarks concerning Roxana's apparently thriving love life—"Let's just install a revolving door, for goodness sake"—but I hadn't realized that she'd harassed her via James. Embezzler though he might be, I was already missing him and his unsung diplomatic skills.

As soon as I hung up, I promptly fell asleep. The phone rang again a half hour later.

"Well?" Mrs. Hannaham's forever-Queens accent punched holes through the remnants of a lovely dream involving George Clooney, me, and a hot-air balloon.

"Helium!" I yelled, trying to clear my head.

"Helium! Did you call the fire department?"

I managed to distract Mrs. H. from her nascent plan to ruin my life by spouting some partially accurate facts about the lightest known element on the periodic table. It was only after I hung up that it dawned on me that had she in fact smelled smoke, I could well have had the worst first day on a job in history and lost my home in the bargain.

So my plan to make space-worthy lemonade had soured by the time Mercedes showed up an hour later, spurring summer on with a tank top and shorts over her long body, beaded mini dreds bouncing around her face. She was irritatingly energetic, ready to help me take on the world even though I just wanted her to let me complain for a while.

Mercedes Kim was my Black Friend. She was all of the Sterling Girls' Black Friend, and if she was particularly ornery after an afternoon battling Shostakovich, she would sometimes make us call her that. On the first day of high school, the ninth-graders, all of us new, joined the upperclassmen in unintentionally segregating ourselves (brochure photos of mingling students notwithstanding). But not Mercedes. The girl with the Latina first name—chosen by her father, who, among his many pernicious acts (including stealing her identity fifteen years after abandoning her), named her for his favorite car—and the Asian last name—courtesy of her beloved stepfather, who adopted her and played Schubert's String Quartet in C Major for her and thus, like a dealer in a schoolyard, got her hooked forever—had carried her tray over and sat down at the table where I huddled with Abigail, trying to remain unnoticed.

She threaded her legs around the bench and announced, "I didn't get a full scholarship to this place just to hang out with morons bragging about how wasted they got every night in the Hamptons this summer." I was so in awe of her courage to denounce the people I was already scared of that all I could do was remain silent. Abigail gripped the edge of her tray and stared at something on the floor beyond our table. But during the next hour, despite the cafeteria cacophony that always sounds like everyone is talking about something you'll never be let in on, Mercedes turned our nervous silence into a comfortable one. By the end of that first week, Lucy and Tag had found us, and we five never ate lunch apart for the next four years.

"None of this is going to help you open the garbage thing," Mercedes said now, snatching back her waffle from my hand. "We need to find the key or call a locksmith."

My first on-the-job challenge, after resisting strangling Mrs. H., had presented itself in the form of the garbage lock-boxes, three wooden containers lined up in the alley beside the building. Monday, as we were beginning to smell, was garbage day, and James had the only set of keys to the padlocks.

I stomped over to the bookshelf, pulled out the yellow pages, and plopped them on top of the toolbox.

"Wait a minute, chickie. Locksmiths charge as much as plumbers and electricians. You're sure no one else has a set of keys?"

I shook my head.

"What about looking in James's apartment?"

I raised my eyebrows at her. Police tape was strung like birthday banners across his door. "It's probably locked."

"You think people remember to lock up and turn off the lights and fold back the bedspread after the cops bust in and take 'em to the clink?"

"Listen to you, Shawshank."

"Seriously. It's probably unlocked and, you know, if he left the lights on . . ."

My own dim bulb started to flicker. "It's my responsibility to make sure we're not wasting the building's resources."

"What if the water's running?" Mercedes said, all wide-eyed innocence.

"Mrs. H. said she smelled something! If his apartment was on fire, there's no way I wouldn't be allowed in . . ."

Mercedes strode through my living room to the front door. I scampered after her out onto the landing. She put her hands on her slim hips and nodded for me to open the door.

"Why me? It was your idea," I whispered.

"Because it should be your fingerprints," she hissed back.

"Fingerprints! Fingerprints doesn't sound good!" I started to back into my apartment, but Mercedes grabbed my arm.

"Open the frigging door, moron." I briefly thought about the night before, when Tag had called me a fuckwad, and wondered if maybe we hadn't all gotten a little too familiar with each other.

I quickly looked up and down the stairs and then tried the handle, hoping it would be locked. It gave way immediately and I jumped back. Even Mercedes looked surprised. The door creaked open slowly as we peered through the crisscrossed tape.

In the ten years he'd been our super, I'd never been inside James's apartment, not even after I'd moved downstairs from my childhood home. If I needed something, I called him or knocked on his door and waited for him to come to my place. From where we stood, it didn't *look* like a split personality's dwelling. It was tidy, if a little dark, well appointed and sleek, if a bit unoriginal. Black leather sofa set, chrome-and-glass coffee table, giant flat-screen TV, plush gray carpeting. Everything screamed Bachelor Pad.

I looked at Mercedes. She put her nose in the air and sniffed. "I definitely smell something." She was not letting me off the hook, and if I was going to be honest with myself, I was starting to get a little excited about the prospect of sanctioned snooping. The police tape was everywhere, but it had been hastily and loosely strung up. I straddled one banner, ducked under another and . . . I was in.

Being in someone else's home alone was the ultimate test

of restraint. Or rather, the ultimate test of *my* restraint. If I had been a dog, I'd have raced in and sniffed every corner. Rooted through the garbage, pawed at the drawers, jumped on the beds. It was only the painstaking evolution of human behavior—and its technological offspring, the nanny-cam—that kept me from opening people's refrigerators, their desk drawers, their medicine cabinets. (Snooping through Hayden's apartment didn't count as a transgression—that had been an act of self-preservation.)

I stood in the middle of James's living room. Looking out his window was a slightly itchy experience because the view was just past what I could see out my own window, like being able to see beyond the borders of a photograph. He could see right into the lobby of the apartment building across the street, whereas I could just glimpse the door opening and closing and the occasional flash of the doorman's brown-and-gold uniform. His window only had the outermost branches of Mrs. Hannaham's apple tree in front of it, but my view was cluttered by leaves in the summer.

I wasn't the only one titillated by unfettered access. Mercedes was on her tiptoes, leaning as far through the tape as she could without actually entering the apartment.

"Oh, for God's sake, just come in," I told her. "Help me look for the keys."

Mercedes put her feet down flat and backed away. "I'm not taking any chances. If Denzel could get pulled over by police, then I can, too."

"You, my friend, are no Denzel Washington. And it wasn't him, it was some other guy. You should keep your peeps straight."

"Don't say 'peeps,' cracker. If you don't start looking around, I'm leaving."

"Okay, okay! Don't go!" I decided to check the kitchen

drawers first, since in my apartment that was where I kept spare keys, expired coupons, and a protractor that had stayed with me since eighth grade geometry class. I practically tiptoed down the hall.

"Do you see anything?" Mercedes stage-whispered.

"Other than the dead body?"

Annoyed silence.

"No, nothing yet." I tentatively pulled out a drawer. Flatware! The next drawer had . . . a bottle opener! I opened some equally unrevealing cabinets with a growing fear/excitement that I'd be required to look around the rest of the apartment. I now knew that James had only four plates, none of which matched, though he had four shelves loaded with glasses.

I opened his refrigerator. An unremarkable jumble of stained take-out containers, crusty condiments, and a stash of film and batteries took up most of the space. But the bottom shelf made my breath catch. On one side were ten perfectly aligned bottles of Brooklyn Lager while the other held ten equally organized jars of Marmite, that noxious, dun-colored yeast spread, beloved only by Brits and likely the real cause of the Revolutionary War.

Here was my first encounter with a psychopath's refrigerator. It made me revise my developing theories about who the real James was. After last night, I had assumed that the British accent was the act, or the secondary persona, but now I wondered. What if no psych researcher had ever done a study of multiple personality patients' refrigerators? Maybe I had before me a crucial diagnostic tool. How many new credits would I need to apply for a doctorate in psychology? I had my dissertation right in front of me. It could be a breakthrough in mental health studies . . .

"Zeph?" Mercedes sounded nervous.

I quickly shut the refrigerator door.

"Nothing in the kitchen. I'm going to the bedroom."

"Okaaay."

"What, you think I shouldn't?" I hustled back to the front door, where Mercedes was still standing guard.

"No, I think you should hurry up." She paused. "Did you find anything?"

"Mismatched plates and ten jars of Marmite."

"What?"

"Marmite!" I was getting antsy and energized. A breeze blew through the apartment, bringing with it the stench of garbage from the holds below, and I realized the window had been left open all night. I went to shut it, kneeling on the comfy window seat James had built for himself. I thought of window seats as furniture for pensive, sedentary people, not psychotic supers. Maybe when he was done caulking the leak in the water heater, the British James took over and read sonnets aloud to himself, looking outside and conjuring up the wind-blown cliffs of Dover.

James had a small fireplace. On his marble mantel were some girly-looking scented candles that accounted for the spicy smell of the living room, and two framed photographs sitting side by side. An innocuous family reunion photo of old aunts with stale smiles gathered on an anonymous porch? A big-haired, underdressed girlfriend? Some slovenly buddies with cans of beer and a big fish on a dock? Oh, how I wished.

They were two identical photos of James. Just James. Big, smiling, identical portraits of just James grinning out at his apartment. Flanked by candles, like a shrine.

"Euww! Euw, euw. Euwwwwww!" Shivers propelled me back toward the front door.

"What?!" Mercedes poked her head through the tape. "What euw?!"

"Photos."

"Of . . . ?" I watched her imagination run wild.

"Himself."

"Naked?"

"No! But just him, two photos of just him. And they're the same photo."

"What!" At that, Mercedes climbed over the tape and headed for the hearth. She stood openmouthed at the little alter ego altar. Mercedes's firm presence and the discovery of the all-bets-are-off photo gallery made me relax. I uncurled my toes, brought my shoulders down from my ears, and started moving through the apartment with more confidence. My parents owned this place. James was a crook. I had a mission. If I didn't look at the yellow police tape, there was nothing wrong with this picture.

Keys, I reminded myself firmly. I needed to find the keys to the garbage hold. I was not snooping.

I left Mercedes to gawk at the pictures and headed for James's bedroom. The stench hit me the second I opened the door. The room smelled like guy. Not the good guy smell, not the kind that makes you think of the spot on his neck where the hair ends in a barber's neat line, and smooth, innocent skin beckons for a nuzzle. Not the smell that makes you think of tendony, tan wrists and a T-shirt hanging just the right way off a trim back. No. This was the smell of yesterday's boxers and last month's sheets. Of solo sex and dank carpet. It brought to mind hair-clogged razors, and toothpaste splatters on the mirror.

I held my breath and picked my way across the sticky carpet, trying not to step on the piles of tangled clothes emitting deadly fumes. The nightstand was strewn with tattered *Hustler*s fighting for space with pulp-encrusted juice glasses. I grimaced and peered under the bed. It was home to dust bunnies and a bowl with once-soggy cornflakes stuck to the sides. Gingerly, I pulled out a couple of plastic bins that looked promising, but they yielded only boxes of screws, nails, tape, and tape measures.

I stood up and opened one of the two closet doors. Or tried to. I gave it another tug before realizing it was locked. A locked closet in a criminal's—well, an *alleged* criminal's—home. What was in there? If I pried open the door and discovered stacks of crisp hundred-dollar bills, would my ethics withstand the test? Here I was, living a life of comfort and health and good fortune. Still, I was pretty sure I might try taking a stack of bills. In my defense, though, after I'd allotted a budget for a ten-minute—no, fifteen-minute—chair massage at a local nail salon once a week—no, once a month; no, once a week—I would do really good things with that money. Rescue abandoned dogs, fund Doctors Without Borders, take out full-page ads warning all women not to date Hayden Briggs.

But how much was actually in the closet? And what if it was marked? The phrase had always brought to mind a big black spot on the corner of the bill, but my keen legal instinct sensed that that was probably an inaccurate image. Was this money planted by cops who had recorded the serial numbers? Oh, the shame that would befall my parents if I was found stealing stolen money!

The bedroom door creaked and I gasped.

"Nervous Nelly. Stealing contraband?" Mercedes asked. She pressed her lips together. "Mmm, I smell vintage pizza somewhere."

"This door is *locked*," I told her ominously. She came over and rattled it. She squatted down and studied the doorjamb. Then she pulled harder and the door flung open. My heart jumped and for a moment I actually conjured up stacks of cash. Then my brain righted itself and my excitement abated. There were clothes in the closet. Shoes, belts, shirts, baseball caps, jeans, work gloves.

"Nervous *and* weak," Mercedes concluded.

"You know, with friends like you—"

"You're so much more interesting. Any keys, Sherlock?"

Just as I was shaking my head, we heard a raspy French voice call from the front door.

"Allo? Ees anyone zair?"

I darted out of the bedroom and found Roxana poking her perfectly messy topknot through the police tape.

"Mrs. Hannaham thought she smelled smoke!" I burbled, my face heating with unwarranted guilt. I had a legitimate reason for traipsing around a crime scene, damn it. "And also, I needed to look for the keys to the garbage hold." I nodded my head toward the window and wrinkled my nose for emphasis.

"What happeent last night?" She furrowed her pretty little brow, scanning the living room nervously.

I shrugged, feeling, as I always did with her, inexplicably eager for some sign that she liked me.

"James was arrested."

She nodded, waiting for more.

"Uh, it turns out he was embezzling? From the oil delivery company?"

She shook her head slightly and raised her eyebrows as if to say, And?

I racked my brain, wanting to appear knowledgeable. "Well, we're going to look into whether he was stealing from the building," I added, realizing at that moment that we should look into whether he was stealing from the building.

"Do you sink I could . . . ?" She gestured at the apartment, and a shock of adrenaline jerked through me.

"No! I mean . . ." Although I was entirely comfortable with my own nosiness, I held others to higher standards. I was the co-heir to these four stories, and now the overseer of them, but Roxana had no business poking around a crime scene. I was disappointed in her.

My disapproval must have shown, because she stepped back and said, "Naw, naw, of course nut. I was jus kewriaus." Her instant demurral made me feel like I had the upper hand at something.

Mercedes appeared from behind me, triumphantly brandishing an enormous ring of keys.

"Roxana, Mercedes. Mercedes, Roxana," I said.

"We've met before." Mercedes nodded agreeably.

Mercedes and Tag and Lucy and Abigail had only ever encountered Roxana while passing her on the stairs, but the Gaul Gal, as Abigail had dubbed her, was a never-ending source of fascination for the Sterling Girls. She exuded a smoky, husky aura that we could only ever hope to achieve via a DNA transplant. We wanted the gravelly voice without having to smoke. The lissome figure without having to forgo Oreos. The cheekbones without getting implants.

But more than her looks, we wanted her air of mystery. She was reserved, private, and, therefore, sophisticated. In contrast, the five of us couldn't keep a secret from one another for more than the time it took to think "I'm going to keep this to myself." We were open books, and nothing was off-limits. Not the unrequited crush Abigail had nursed for her married thesis advisor. Not the gruesome details of Lucy's father's fatal cancer. Not the description of the stomach virus Tag acquired during a twenty-four-hour journey to the east coast of Africa. Not the blow-by-blow accounts of the shedding of our respective virginities.

We also never hesitated, with Lucy's embryonic expertise at the helm, to analyze anyone's relationship with her mother, or her approach to dating, or to make sweeping declarations about how each of us ought to approach life.

"Abigail, you spend a lot of unnecessary energy trying to be the academic star your mother is. Just be good to yourself."

"Mercedes, you spend a lot of unnecessary energy trying to be someone your father wouldn't have left, but it was his fault, not yours. Be good to yourself."

"Lucy, you spend a lot of unnecessary energy telling people to be good to themselves. Some of your clients really are homicidal criminals who don't deserve to be good to themselves."

To anyone else, we would be deathly repetitive and unforgivably self-involved. But we never tired of ourselves. I was pretty sure, on the other hand, that Roxana and her friends didn't analyze one another ad nauseam and without a license. Come to think of it, I'd never seen her in the company of anyone else, Mrs. Hannaham's accusations of promiscuity notwithstanding. Did you have to drop all your friends to be sophisticated? *Was* it immature to have so many people to keep track of, as though you weren't discerning enough? Was I guilty of quantity and not quality? Which of my girls could I possibly live without?

"Ah, yis, how are you?" Roxana said now, eyeing the jangling tangle Mercedes was clutching. There were about twenty keys on the ring.

"One of these has to be for the garbage bins, right?" Mercedes asked.

"Are those James's?" Roxana asked.

I nodded, but Mercedes said, "Well, technically, they belong to the building. They belong to the Zuckermans."

Roxana raised her arm as if she was going to ask something else, but changed her mind.

"Aw kay. Well," she gazed at the keys, "keep me on zuh post."

Mercedes looked confused, but I answered, "We will, we'll keep everyone posted."

I should get a job at the U.N., I thought. I was really good at bridging cultural divides. I could start out as a hostess of some sort, shepherding the wives of foreign leaders around the city, showing them the true gems. Not the Olive Gardens and the Gaps and the other insidious chain predators that had tragically devoured New York. Not the stifling department stores or the Empire State Building, but the excavated, 17th-century ruins beneath Broad Street and the spice markets in Jackson Heights. The hidden gardens behind the Church of St. Luke in the Fields on Hudson Street and the peaceful, abandoned stretch of Pier 40's western end, one of the few places a New Yorker could be alone outside. The ex-cons playing chess with the stockbrokers in City Hall Park and the sunset on the Brooklyn Heights promenade. The aquatic memorial of the Merchant Marine who drowned over and over, each time the Hudson River lapped over his head.

The first lady of Iran/Iraq/Libya would confess during a stroll past the Chelsea Market waterfall how refreshing it was to speak candidly—a decade and a half with the Sterling Girls would turn out to have been training for my true calling—and we'd forge a plan for peace between our countries. I would pitch my idea to save the world by getting young boys in aggressive countries to read novels. If these potential terrorists could only read something besides the Bible or the Koran, all the energy spent learning how to blow themselves up would instead be spent blowing their minds with Steinbeck, Defoe, Marquez, Dickens, Lahiri, Eliot, Fitzgerald, and Patchett. We would share the Nobel Peace Prize.

Roxana took a last glance around the room, studied Mercedes

and me carefully for a moment—which I found immensely flattering—and then headed upstairs.

"You think we'll ever be that hot?" Mercedes wondered. I shook my head.

"Ready to be super?" Mercedes asked, and slipped through the tape and out onto the landing.

"No. Not at all." She laughed, but I wasn't kidding. I wanted to go stick twenty keys into a garbage hold about as much as I wanted to be a lawyer or a doctor.

Mercedes considered me across the police tape. For the first time in the fourteen years I'd known her, I detected the faintest hint, the barest trace, the most infinitesimal squeak of . . . disapproval. My heart sank. Since the age of six, she had sawed away at her viola for an hour every morning before school and then for four hours—*four hours*—every day after school and what seemed like all day on weekends. Summers were filled with music camps and competitions and auditions and more practicing. At every turn, from her auditions for conservatory to her acceptance as third chair violist in the New York Philharmonic, she had battled the subtle prejudices that no one in the music world would ever admit to harboring. And not once had she complained.

I sighed. I could live, just barely, with my parents' disappointment, but I could not wake up in the morning if I thought my friends were disgusted with me.

Lemonade. I had to go make lemonade. Out of garbage.

FIVE

ONE WEEK LATER, I'D NOT ONLY BECOME AT EASE IN JAMES'S apartment, I'd begun to think of it as my office. Every inch of the living room was covered in crumpled, smudged paper, and not one single scrap reflected anything I'd ever, in my dullest, tamest dreams, given a second thought to: receipts for washers and extension cords and faucet handles and drill bits and plywood and Sheetrock. Old invoices and canceled checks to electricians, exterminators, the fire department, an ironsmith. Tax assessments, water/sewer bills, battered repair logs, sprinkler inspection reports, fuel oil storage permits.

In the few moments that weren't riddled with panic, anxiety, and confusion, I sometimes felt like I was perusing the unearthed papers of an old friend and discovering clues to the parts of him I didn't know. Finding an old engineer's report was like coming across an EKG—I didn't know Joe had a heart murmur! I didn't know the bricks of my building's east wall needed to be repointed! Occasionally, sifting through James's questionable record-keeping meant learning about the essence of my childhood home. But mostly, it meant a passionate new relationship with antacids.

Before I'd spread them across the floor, the tatty records had lived in close quarters in three large file boxes, all jumbled together. When Lucy, who admitted she probably had just a soupçon of OCD, heard about this, she snuck out of her office and was at my door an hour later to minister to me. She arrived dressed for work: sweatpants, one of her father's old army T-shirts, and her thin blond hair pulled back in an eighties-era terry-cloth headband.

Lucy had insisted on helping all the Sterling Girls move into their respective apartments, and she was still peeved she hadn't been able to fly to California to help Abigail unpack out there. We all knew where to find things in one another's homes because they were organized in almost precisely the same manner. Our dressers held underwear and bras in the top drawer, sweaters and foldable shirts in the next drawer, and jeans in the bottom one. In our closets, from left to right, were pants (by weight), skirts, dresses, and at the far right were blouses and random unfoldables. Sweaty workout clothes aired out on permanent hooks on the back of the bedroom door. It was the same story with the kitchen, the bathroom, the bookshelves, and the CD racks.

"Here's another plumbing-looking thing," Lucy said, handing me a coffee-stained yellow carbon copy to put in the "plumbing stuff" pile. Only after every last scrap had been laid out and organized would Lucy let me start putting papers away in the color-coded folders with color-coded labels to store in the color-coded rolling storage crates she had bought. Lucy was the only non-CPA I knew who had her own personal stash of "sign here" stickies. She wandered through the aisles of stationery stores the way some women haunted shoe stores: longingly, lovingly, and always leaving with something she didn't need but couldn't live without.

I surreptitiously glanced at my watch. Tag had promised to

unexpectedly stop by to tell us how gorgeous it was outside and suggest we go kayaking from Pier 66.

"Do you or don't you want me to help you?" Lucy demanded, following my glance.

"No, I do," I assured her. "This is great. I don't know what I'd do without you."

"You'd still be sitting here in a near-catatonic state." She handed me an invoice. "This goes with tax records. Do you have any snacks?"

I jumped up. "I'll go get some!"

"Sit *down*. We'll take a break at two-oh-five."

Deep breath. "Okay." I reluctantly grabbed another mush of papers and started smoothing them out. We'd been at this for two hours already. But just as I started running a bored eye down a tax assessment, the intercom buzzed.

Tag!

"I'll get it!" I yelled, jumping up. Lucy just shook her head in disgust. I bounded down the creaky, carpeted steps to the front door.

On the stoop was a tall man who immediately scrambled my social sensors. He wore a navy blue jumpsuit embroidered with the name "Ridofem" and an image of a cockroach and a rat holding their antennae and paws to the sides of their faces in a Munch-like *The Scream* pose. He was carrying a spray can with a long hose. I would have confidently concluded that he was an exterminator, but, all avowals of class-blindness to the contrary, I knew blue collar from white collar, laborer from lawyer, and something about this young verminator didn't compute.

He was angular and pale, but not unattractively so. His nose was just big enough to keep him from being vain—I guessed—but not so big as to be a deal-breaker. He had a mop of chestnut hair that needed a trim, a brooding brow, and big eyes—ish-colored, like mine—fanned by thick black lashes. The long, bony fingers wrapped around the nozzle looked like they should be covered in paint splatters, caked in ceramics mud, or leafing through precious, rare books. He looked, I realized, Jewish, and I didn't know Jews could be exterminators.

I must not have been the first person to regard him with some degree of surprise, because he sighed as if he was waiting for me to finish my mental computations.

"I thought I rang James's bell," he said a little impatiently.

"You did, you did. But James isn't here right now. Can I help you?"

Now *he* looked confused, and I realized he was trying to figure out what I was doing in James's apartment. Was he wondering whether I was James's girlfriend? Did he deal with Brooklyn James or English James? Which one did he think I dated? What would it be like to date James anyway? Did he escort his women to Hooters or did he invite them to swirl mojitos at Gotham? I was finding a fleeting satisfaction in presenting this oxymoronic Jewish exterminator with a mysterious front. I was rarely—no, never—mysterious to anyone.

He lifted up his spray can. "I'm supposed to do this building today."

I had no reason not to believe him, especially since I'd seen bills from Ridofem in the mess upstairs. But the new me, the responsible, lemonade-making, Super me, figured I should ask some questions before allowing a stranger to spread poison throughout my building.

I nodded at his canister. "What do you use?"

He looked at me squarely. "Are you familiar with pesticides?"

"Somewhat," I lied.

"Will it make a difference if I tell you we use cypermethrin instead of bendiocarb?"

Now, I could have been a chemist for all he knew. Or a public health researcher, or maybe my best friend in grade school had been a DDT baby. My hackles were up, but rather than directly address his impudence, I chose instead to take my pique out on a passing double-decker tour bus that had turned illegally onto our narrow street.

"Sign on the corner says no commercial traffic!" I shrieked, bolting out onto the stoop in my bare feet. "Get out and walk, you fat Americans!" Carl, a neighbor who ran a biofeedback therapy clinic out of his living room across the street, waved cheerfully to me.

The exterminator stepped back and pretended to wipe spit from his cheek. "So you're doing *your* part to improve New York's image."

"We're the most helpful people on the planet," I retorted, self-conscious about my outburst, which, on some very uncomfortable level, I immediately knew to be a show of bravado for this guy I'd just met. Why, Zephyr? *Why?*

"As long as other people don't drive down your block."

"Not when they should be walking, no. Not when those polluting buses wreck our air and break the branches on our trees. If they want to sit on their asses, they should stay back in Idowa. I mean Idaho."

The exterminator grinned. "You don't know the difference between Idaho and Iowa."

"Of course I do." I sneered unconvincingly.

"Where's Idaho?"

"I can't *explain* it."

"Sure you can." He crossed his arms.

"There are three 'I' states in a row in the Midwest," I said impatiently. "It's one of *them*."

"You mean Illinois, Iowa, and Indiana?"

"Yeah."

"Idaho isn't any of those." He looked so smug I wanted to smack him.

"What . . . ? Why are we— This is ridiculous!" I waved my hands as if to erase the conversation.

"I'm from Idaho," he said victoriously.

"You are not." I inspected his face for signs of Idaho-ness, but I realized that I had no clue whether he was really from the potato state, and that we both knew I had no way of figuring that out.

He looked directly at me and before I could stop myself, I pictured myself kissing him. A delicious flutter hit my belly and I jumped back, as surprised as if we had actually locked lips. He raised his eyebrows in a question and then pointedly looked at his watch.

"Well, look, I *am* from Ridofem and we have a standing contract with James to do your building once a month. Would you like me to come back another time when he's here?"

I shook off the hazy aftermath of our non-kiss. "No, no, he's not gonna be here anytime soon." I didn't want to admit to this guy that our super had gone to jail. "Just tell me what you need and we'll set you up," I said, trying to sound on top of things. I motioned him inside with as much dignity as I could muster.

He followed me into the foyer and I bolted the door behind him. The sudden quiet felt intimate.

"Who are you?" he asked bluntly.

I extended my hand officiously. "Zephyr Zuckerman."

He took it and laughed. "Seriously?"

I pulled my hand away, flabbergasted.

"I'm sorry, I'm sorry." He was still laughing. "It's just an unusual name."

"What's *your* name? John Doe?" I spat.

"Gregory. Samson. I mean, Gregory Samson."

I frowned at him for a moment, then broke into a triumphant grin.

"Don't say it," he warned.

"Gregor Samsa was the guy who turned into a bug in *The Metamorphosis*!" I crowed. But my next thought was: how many vermin protagonists can there be in literature, and why do I keep meeting men who share traits with them? I was pretty sure that in the annals of romantic turbulence, this was an unprecedented pattern.

"Do you live here?" he tried again.

"I own the building," I said pompously. "My family does. And James, as I said, isn't here right now, so why don't you just tell me what you need from me."

I thought I saw a brief flicker of remorse cross his face, but just as quickly, it was gone.

"I need access to all the apartments. And, legally, if you are who you say you are, you need to accompany me."

"Why shouldn't she be who she says she is?" Lucy was on the landing above, sliding her hands and upper body down the banister so that she was, effectively, upside down.

Gregory looked up and I snuck a long peek at his profile. Was he really a Jewish exterminator? Maybe he was an undercover cop *posing* as an exterminator! (Were there many Jewish cops?) What if he'd been sent by the NYPD to investigate whether my family played a part in James's nefarious activities? Oh my God, *had* I done anything illegal? At the very least, I'd been treating a crime scene as a home office.

But maybe Gregory had been sent to protect me, not investigate me. Maybe someone James had stolen from was after him, and Gregory had been assigned to cover me night and day. Where would he be stationed? In my living room? I tried to remember the last time I'd vacuumed.

Both Gregory and Lucy waited for me to say something.

"Sorry, Luce. I'll be right up."

Lucy looked at me pointedly.

"Oh. John Doe, this is Lucy. Lucy, this is John Doe," I said.

"Seriously?" Lucy raised her eyebrows, in a refreshing moment of unprofessional insensitivity.

I laughed and Gregory rolled his eyes.

"I mean . . ." Lucy hurriedly straightened and came down the steps to look Gregory in the eye, as she did all her clients, as well as salespeople, waiters, and anyone else who might need to feel validated, to be *seen*. "I mean—"

"I'm the exterminator," Gregory interrupted. "Are you also an owner of the building? Do I need your permission to spray, too?"

"What? No. Just Zeph's." I saw Lucy giving Gregory the same once-over I had, trying to mentally catalog him and being thwarted by his contradictory indicators. Suddenly her eyes lit up. "Hey, which apartments are you doing?"

"All of them," said Gregory.

"Oh, yay!" Lucy clapped her hands. "Now we can label all those keys!"

Lucy jogged up the steps, looking back over her shoulder to throw Gregory a flirtatious little half smile that purposely forced the dimple in her left cheek to appear. She was shameless! Gregory followed her up the stairs and I stomped after them, trying to imagine the toast I'd give at their wedding. Instead, I envisioned myself tearfully telling my children about my perfidious former friend named Lucy.

We reached the first landing and Gregory's eyes widened slightly at the police tape. Exhibiting a self-restraint I could never hope to cultivate, he said nothing and continued up the stairs.

"I usually start at the top and work my way down." He passed Roxana's and Cliff's apartments and headed for the top landing, which my parents shared with the Caldwells, a surgeon/sculptor couple who threw elaborate Martin Luther King, Jr., Day celebrations even though they were paper-white WASPs who hailed from New Canaan. Gregory turned to Lucy and me, whereupon we embarked on a silent competition to flash him the most winning smile. I rolled my shoulders back, sucked in my stomach, and tried to convey that I was intelligent, interesting, funny, and self-knowing.

He looked back and forth between us, a hint of fear creasing his brow. He was alone at the top of an empty house with two strange women, one of whom randomly spewed imprecations at passing tour buses, and both of whom were grinning at him like asylum residents. Meanwhile, the one person in the building he did know was missing, his apartment decorated with dingy police tape.

Gregory bounced the canister hose in his hand, perhaps to remind us that he was armed.

"Keys?"

"Oh, right! Keys!" Lucy and I giggled. We turned to each other expectantly.

"I don't know where they are," I said before she could say it. She struggled to look angelic to Gregory while shooting me darts of venom.

As she raced down the stairs, I almost felt sorry for her. Lucy was an inveterate hopeless—no, hope*ful*—romantic. She regularly defaced U.S. government tender in the hopes of finding true love. She used to write "Middle of Brooklyn Bridge, Sun, noon" on all her ten-dollar bills before putting them into circulation, hoping the money would fall into the hands of some equally lovelorn and optimistic man who would then go linger at the appointed spot. Every Sunday, rain or shine, she would Rollerblade back and forth to eye potential bait, but things got confusing when she realized two other women were doing the same thing. After that, she started writing "3 Lives Books, Sun, noon," which was an improvement, as the Tenth Street bookstore was, first of all, indoors. It also deterred illiterates, as well as uptowners who wouldn't deign to go below Bloomingdale's for a date.

So far, she had gotten two dates out of the scheme—a bald performance artist and a married man—and gently let down a handful of women, after which she started adding a "♂" to her missive. But she also cheated at fate: Lucy was not above spotting an artsy cutie through the window of Jamba Juice and going in to ask if he had a twenty for her two tens, which was, of course, patently absurd. Who needs *bigger* denominations? Still, Lucy was a wide-eyed bundle of cute, and few men balked at her questionable currency maneuvers.

Lucy returned in a flash, bearing not only the keys, but colored tags and a pen.

"Let's do it!" she said, her organizational zeal momentarily overshadowing her quest for love. We had already identified the keys to James's apartment, the front door, the garbage hold, and my apartment, but there were still about seventeen motherless keys left. Lucy started jamming them into the Caldwells' lock one by one. Gregory put down his poison and leaned against the pale yellow wall. I tried to look like a super.

It suddenly occurred to me that I had the key to my parents' apartment. Gregory and I could go in there *alone* and he could start working. I opened my mouth, then stopped. I wasn't cruel enough to leave Lucy by herself, crouched on the floor in front of the Caldwells' door. I didn't need Gregory that badly: I was confident that I would one day soon find a true love, and that Lucy, in that classic irony that besets so many therapists, was going to have a tougher go of it. Poor Lucy!

"Hey, Luce," I offered, "give those to me. You shouldn't have to do that." She looked at me suspiciously, as if there was a way to Gregory's heart she hadn't considered that involved sticking a mess of keys into a lock. She reluctantly switched places with me.

"What's with James's apartment?" Gregory finally inquired. Aha! He wasn't as detached as he was pretending to be. I thought for a moment, but there wasn't really a lie that would be either more interesting or less embarrassing.

"He was arrested for embezzlement."

"No shit?"

Lucy and I traded quick glances. Casual cursing: unsexy. Colorful, vigorous, articulate cursing at appropriate moments: manly. A guy had to know the difference. I was suddenly less interested in Gregory. Apparently, so was Lucy.

"Hey, you guys could start on Zephyr's parents' place," she said cheerfully. After all I'd just tacitly done for her. I blew her a mental raspberry.

"Who was he stealing from? You guys?"

"The oil company. Kickbacks."

"How was James in a position to offer anyone anything that might merit a kickback?"

Lucy and I looked at each other again. That might have been articulate enough to redeem the "no shit."

"What do you mean?" I asked.

"Well, he wasn't running some big operation. I mean, what could he offer anyone that they'd be willing to pay for? A fixed bid on an oil delivery contract for a seven-unit house?" He laughed.

Gregory's entire body lit up when he laughed. His stooped shoulders righted themselves. His arms and hands relaxed. His smile was enormous. It took over his face, and his features abandoned the surly layout they maintained in repose. For just a few seconds, his guard came down and his eyes generously let me far inside.

For just a few seconds, Hayden Briggs was out of my system.

"Hey, Gregory," Lucy said, "do you have a twenty for two tens?"

SIX

Six o'clock on a Saturday night in April is an excellent moment to be twenty-seven, single, and living in New York City.

I was standing in my underwear—sexy, uncomfortable, *matching* underwear—with a new thrift-shop find freshly steamed and hanging on the bathroom door, experimenting with my hair up/down, earrings long/short. All the lights in my apartment were on and *Abbey Road* was blasting on the stereo while I prepared to crash a party with Tag, Mercedes, and Lucy.

It had taken a while to get back to this point. That first year after the towers fell, I'd stopped wearing contact lenses because the smoke blowing up from Ground Zero wrecked every pair after a day or two. I'd carefully kept my gaze cast downward when I crossed Sixth Avenue because the skyscape was too brutally unrecognizable. And I woke up every morning with a gasp, unable to purge my memory of the flames and the jumping bodies I'd witnessed from the rooftop of Tag's father's

Tribeca loft, where I'd been studying for a post-bac organic chemistry test. In those twelve months, there was no night-out anticipation, no belting out "Maxwell's Silver Hammer," no accidentally crashing an infanta's birthday party. First-world moments seemed to be a thing of the past.

But I was secretly shocked and a little ashamed by how normal life had become after the first anniversary. Even the small residual effects on our lives, like Tag's heart palpitations, had evaporated. When her syncopated valves started interfering with her ability to sketch a tapeworm, she finally went to a doctor. He made her wear a diagnostic heart monitor for what was supposed to be twenty-four hours, but when a security guard at the museum spotted the wires hanging out of Tag's shirt, a brief lockdown had ensued. Being Tag, she'd found the irony of the whole incident so hilarious that her palpitations had stopped instantly.

I tried to keep the enormity of the attacks fresh in my mind, out of respect for the mourning families. But I was a fourth-generation New Yorker and, except for the occasional fantasy in which I alerted the police to a bomb in the subway, was interviewed on the news, and was subsequently offered my own PBS talk show because Charlie Rose's producers had just that morning decided he had interrupted one too many guests, I wound up going back to living the only life I knew.

Which, at the moment, consisted of balancing on a chair in my living room in front of a mirror, gauging whether my black bra and panties looked good or whether they just highlighted my end-of-winter pastiness. I had never bought a full-length mirror, out of fear that it would make me vain (a favorite subject of analysis and ridicule among the Sterling Girls). As a result, I could only see from my thighs up to my hearty arms, round face, and rebellious hair, a disproportionate view that allowed me to be pleasantly surprised whenever I caught my full reflection in a store window. I peered into the mirror and wiped a smudge of peanut butter off the corner of my mouth.

Tag had managed to persuade Lucy, Mercedes, and me to crash a book party at Soho House, the private hotel in the meatpacking district favored by movie stars, moguls, and anyone who wore a size zero. I was still recovering from the fiesta fiasco at the St. Regis two weeks before, but Tag insisted we get back in the saddle.

"So maybe once a year—"

"Uh," I interrupted.

"Okay, twice a year, even three times, we get caught. Is that a reason to give up our only window into lifestyles we'd otherwise never encounter?"

Oh, she was good.

I watched myself dance on the chair, grunting and scowling to "She's So Heavy" and suddenly realized that I was dressing for Gregory. Usually, my primary source of fashion guidance was whether if I encountered Hayden he would drool with regret at botching his chances with me. But tonight, I was imagining bumping into Gregory. He was a sourpuss in a jumpsuit with a rat and a roach on it, and I still wasn't sure whether he was an undercover cop, but there it was.

The revelation made me freeze mid-gyration. I didn't know which part of the equation was more shocking to me: that Hayden was, at least momentarily, out, or that the sullen exterminator was in.

The phone rang, and I made a mental note to run this new development by the Sterling Girls when they arrived.

"Sweetie," came my mother's brisk, efficient voice. "We're just headed out to meet the Lowells for dinner and the ballet . . ."

She paused. My mother and Derek Lowell's mother had

unsubtly waged a campaign since he and I had been in kinder-
garten to get us married to each other. It had been intensified
(by my mother) when he had gotten into Harvard, relaxed
when I was dating a Legal Aid lawyer, intensified (by his
mother) when he had broken up with the actress, and then intensified some more (by my mother) when I had dropped out
of med school. If I wasn't going to make anything of myself
professionally, she must have thought, let's at least get her
safely married.

"Uh-*huh*," I said warningly.

". . . and our dryer isn't working. When you press START, it
makes these noises that sound like 'O Canada.' "

I laughed. "Bummer. Do you want to use mine?"

There was an awkward pause.

"Uh, well, actually, Zeph, we need you to fix it. Or have it
fixed."

And there it was. It had been no problem escorting
Gregory around the building while he fumigated apartments—
practically a first date. It was annoying but tolerable to humor
Mrs. Hannaham and her phantom odors. I found it downright
educational to help the Caldwells measure their bathroom
windows for new blinds. (It turned out that the retired surgeon
and her effete sculptor husband slept in separate beds, a fact
I'd wasted little time in relaying to Lucy, who chewed over the
information intently, even though she'd never met them.)

But I had avoided thinking about the moment when I'd be
called on to act as my parents' super. It shouldn't be any different, I advised myself quickly, as my mother breathed over the
phone, from someone who worked in a family business. After
all, 287 West 12th Street *was* a family business. How many
hardware stores, accounting agencies, medical practices, and
bagel shops were So-and-So and Sons? Or Zuckerman and

Zuckerman, LLP. How many Korean grocers had made their kids pause during their calculus homework to ring up my order of Ben & Jerry's?

But the difference was that in those businesses, Junior was *working* for his parents, but *serving* other people. If I had been an accomplished forest ranger living downstairs from my mom and dad, and they'd called me to help them with their dryer, I would have been performing a familial favor. My position as super, on the other hand, required me not just to work for Ollie and Bella Zuckerman, but to serve them.

I twirled my earring nervously and fought off a wave of anxiety, the kind that comes from realizing one has made a very bad decision.

"Zeph?"

"Yeah, no problem," I squeaked out. And then I had a terrible thought. "Does it need to be taken care of . . . tonight?"

My mother chortled loudly and I had to hold the phone away from my ear. "Sweetheart, no repairman works on a Saturday night. Just take a look at it tomorrow and . . ."

Then, I believe, Bella Zuckerman had a similar realization to the one I had just entertained, though it probably flashed up on her brain as a spreadsheet. In one column: money invested on four years of private high school and four years of college plus additional pre-med classes, med school itself, and law school applications—multiplied roughly by two to take into account her wayward filmmaking son. In the other column: zero ability of any child of hers to repair a Frigidaire dryer that was humming the Canadian national anthem.

"Well, just take a look at it, then look in James's files for a repair person and call him. Or her," she quickly amended. "Of *course*. With the money we're saving on James's salary, we'll have no problem covering fees to outside sources." Her mental spreadsheet was in the black once more.

I hung up dejectedly. It felt like the end of the evening instead of the beginning. My strapless bra felt saggy, my thighs suddenly looked pale against the black lace, and I was tired. The phone rang again. Did her toilet need plunging, too?

"Yeah," I answered.

"Um . . ." came a male voice.

I perked up. "Oh, hello?" I ran the voice through my audio inventory, first stop Hayden. Hayden?

"This is Gregory Samson."

My bra rose up, my thighs grew a shade tanner.

"Hi!" I said. "How are you?" I chirped. I was glad that, in my official capacity as super, I'd thought to scrawl my phone number on an old hardware store receipt for spackle and caulking.

"Fine. I was wondering if you were free tonight," he said brusquely.

I looked in the mirror to see if my reflected self knew what to make of this.

Gregory's tone was rude, though I reminded myself that some people were challenged by phone performance. And even though this wasn't the 1950s and it was perfectly cool for a woman to admit she didn't have plans for a Saturday night, I was still offended.

"Did you suddenly remember a corner you forgot to spray?" I said meanly, and regretted it instantly. Why were Gregory and I—ooh, that sounded nice—so snippy toward each other?

He said nothing.

"Actually, I'm about to head out. What's up?" I tried to sound lighthearted.

"I wanted to see if you'd have dinner with me, but forget it."

I sighed loudly. What a pain in the ass. But at least we were dispensing with game-playing. Except that I *liked* the game-playing.

"Look, I'm sorry, but you just asked me kind of . . . abruptly."

"So come out to dinner and teach me some manners." Again, this Jewish exterminator was confounding me. Was he obnoxious or refreshingly direct? Sexy in his confidence or a geek with no social graces?

Just then, someone pressed hard on the intercom buzzer, someone else threw something at my window, and, just in case I didn't know my friends had arrived, Tag bellowed my name from downstairs. If he was going to be direct, so was I.

"How about you come over here tomorrow afternoon and help me figure out what's wrong with my parents' dryer, and then I'll take you out to coffee?" I held my breath. What kind of alternative mating dance was *this*? Fumigation and busted dryers?

"It's a deal."

I raised my eyebrows in surprise.

"Okay."

"Okay."

This relationship was never going to work.

"See you tomorrow at . . ." I did a quick calculation of how good the night might be, and how late I'd want to sleep, "noon."

"Twelve-thirty," he said. What a creep.

"Twelve thirty-five," I rebutted and finally got a laugh out of him. I remembered what he looked like laughing and was suddenly eager to get through tonight so I could see him again.

I hung up and buzzed the girls in. Their faces fell when they saw my state of undress.

"No, no, I'm ready—see?" I stepped into my dress, and slid my feet into the Nine Wests I'd worn two weekends before.

Mercedes looked at me suspiciously. "You're always ready twenty minutes early. What happened?"

I felt a rush of affection for my friend who knew me so well, followed by a twinge of irritation at being pigeonholed.

"I'm a minute behind," I assured her, replacing a mismatched earring and putting my hair up one last time. "My mother called. About her dryer." I looked at them to see what they thought of this.

"And did anyone else call?" Lucy asked shrilly.

I bent down and pretended to adjust my shoe. That afternoon on the landing outside the Caldwells' apartment, Gregory had fished a twenty out of his wallet and accepted Lucy's two ten-dollar bills with a puzzled expression. She and I then waged an exhausting battle of wits as we escorted Gregory to each of the seven apartments. The result was that the two of us chattered animatedly to each other and left no opportunity for Gregory to say anything. After he left, we finished sorting paperwork in James's apartment, and the pink elephant in the corner of the living room grew pinker, until Lucy finally went home.

I didn't know how to break the news to her. None of the Sterling Girls had ever been interested in the same guy: we had vastly different taste in men. I had weakly hoped that in the few days since I'd last seen Lucy, she'd gotten over her infatuation. Apparently, she'd been hoping the same for me.

I looked at her now, my tiny friend, standing in her electric blue halter dress, her sheen of blond hair brushing her bony shoulders.

"Gregory called," I said carefully. Mercedes and Tag stopped making hurry-up noises, sensing a delicate matter at hand. They looked back and forth between us.

Lucy's face fell, and I lost my courage.

"He said he noticed mouse holes in Mrs. Hannaham's apartment. He wants to come back and stop them up." The lie was worth it. Lucy relaxed and the whole evening veered back onto the right path.

"Who's Gregory?" Mercedes asked.

"Oh, just this exterminator," Lucy said disparagingly. She shouldn't talk that way about my future husband, I thought before I could rein in my brain.

"Or an undercover cop," I joked. Half joked.

"What!" Lucy was wide-eyed. And that, I realized, was my way out. If Gregory was investigating James's embezzlement, he would of course need to talk to me regularly. Sometimes over lunch or dinner. And if later, we happened to fall in love— assuming we could first achieve a civil exchange—then Lucy would understand the natural progression. It wouldn't be about him picking me over her after just one afternoon of spraying for vermin.

"Well, think about it. He doesn't *look* like an exterminator. He might be an undercover cop checking out James's background."

"What exactly do exterminators look like?" Mercedes challenged, an instant member of Fumigators Against Stereotyping.

"Black," Tag shot back at her. "They're all black. Zephyr is secretly racist and thinks black people can't do anything more than become exterminators. Or musicians."

Mercedes abruptly put Tag in a headlock.

"Her hair!" Lucy and I shouted at Mercedes. "Don't mess up her hair!" Mercedes let Tag up and studied her gorgeous tangle of black curls.

"As if anyone could do anything to that mop. Hey, wait, there's a tapeworm dying in there . . ."

After a small scuffle, a round of last-minute peeing, and an extra application of deodorant, we eventually got ourselves out the door. As I locked my apartment, we heard the front door buzz open.

Senator, was my first thought when I saw the perfectly coiffed, gray helmet of hair ascending the stairs. The 'do was followed by an impeccable, absurdly *L.A. Confidential* pin-stripe suit and shiny black lace-up shoes.

He stopped abruptly when he saw us on the landing. He looked startled and then delighted.

"Well," he said, giving each of us the once-over. His voice was oily, with a hint of the South, and he reeked of cigar smoke. As he appraised us, his smile grew. He was truly repugnant.

"Can we help you?" Tag scowled at him, her arms crossed.

His smile grew wider and he looked like an animal that could swallow us whole. "Why, yes, I do believe you can." He looked at Mercedes. "You, in particular, could be a big, big help." He turned to Lucy. "Although you could help me in many ways, too, my dear. How old might you be?"

"Meester Smeet? Meester Smeet?" Roxana hustled down the stairs and froze when she saw all of us.

"Aw, Zepheer, hallo."

All I could think was, Roxana has a boyfriend! Roxana has a boyfriend! Finally, some dirt on Roxana.

Mr. Smith from Washington looked at her happily, as if she were about to tell him the dessert specials.

"Ah, well yis, Meester Smeet, zees iz my neighbor, I mean, my zooper, yis Zepheer?" She laughed throatily, but it caught halfway. "You and your friends are out for a night wiz duh town, no? Zees is Meester Smeet. We do zuh eBay togezer, yis? We must deescus a problem we are hafink wis zuh eBay. Come zees way Meester Smeet, right zees way!"

"But . . ." he protested, as she took his hand and led him upstairs. He looked longingly at us. "I was just making the acquaintance of these fine ladies."

"Ew," Mercedes said to his face.

A storm cloud instantly closed in on the senator.

"How *dare* you speak to me that way!" he sneered. "You little nigger!"

Roxana pulled him into her apartment, threw me a distraught look, and slammed the door.

The four of us stood in shocked silence.

Mercedes pressed her index finger to the bridge of her nose, as if she were thinking hard, but I knew it was a trick she'd developed at auditions to keep from crying.

Finally, Tag put her arm around Mercedes and said, "The thing is, you're not little. You're really very tall."

SEVEN

"Oh, you were right, Tag," Lucy cooed, sipping something pink and frothy and lying back on a deck chair. She tossed one calf up in the air and seemed to be admiring her kneecap.

"I'm sorry, would you repeat that, please?" Tag demanded.

"You were really, really right," Mercedes murmured, looking out from the safety of our little coterie, toward Soho House's rooftop pool, which was filled with floating lily pads and candles, and surrounded by tiki torches and B-list celebrities. She downed a glass of champagne and exchanged it for a full one floating by on a waitress's tray.

"This was the right move."

After our appalling encounter with Roxana's swine, none of us had been in the mood to crash the book party at Soho House, but Tag insisted that it would be the perfect anodyne. So we made our way reluctantly along the five blocks to the club, parsing the incident the whole way.

"He so clearly wasn't a business partner, but why would

she lie?" I said, sidestepping a delivery guy who was biking on the sidewalk to avoid the cobblestones.

"Wouldn't you lie if he was the guy you were fucking?" Tag retorted.

"She's in an abusive relationship," Lucy concluded sadly. "We can get her help, you know." We turned onto Gansevoort Street and a warm breeze greeted us.

"What we could get her is a hit man," advised Mercedes. "But I don't think he was her boyfriend. She's smarter than that."

"You don't even know her," I pointed out. "How do you know she's smart? Just because she has a cute French accent?"

"And really great clothes," Lucy added.

"I just want any woman to be smarter than that, okay?" Mercedes stopped short outside the microscopically marked door to Soho House and looked at us, annoyed. "Can we drop this? If we don't, I'm going home."

A PR chippie with a clipboard who was hovering at the red velvet rope—behind which exactly nobody was lined up—overheard Mercedes and suddenly looked anxious. Were four age-appropriate, correctly gendered pieces of eye candy about to turn their backs on her party?

"Ladies, ladies, welcome!" she crowed, teetering on skinny legs and even skinnier stilettos. "You're *just* in time! There's almost no more room upstairs." She tossed her slippery blond hair conspiratorially. "Grab a goodie bag—there's *amazing* stuff in there—and head up to the pool! Walter is serving up the best caipirinhas you have ever, ever tasted! Hurry, hurry, hurry!"

Tiffany (why not?) shooed us inside and hustled us onto the elevator. As soon as the mirrored doors closed, we all started yelping with laughter.

"This is makeup karma for last weekend," Tag said to me.

And now here we were, huddled together in a moonlit corner, with no one bothering us except for the circulating waiters who snuck glances at us, trying to assess whether we were important, as we speared their crab-filled dumplings. A morning talk show host, a tennis champ with his singer/songwriter girlfriend, and a pair of twin teenage stars with raccoon eye makeup all strolled by, smiling prophylactically at us in case we *were* important.

"Who's this party for?" I asked Tag, as peals of laughter rose up from the bar.

"It's for Renee Ricardo's book," she answered.

"She's on some show?" Mercedes asked vaguely, her nimble fingers rapidly fingering a piece on air viola.

"One of the morning thingies."

"Anyone know what the book is about?" I pressed, feeling a tad cretinous that someone had slaved away at an entire tome in order for us to suck down free seafood, and we didn't even know the title.

"She's a psychic," Lucy informed us. "She does a segment every week on *Hello, America!*"

"You said you'd quit watching morning television," Tag said suspiciously. "Learning to love your quiet spaces and all that."

"My clients?" Lucy replied with the intonation of a seventh-grader stopping just short of "duh." "*They* watch her. They say she's really accurate."

"Like?" the scientist prompted.

"*Like*, she predicted for this one woman that she would find a buyer for her line of handbags, and that the buyers would be an Indian couple. And they were, and they did!"

"And don't you think that by airing what was essentially a promotion for the handbags, she was making the future happen?" Mercedes gently challenged.

"She *acknowledges* that in telling someone their future it *of course* helps shape it," Lucy said defensively. "She's very down to earth and realistic. But she predicts the sex of people's babies—"

"Fifty-fifty shot," Tag interrupted.

"Look, I'm not Renee Ricardo's lawyer! Go have your future told by her. If you dare," Lucy added dramatically. She pointed to a kitschy gauze tent that was set up in a far corner of the roof.

"Oh, please." Tag fluttered her hand at the suggestion and polished off her martini.

"I'll go!" I volunteered, jumping up. A fortune-teller? Why hadn't I gone to one before? Just because I was raised to believe only in what I could see, touch, taste, hear, smell, or prove, and that among my family and friends throwing money away on a hoax was a clear indication of a weak character?

But this was free! And the woman was on national television—she must have a good track record, otherwise wouldn't angry viewers demand she be taken off the air? She could tell me what I was going to do with my life. If I knew that I was going to relent and join the legal establishment in five years, then I could relax and enjoy being a super now. Or, at my college reunion, I could confidently say that I was taking time off to help my family and would be heading back to medical school. A fortune-teller could put the sugar in my lemonade.

"We're supposed to keep a low profile, Zeph," Tag reminded me ominously. "Or did you just love being chased out of the St. Regis?"

"Hey, I got chased out of the St. Regis, too!" said a deep, familiar voice. We all looked up and there, close enough to stroke the stubble on his perfect cheek, was the one and only Dover Carter smiling down at us from his awesome height.

I was used to seeing celebrities on the street, but I rarely looked them in the eye, because I wanted to demonstrate that we New Yorkers were sophisticated enough to grant them the privacy they sought . . . and I hoped one day to be rewarded for my self-restraint. Maybe I'd be doing some good deed like helping a family push their stalled car, when a celebrity—ideally Jill Amos from *Getting Warmer*—would fall into step beside me and together we'd push the car to a garage. Something sitcomishly funny would happen—a shoe lost in a pothole, uproarious miscommunication with the car's owners—and we'd have a good belly laugh together, and then she would comment on how great it felt to be a real, regular person for a brief time, and our friendship would blossom as she sought refuge in my refreshingly unglamorous life. I'd introduce Jill to the Sterling Girls and we'd be the genuine friends she'd always wanted, refusing to be interviewed by the press and remaining reliably unimpressed by her fairy-tale lifestyle.

But if my current reaction to Dover Carter's proximity was any indication, I had a long way to go before I qualified to become Jill Amos's best friend. As I gazed up at the star of *Last Call, The Ecstasy,* and *Who Needs Mo?* and the voice of the kingly grasshopper in *Squashed!* my heart rate doubled and my vision narrowed.

Why was Dover Carter slumming it at a B-list bash? Dover Carter only made films that were historically or politically important. He showed up at Democratic fund-raisers and was unafraid to tout liberal ideals. He was the first guy in Hollywood to drive a Prius and install solar panels on the roof of his Malibu mansion. If someone had asked me for which movie star I'd most want to bear children, there was really only one answer. And now he was standing next to us, smiling sheepishly. I sank back down onto the lounge chair I'd been sharing with Lucy.

"Oh, yeah?" Tag looked up at him dubiously. "Why'd *you* get chased out?"

Lucy and I exchanged nervous glances. It was entirely possible that Tag had no idea who she was talking to.

"Paparazzi," he said simply. No false modesty there. "You?"

Tag looked at him quizzically, trying to place him. Lucy and I groaned.

"We crashed the Princess of Spain's birthday party."

"Really?" Dover Carter said, crossing his arms and holding his elbows, a sweetly insecure gesture, like he was protecting himself. "Do you make a habit of doing that?"

"Yes," Mercedes interjected. "We're doing it now."

Tag whirled around, furious. Mercedes shrugged and sipped her champagne.

"I'm glad you did." Dover looked . . . shyly? . . . at Mercedes.

"Why?" Tag demanded. "You don't know the first thing about us."

Lucy and I watched mutely, like slow-witted spectators at a tennis match. I kept trying to think of something droll to offer up, but wisely continued to censor myself.

"Yes, I do," the movie star said.

Oh, here it comes, I thought, already disappointed. A feeble pickup line revealing Dover Carter to be as gormless as the bulk of the single male population.

"You're the third chair violist for the Philharmonic," he said to Mercedes.

As exciting as it was to be in Dover Carter's airspace, it was nearly as thrilling to see Tag speechless.

"How could you possibly know that?" Lucy blurted out. He smiled at her, and she leaned back, as if the sheer force of his gaze required her to seek shelter.

"I'm a groupie." He spread his arms helplessly. "I try to schedule my shoots around your performances."

"You're bullshitting us," Tag said, recovering quickly.

"Ta-aag," I managed to say.

Dover Carter, to his everlasting credit, just laughed. "Well, I purposely skipped some of last season. Too much Rock and Shostakovich. Maybe it's unoriginal, but I'm a Mozart man. I think you guys are better at it, too."

Mercedes nodded intently.

"Rock?" I asked, bravely trying to be a part of this historic conversation.

"Rachmaninoff," Mercedes and Dover said together. I turned red.

"Did you catch Josh Bell's concerto? You think he's the real thing or an overrated pretty boy?" Mercedes asked earnestly.

And they were off. It would have been surreal, except that Dover seemed more in awe of Mercedes than she was of him. He was a genuine nerd, in the best sense. He knew the names and stats of nearly every member of the Philharmonic, savoring this bulk of largely unimportant information as if he were a baseball junkie. He knew who had joined when, and where they had played before, and what pieces they were best at. All he needed was trading cards.

"Let's check out that fortune-teller," Tag said in an uncharacteristically considerate gesture.

Mercedes and Dover didn't notice the three of us sidling away.

"Is that really happening?" I asked, looking back at one of my oldest friends in an intimate tête-à-tête with last year's sexiest man of the year (according to scientifically rigorous periodicals).

"Are we really going to a fortune-teller?" Tag asked disdainfully.

"I am," Lucy told her firmly. "I need to know when I'm going to meet my soul mate." She steeled herself. "I'm prepared for her to tell me it's never going to happen. I'm strong. I'm independent. I'll be okay."

Tag looked at me.

"Aren't you curious?" I asked sheepishly.

Tag gave us a look of disgust and headed for the bar. Lucy and I got on line behind a square-jawed network weatherman who had a woman clinging to each arm.

A warm breeze rolled across the roof deck, sending the Chinese lanterns fluttering, and blowing the women's hair across their faces, making it catch in their lipstick. This made the three of them laugh riotously, and I imagined the women recounting the incident the next day to other friends and laughing again with equal gusto. I was on the verge of a moment of snobbish superiority—windblown hair is what these people find funny?—when one of the women caught my eye and gave me a sweet, conspiratorial smile that belied her high-pitched giggle. I decided she was savvier than anyone I knew and that she would probably be anchoring the evening news long before I learned how to fix a running toilet.

I looked impatiently toward the front of the line and was rewarded by the sight of Adam Mason, one of my earliest objects of desire, emerging from the tent. He gave all of us waiting on line a thumbs-up and a white-toothed grin. I elbowed Lucy frantically, instantly awash in the same desperate longing I used to feel when I was ten, watching him cavort around a soundstage kitchen. Adam was not aging well, but Lucy clutched my hand and gasped, apparently also in thrall to our childhood crush. Dover Carter *and* Adam Mason, moonlight, free food, lily-pad-filled pool . . . this was turning into a stellar evening. And tomorrow I'd see Gregory. First-world moment approaching.

After the weatherman and his arm candy made a quick trip into the tent together, a hand beckoned from inside, and I grew jittery. I was afraid of being outed as a party crasher for the second time in a month. I started to veer off the line, but an assistant pretty boy in tight black jeans parted the curtain and led me into the tent.

Seated at a table covered in candles and a pile of books (at thirty percent off the cover price) was a woman I vaguely recognized from the sides of buses. She was plump—as plump as you could be and still hold a job on network television—with a red bob. She wore Mardi Gras beads and exuded an unthreatening, matronly aura. I could see why people believed what she told them.

"I'm Renee Ricardo," she said in a voice that was higher than I expected. "Thank you so much for coming out tonight to share *my* good fortune." She gestured to a seat across the table. "Won't you please sit down?"

The chair was warm, and I indulged a tingle at the thought of Adam Mason's molecules clinging to my dress.

"Before you ask me your question, I'd like you to give me something to hold, preferably a piece of metal that's always on your hand, maybe a ring or a watch. I can learn a lot about you from the energy."

So this was all going to be a circus act. Politely, I pulled off the garnet ring my parents had given me on my twenty-first birthday and handed it over. I wondered how fast I could get out of there without offending her.

Renee held the ring between her palms in a prayer pose. I looked over at the assistant. He was thumbing through a copy of Renee's book and chewing his fingernail.

"I'm getting a vibration, but it's not strong enough. Do you have anything else? Let's try your watch."

I unclasped my watch, certain I was about to be outed as an imposter. It had to be the only Timex in the whole building.

"Oh, much better," she said with her eyes closed, smiling. "I'm getting a lot. You have a very solid character and that's making this easy."

Well, I *am* pretty solid, I thought hopefully.

"Your guides are speaking to me. I'm getting a very strong maternal voice. Do you have a mother or grandmother who just passed over?"

"My aunt died this year!" I said excitedly.

"Oh, boy, does she love you. She is watching over you and she is so happy about something." I tried not to think about the fact that I had talked to my aunt about twice a year while she was alive.

"She's saying you recently switched jobs? Or, it's hard to hear exactly . . . she thinks your current job is not exactly right for you."

Why hadn't I gone to a fortune-teller before?

"Both," I shouted. The assistant looked over at us. I lowered my voice. "Both. I recently switched, well, yeah, switched jobs *and* I don't think it's the right job for me!" I could barely catch my breath.

"Okay." Renee opened her eyes and looked at me, smiling. "What would you like me to ask your aunt?"

My mind was reeling. This was a momentous opportunity. What did I most need to know?

How long will I be a super?

Will I ever stop looking for Hayden?

What am I going to be when I grow up?

"Am I supposed to get involved with Gregory Samson?" I blurted out.

Renee smiled at me.

"Wait!" I said. "I don't want that to be my one question."

"You can ask more than one question," she said kindly.

"I can?" I thought about how to phrase what I wanted to know without letting on that I was responsible for disposing of people's garbage and had no right to be at her book party. "Am I ever going to . . . to . . . find work that makes me happy?"

Renee closed her eyes again and furrowed her brow.

I fidgeted. The assistant spit out some chewed-off finger-nail and looked over at us.

"Yes," Renee said quietly. "You will be very happy. Some-time soon, you will discover what it is you want to be doing—"

"How soon?" I interrupted. Was I imagining it or did a look of impatience flicker across her foundation-saturated face?

"In the next two years," she said crisply. "And actually, you are going to spend your life with Gregory Samson. Con-gratulations! Would you like to purchase a copy of my book at thirty percent off the cover price?"

EIGHT

AFTER JUST TWO WEEKS, I WAS ALREADY RESIGNED TO Mrs. Hannaham's wake-up calls. When the phone rang the next morning, I wondered whether the sententious "early to bed, early to rise makes a man healthy, wealthy, and wise" had in fact been coined out of resignation: perhaps Ben Franklin just lived next door to Mrs. Hannaham's annoying ancestors.

"There are strange people going into her apartment," Mrs. Hannaham croaked into my ear at seven-fifteen.

My bladder was about to burst. I took the phone into the bathroom and sat down on the toilet.

"I'm sorry, who's speaking?" I couldn't resist needling her.

"Zephyr, this is Mrs. Compton Hannaham, your tenant on the garden level. What is that sound? Is something leaking?"

I was leaking and I didn't plan on stopping. I hoped my hearing was that good when I was her age.

"It's the faucet," I told her. "I'm doing dishes."

"Make sure you use the Joy and not the Ivory. The Ivory doesn't get the china as clean."

"Gotcha," I said, thinking about my chipped IKEA "china." I rested my elbows on my knees and closed my eyes.

"So?"

"So what?"

"So there are strange people in her apartment," Mrs. Hannaham growled.

"Whose apartment?" I said, cementing my place in hell for needlessly tormenting a lonely old woman.

"You know," Mrs. Hannaham said ominously. *"Hers."*

I said nothing.

"Mrs. *Boureau.*"

"What kind of strange people?" I was too tired to get off the toilet so I paged through an old water-stained *New Yorker*, skimming for cartoons.

"Men, women. Un*seem*ly men and women. At all hours of the night."

I suspected that Mrs. Hannaham construed any hour after eight as "all hours."

"Okay. Well, I'll talk to her about it." I yawned loudly.

"You should take something for that cold," she instructed before she hung up. For a moment, I pictured her shuffling around her white apartment, straightening the white feather boas she sometimes wore, looking through photos of Compton (no doubt in white frames), and I tried to feel sorry for her. I really tried.

I flushed the toilet and hurled myself back into bed. Now I could go back to thinking about Gregory and our definite future together, beginning with what I would wear when he came over to help fix my parents' dryer that afternoon.

Renee Ricardo's predictions the night before had been met with a certain amount of skepticism.

"You're a damned fool," Tag said. After Lucy had taken her turn inside the fortune-teller's tent, we reconvened on a corner of the roof that had an unfettered view of the Hudson River.

"But how can she say things that aren't true?" I insisted, swirling the ice in my glass. "She'd be out of a job. Mobs of people would be pounding down her door demanding a refund."

"She's paid by the network."

I shook my head. "I'm sorry, she *knew* things about me. And she was so certain about Gregory and me." I really did love saying our names together, so much that I forgot my promise to myself not to talk about Gregory in front of Lucy.

"What did she know about you?"

I didn't want to repeat the bit about my strong character. Tag would rip me to shreds.

"She knew my aunt had died." It was practically true.

Tag frowned.

"She knew I was in a job that wasn't right for me."

"That's fish in a barrel. Most people think their job isn't right for them."

"You don't," I shot back.

I ran my hand along the smooth copper railing. "She had so much confidence. In me. No one is ever willing to say things with any certainty, not even my parents. We're all so careful and realistic."

Tag opened her mouth, but I interrupted her.

"Look, I'm willing to accept that she's not really a psychic, but what if she's unusually talented at sizing up a person quickly and knowing what they're capable of? I feel like I should do everything possible to make something happen with—" I stopped short, glancing at Lucy. "With any guy that might come along. I'm more certain that it's worth trying, is all."

"She said you'd spend your life with Gregory," Lucy finally piped up. "She didn't say *how*, Zephyr. He might be your exterminator forever, not your husband."

Lucy was bitter because, she claimed, Renee had told her she was going to die.

"Exactly," Tag said to Lucy. "So why can't you apply that logic to what she said to you, dipshit? You asked her whether you're going to die. Why, I have no idea, but you did. And she said yes, you are. I could have told you that."

"If it wasn't going to be soon, she wouldn't have said it," Lucy said, feeling—understandably, I thought—sorry for herself. She had downed two caipirinhas after emerging from Renee's tent and was getting pretty droopy.

"You two are getting on my nerves," Tag announced. "Where's Mercedes?"

We looked over to where we'd left her, but there was no sign of her or Dover Carter. We scoured the deck and then searched the ladies' room. We went downstairs and asked Tiffany, who was sitting on the bouncer's stool rubbing her feet.

"What does your friend look like?" she asked in a bored voice, her enthusiasm for our attendance apparently a thing of the past.

"Tall black woman in a blue-and-green strapless dress," I told her. "Head scarf, too."

Tiffany perked up.

"Oh, she left with Dover Carter!"

"Willingly?" Tag asked suspiciously. Tiffany looked at her like she was insane.

"Call her," I instructed Lucy. She punched Mercedes's number into her phone and immediately my handbag started ringing.

I remembered. "Shit. She gave me her phone to hold because it didn't fit in her bag."

"What kind of asinine purse doesn't have room for a phone?" Tag demanded.

"A really pretty beaded one," Lucy slurred admiringly.

Now, as I lay in bed, I remembered guiltily how quickly we had convinced ourselves that Mercedes was fine, using the same logic I had used to validate Renee Ricardo's credentials: Dover Carter couldn't afford any bad publicity and therefore Mercedes was not in any danger.

I grabbed my phone again and dialed Mercedes's home number. Her machine started to pick up, but then she answered, cutting off her recorded voice.

"It's seven-thirty in the freaking morning," she snarled. Mercedes had trained herself not to curse, arguing that a black woman trying to make it in the world of classical music had to hold herself up to a higher standard. It was a favored pastime of the rest of the Sterling Girls to see if we could make her slip up.

"Seven-forty and I was *worried* about you," I said, trying to make her feel guilty.

"It's a little late to worry," she replied haughtily.

My stomach clenched.

"Why?" I sat up. "What happened? What did he do to you?"

I imagined Mercedes tearfully telling her story on *Dateline*. I'd sit beside her, holding her hand for strength as she recounted how devastating it had been to have no one believe her except, of course, for her closest friends. We would start a foundation for the victims of celebrities. What would we name it?

"Nothing. I'll call you later." I heard the ping of her viola.

"You big fat liar! You've been practicing for an hour already, haven't you?"

Then I heard muffled voices.

"Mercedes," I enunciated slowly. "Is Dover Carter in your apartment *right now*?"

"Wait, what? Sorry, I dropped the phone."

I stood on my bed. "ARE YOU GIVING DOVER CARTER A PRIVATE CONCERT AT SEVEN-THIRTY IN THE FUCK-ING MORNING?!" I screamed.

"Seven-forty," she said, and hung up.

I looked at my phone in disbelief and jumped down to the floor. This is huge, was all I could think as I stomped into my living room. Huge. Huger than huge, and it's too early to call anyone. *My* friend spent the night with the man of, literally, my dreams. Which of us would be her maid of honor? The right thing would be for all of us to be bridesmaids and have no maid of honor, I decided.

I looked out the front window and congratulated myself on not feeling jealous. Not exactly jealous. Well, I was jealous, but only because my current career would never, in this three-dimensional world, capture a movie star's interest. There was no scenario in which Dover Carter would have spotted me across a crowded roof deck and recognize me as the object of his obses-sion. "You take care of your parents' building? I arrange my shoots around . . ." Around what? The tax assessor's schedule? Street-cleaning hours? I waved away the depressing thought.

My phone rang and I raced back to it.

"Mercedes?" I said.

"Abigail," Abigail said grimly.

I looked at my clock yet again.

"Isn't it the middle of the night for you?"

"Men suck." She was trying to sound annoyed, but I heard a quiver in her voice.

"Oh, no." Damn. Now there was no way I could share the news about Mercedes and Dover. Not this minute anyway.

"Honey, what happened?" I padded into the kitchen and filled up the teakettle. I wiped at a stain on the counter, calcu-lating that it would take about an hour to clean the apartment before Gregory showed up.

"What happened is, my sister finished her dissertation, landed the Yale job, and then found her husband within a year. It worked for her, it was supposed to work for me. But it's been *two* years since I finished!" I almost laughed at how surprised she sounded that life didn't adhere to the Greenfield family syllabus, but she sounded too wounded to joke.

"Ab, what *happened*?"

"Darren."

"The guy from JDate?" I dug around the drawers of my fridge and came up with a block of cheddar cheese. "But I thought he lives here."

"He's out here for a week for a conference. We went out three times, but only fooled around for the first time last night. I mean tonight."

I heard a door slam on her end.

"Cat out," she explained dejectedly. "So we've been having a great time. He's cute, Zeph, really cute." Her voice faded away.

"And?" I prompted, biting into the cheese.

"And really smart. He's the step-grandson of Athol Baron."

"Abigail, I don't know who that is, but does that mean your guy's name is Darren Baron?" I watched the flame flicker beneath the kettle and wondered whether I was responsible for forming an evacuation plan in the event of a gas leak.

"He's not my guy and his last name is Schwartz. He's so smart and he gave this phenomenal paper on theoretical linguistics . . ." She paused, not wanting to insult my intelligence. "Well, he gave this great paper and I thought we were clicking. He really listened."

"Uh-oh."

"So we're messing around—"

"How much?"

"Shirts off."

"Bra?"

"Still on."

"Prude," I said, as the kettle whistled.

"You know, I can't even find Bengal Spice tea out here," Abigail whined.

"So you're fooling around . . ." I prompted.

"And . . . I still can't believe this. You know, the more I think about it, the more I'm just livid. What a shit! What kind of man says things like that?"

"Abigail!" I said. "What *happened*?"

"He told me I was too Jewish-looking," she admitted.

I slammed down my cheese. "The guy you met on a Jewish dating site said you looked *too Jewish*?"

"And he said I was too chubby. He said he likes thin Asian women."

I had never met this guy, but I wanted to make him walk naked down Broadway in a blizzard. No, that was too irrelevant. I wanted to publicly humiliate him, break his heart, get him to beg for Abigail's love. I wanted to string him up, kick him in the guts, and watch him bawl like a baby. My throat closed up with bile.

"What did *you* say?!" I sputtered.

"I told him he was an insensitive prick and kicked him out. About a half hour ago." I heard her door open and close again. "How can an educated, normal-seeming man . . . ? Zeph, I really liked him." I pictured her in her spacious, faculty-subsidized kitchen: shoulders hunched, an oversized Near Eastern Language Association T-shirt hanging to her knees, one finger yanking at her curls. It made my heart hurt and I loathed the three thousand miles between us.

"So who's next?" I wanted her to move on.

Abigail groaned. "It's slim pickin's out here in the mild, mild west. The sun's deep-fried their brains. That's why I was trying to import." She sniffed. "When I told him he was a prick, he didn't even understand what he'd done that was so bad."

"Oh, Ab."

"Forget it. He's headed back to New York tomorrow anyway. I'm going to do one of those eight-minute speed-dating things. It sounds extremely efficient." I could hear her psychically picking herself up and brushing herself off. "So what did you guys do tonight? I mean last night. Tell me how much fun you're having without me."

"It's never fun without you!" I said automatically. I dunked the tea bag in a mug I'd picked up in Mexican Hat, Utah, during a cross-country drive with Abigail and Tag to celebrate the acquisition of their respective Ph.D.s. The cup was a reminder of one of the best trips I've ever taken; it was also a stained porcelain memento of how undereducated I was compared to my friends, who, among the four of them, were an alphabet soup of advanced degrees. But they loved me and I wanted to torture any guy who mistreated any one of them.

"Liar."

"We crashed a party at Soho House. A fortune-teller told Lucy she's going to die," I said offhandedly. An idea was beginning to needle the back of my brain.

"Soon?" Abigail sounded worried.

"Unclear." I sipped at my tea. "Abigail, wait. There's something that might be worth trying. How do you post a profile on JDate?"

AT NOON, CLAD IN MY PERFECTLY PAINT-STAINED LEVI'S THAT suggested a can-do kind of gal (Zephyr helps her friends paint murals, stage sets, and kitchens!) and a long-sleeved, low-plunging white shirt that clung in the right places and miraculously made my tummy roll go on furlough for a few hours, I did a privacy check of my apartment.

I started in the living room, removing all issues of *Us Weekly* and strategically tossing a couple of *National Geographics* and yesterday's *New York Times* on the coffee table. I peered into my basket of mail and bills and covered my bank statement with a donation solicitation from public radio. On the pad next to my phone, I scribbled "Pete" and "Mark" so it would look like I had a flock of men in my life. I added "Hayden." Then I crossed it out. Then I wrote it in again.

I rearranged some framed photos on the bookshelf, remembering James's creepy portrait duet still holding court across the hall. I put the picture of the five Sterling Girls looking like a Banana Republic ad in front of the others. Tag's half brother—son of trophy wife number one—had taken it the year before when we'd spent the better part of an autumn Saturday raking leaves at her father's country house. We looked downright enviable in our twiggy, tousled joy.

In the kitchen, I hid the Entenmann's devil's food cake that was ragged with fork furrows and put the cheddar cheese riddled with teeth marks at the back of the fridge. I pushed the box of Corn Pops behind the granola.

In the bathroom I hid the plaque rinse, but left out the fluoride rinse. I didn't want him to think I was obsessive about keeping my teeth clean (which I was). I debated about the box of condoms. Sexy or overkill? Sophisticated if it was in the right place. I tucked it inside the medicine chest, off to the side, so he'd see it if he opened the cabinet, but where I couldn't be accused of flaunting it.

At twelve-fifteen the intercom buzzed. I looked out the window and saw the top of Gregory's head, the mere sight of which made me inexplicably happy. He stepped back and looked up at my window. I threw myself onto the floor.

Fifteen minutes early? I thought as I jungle-crawled out of his line of sight. What kind of sick game was this guy playing?

"I'll be right down," I shouted through the intercom. I stood there a moment, pissed off and excited. Excited the way I used to be before sixth-grade dances, which is to say achingly and irrationally so, because the objects of my affection were inevitably huddled in a corner fervently recounting to one another what David Letterman had thrown off the studio's roof the night before.

I went downstairs and opened the door, which was unbolted. I'd have to put up a safety notice reminding everyone to double lock the door. That thought made me feel professional, responsible, and instantly more attractive, like a streak of eyeshadow for my ego.

I immediately got what Lucy calls the yummies when I saw him. His hair looked more golden than it had the day before and he gave off a woodsy scent. He wore jeans with a deep red button-down shirt that set off his olive skin. I wondered whether he'd dressed as carefully for me as I had for him.

He smiled at me tentatively. He was nervous! Ha.

"How was the trip from Idaho?" I asked, proud of hitting the right note. Flirtatious, witty, able to acknowledge my own foibles.

"Idowa," he said with a trace of a grin.

"Idowa," I agreed.

He was still standing on the stoop.

"So, where do you want to go?" he asked.

"Um," I hesitated, "the dryer?"

"Never heard of it, but sounds fine." He glanced down at my bare feet. "I'll wait here."

Suddenly I was embarrassed that he was being decent and date-like while I'd been planning on holding him to a proposal I'd made in a moment of anger. I lost my nerve.

"Okay, I'll be right back."

I ran upstairs. I was hunting around for my wallet when Gregory appeared at my apartment door.

"I just realized what you meant by 'dryer,' " he said coolly. "You meant *dryer*." I saw the surly look from our first encounter start to creep back into his face.

"No." I waved away the idea. "No, let's go have coffee. You don't have to look at my parents' dryer." I tried to make it sound like some irrational third party had suggested it.

He nodded up the stairs.

"C'mon. It was part of the deal."

He's very moody and very intense, I heard myself reporting to the Sterling Girls. I really did want to go on a date with this guy, especially if I was going to wind up marrying him. I opened my mouth to plead with him to let it drop, but he just crossed his arms and arched his eyebrows at me.

Fine. I grabbed my keys and stomped up the two flights to my old home. Just as I turned the knob, I realized I hadn't called ahead to see if my parents were presentable to a non-Zuckerman. I offered up a quick prayer that they weren't there.

"Zephy!" my mother trilled before I could even wrestle the key out of the lock.

"Darling daught!" my father bellowed cheerfully.

"Are you guys decent?" I called out, smiling weakly at Gregory. I peeked around the door.

"Wow," Gregory said quietly from behind me.

It's no small miracle that my parents were able to locate Gideon and me and send us to school every day for eighteen years. Their home is an homage, my mother likes to say, to their limitless engagement with the world. Others might say it is the outward manifestation of their inner psychosis.

Ollie and Bella Zuckerman had never met a hobby they wouldn't try, and their apartment contained elements of all of them. By the window were some desiccated, crumbling branches from their forest-furniture-making phase. Next to the quilting corner were the metal jewelry-making tools, acquired at no small expense. Stuffed under an armchair were Renaissance instruments whose names I did not know and it didn't really matter anyway because they were mostly obscured by the footprint maps for traditional Greek dances. I loved my parents dearly, but their enthusiasm was oppressive.

Still in their sweaty biking clothes, Bella and Ollie were sprawled across the sectional couch, their collection of American folk crafts looming in wicker chaos on shelves above them. Empty cups of coffee and glasses filled with green energy drink made wet rings on the glass table. My mom's feet were in my dad's lap and it looked like the Sunday paper was holding them hostage. The dining room table held the picked-over remnants of lox and bagels and what appeared to be my father's homemade apple strudel.

"Why didn't you call me for brunch?" I asked petulantly, forgetting for a moment that a strange man stood beside me, awaiting an introduction.

"You missed the most fabulous bagels! Chewy inside, a little tough on the outside. A perfect morning!" My dad pushed aside my mom's feet, peeled off a few sections of newspaper, and rose up to his full height. He held his arms out and I dutifully let myself be enveloped.

From the crook of his arm, I could see my mom giving Gregory the once-over.

"Aren't you—?"

"This is Gregory," I interrupted, disentangling myself from my father. "He's going to help with the dryer." I felt like I was insulting him, but really, what else was I supposed to tell my parents? I met this guy Monday and we're going to try to go on a date if we can manage five minutes without bickering?

"But aren't you the exterminator?" my mom persisted, looking at him over her reading glasses.

"I am," Gregory told her, not volunteering anything further. The man had the social graces of a sewer rat.

"Really?" my dad piped up, squinting at Gregory. "You don't—"

"No, I don't look like one," Gregory said quietly. "I don't look like a dryer repairman either, but that's what I'm here to do."

My mother glanced over at me questioningly and rubbed her fingers together: is this going to be expensive?

"Ah," said my dad, pulling his chin. He studied Gregory openly, and Gregory met his gaze.

"Da-ad." I pulled at his sleeve, trying to think of a way to end the uncomfortable encounter.

"Let me tell you what *I* think is wrong with the machine." He gestured to Gregory to follow him. I watched them push through the swinging door together. Son-in-law! I thought involuntarily.

I looked at my mother, who was frowning in spite of the single Botox treatment she wouldn't admit she'd had.

"He really doesn't look like an exterminator." She sucked in her breath. "Maybe he's FBI! Oh, Zephy, do you think he's investigating Daddy? After the Wheeler nightmare, I bet they're on the lookout for other bad eggs in the bureau . . ."

"Mom!" She was so absurd sometimes that I was embarrassed for her. I shoved my own undercover cop theory to the back of my mind and grabbed a plate from the rough-hewn cabinet they'd picked up two years ago during an antiquing weekend. For nearly every weekend since, my mother had been planning to refinish it.

"Speaking of bad eggs," she said dramatically as I piled a bagel with the smoked fish that was, by all rights, mine. "Did

Officer Varlam reach you?" I shook my head. "James pleaded guilty right off the bat. Three counts of mail fraud."

"Wow." I scooped up some pastry crumbs with my fingers and shook my head, still unable to connect the American thug with the British charmer who'd laughed at all my jokes and taken out my garbage for the past decade. "I wonder how much time he'll get."

"Do you think we really had a psychologically unsound man going in and out of our apartments all these years?" my mom wondered. "I mean, did you get a load of that Brooklyn accent?"

"Well, either way," I said with feigned confidence, "I've been looking through his paperwork to see whether James was stealing from us." It was going to be true soon. I glanced over at my mother to see if she was impressed.

"Oh, I checked the books from time to time," she said, nonchalantly uncoiling herself from the couch. "If he stole anything from us, it had to be minimal. Cost of business." She waved away the idea. "Make sure you try the sable."

"There's none left," I said pointedly as I pulled a chair up to the food.

A loud crash came from the other side of the door. "We're fine, we're fine!" my father yelled.

My mother beamed proudly. "He can fix anything."

So why didn't you ask him to do it instead of me? I wanted to ask. What is this test I'm taking and when will I know whether I've passed it? But I kept my mouth shut because I am like a Mormon with caffeine when it comes to confrontation: I just don't do it.

And anyway, I knew the answer. I would pass the test when I found a real job.

No, not a job.

A career.

Fair enough.

While I had an entire argument with my mother inside my head—which I ultimately lost—she said carefully, "So now we, I mean you, can rent out James's apartment." She began to pile up dishes.

I grabbed a cream-cheese-caked knife before she could take it away.

"Eva Lowell knows a great real estate agent," she offered. So much for my scheme to handpick a hottie to share my landing.

A rushing-water sound followed by a slam reminded me that Gregory was still on the premises. Here was my plan: first, have coffee with him. Second, see whether we could have a conversation. If not, then third: fill James's old apartment with a new contender for future love of my life, someone whose work as a developer of clean water systems in India, a designer of flood-proof homes in Louisiana, or a foe of the plastic-bag industry would illuminate new professional paths for me.

"First," said my mother, "you'll need to get James's stuff out of there. Then you'll need to get the place cleaned. Then you can call Eva's agent to see what you can get for it."

I preferred my plan.

"Zephy?"

She paused outside the kitchen door, her arms filled with plates, and studied me. I licked my knife, something I knew drove her up a wall. ("You can't put a Band-Aid on your tongue!" she used to yell at Gideon.) She shook her head, her thick, silver French braids brushing stiffly against her shoulders, and chose not to take the bait.

"How's it going?" she asked gently. I shoved a piece of bagel into my mouth and shrugged. I had hoped to avoid directly acknowledging the fact that my life was in limbo for the foreseeable future. I had hoped that one day very soon, before I became too identified as the new James, I would come upstairs and announce that I had found my true calling as a . . . a . . . psychologist? Stevedore? Sewer builder?

She nodded, then looked away, something the CEO of MWP did not normally do.

"Daddy and I decided that whatever you're able to rent James's apartment for will be your salary. It's not income we ever had before anyway, and, well, you need to earn cash," she added, delicately broaching the subject we had all sidestepped for the past two weeks.

I stared at her. Forget the hottie with the heart of gold. I was going to find a stockbroker and milk him. Or her. How much could I get? It didn't even matter. I would have steady income. When was the last time I'd had that? Never. Never was the last time I'd had a steady income. My one year of med school qualified me to tutor the over-scheduled children of anxious, wealthy parents, and while it provided me with enough money for cheese and subway fare, it was hardly the stuff on which great fortunes are built.

I swigged some green juice to hide my excitement and promptly gagged. I looked at my mother accusingly.

"Beet greens and lime," she explained. "So, what do you think?"

I nodded casually. "I think that could work."

"Excellent." She seemed relieved. "By the way," she nodded her head toward the door and adjusted her stack of plates, "the exterminator, who I really don't believe is an exterminator, is very cute."

Gregory pushed open the door.

"Oh, crap," was all I could mutter as I hid behind another sip of mossy elixir.

"Thank you," Gregory said to my mother.

"You're welcome," she replied, not missing a beat. "Did you fix my dryer?"

My father emerged from the kitchen, which is when I noticed that both of them were damp from the waist up, their hair plastered to their foreheads. He clapped a hand on Gregory's shoulder.

"Did he ever!? This lad is amazing. Amazing, I tell you!"

"Why are you wet?" I asked, unable to look Gregory in the eye. I felt myself turn red as soon as the word "wet" escaped me.

"Because the washing machine also needed our attention," Gregory answered. I glanced over to see whether he was being nasty, but his expression was deadpan. How could I spend my life with someone I couldn't read?

"I need you to let me into the alley so I can see where the dryer's venting," Gregory said in my direction.

Alley. Venting. Gregory pushing me up against a wall, determined, gentle, taking my face between his hands, forcing me to lock eyes with him. Taunting me with the nearness of his full lips. One hand sliding down over my hip and lingering. His exposed collarbone begging my fingers to unbutton his shirt.

My brain might have been scrambling the words "venting" and "panting," but there I was, standing in my parents' dining room, suddenly flushed and short of breath.

"He thinks it's stopped up, and hot damn, I think he's right!" my father said proudly. "The pipe's not fully penetrating the wall."

Penetrating. Oh, no.

NINE

I FOLLOWED GREGORY DOWN THE STAIRS WITH IMPENDING First Kiss Shakes. I reminded myself that *he* didn't know he might be making out with me in the alley just a few minutes from now. He had not expressed any interest in such an activity at all.

But *he* had called *me* yesterday. He'd asked me to dinner. Which I had turned into "dryer."

None of this meant he wanted to kiss me. But why not? I was kissable. Was he a religious fanatic? Did he not believe in sex before marriage? Did he know that when I sat down my naked thighs looked like a profile of two Mr. Potato Heads kissing? Didn't he at least want to seduce me to get closer to the James case?

But James's case was closed, my mother had just told me. Which meant Gregory wasn't an undercover cop.

Before I could fully process this new information (new to me, not to him), Gregory stopped short on the landing to avoid barreling into Roxana and a busty little fireplug of a blonde.

My boiling libido didn't prevent me from torquing like Rubber Man to get a peek inside Roxana's apartment, an enclave of French mystique I'd never been inside, not even the day that Gregory sprayed the apartments—Lucy and I had been too busy silently squabbling over his attention on the landing. For my efforts, I was rewarded with a quick view of a framed print of something minimalist hanging above a low, hard-looking sofa slipcovered in a tallowy yellow, which was set before a thick Turkish rug.

That was all I got before Roxana pulled the door closed and locked it. I felt vaguely disappointed. On the other hand, there was Roxana's companion to feast on. In less than twenty-four hours, I had now encountered two of my neighbor's acquaintances, which was two more than I'd seen in the three years she'd been living at 287 West 12th.

The blonde looked like an even shorter Dolly Parton minus the I've-got-millions-in-the-bank-and-Jesus-on-my-side joy. Mini-Dolly was Soviet steely, though her eyes brightened predatorily when she looked up at Gregory, an act that apparently required her to arch her back. She was everything Roxana wasn't: zaftig, garishly dressed, excessively accessorized.

Roxana's face fell when she saw me, and I immediately felt apologetic, as if I were on a mission to invade her privacy.

"Hallo, Zepheer," she said dejectedly. She offered no frenzied introduction as she had with Senator Smith the night before.

No one really wanted to be on that landing except, creepily, Mini-Dolly, who was still sizing up Gregory. I flashed what I hoped was a reassuring "I'm not spying on you" smile at Roxana and continued down the stairs. Gregory followed me outside.

On the stoop, in the newly warm, sweet air, Gregory gave

me an amused, conspiratorial look that said: "What was *that* about?" Which meant he was emotionally sensitive, tuned in to subtle interpersonal nuances, and had a sense of humor.

I couldn't wait to get into the alley.

I COULD IMAGINE LOSING OUT IN ROMANCE TO AN ESTIMABLE competitor like, say, Roxana, but I never predicted I'd be in competition with a Frigidaire dryer for a man's attention. Whereas Mini-Dolly had elicited nothing more than a raised eyebrow from Gregory, my parents' sonorous appliance was completely monopolizing his attention.

We stood in the alley behind my building, a place I had only ever visited a handful of times. I generally tried to avoid the rank, narrow space, which was really no place for a first kiss. Gregory craned his neck to examine the line of exhaust vents at the base of each floor.

I glanced at the shriveled, graying cigarette butts littering the ground like desiccated worms—who were the philistines chucking their crap into our alley?—and felt my skin crawl with an urgent desire to get out of there. My desire to kiss Gregory was rapidly dwindling, and without it, I was just wasting a beautiful Sunday afternoon in an alley with an exterminator.

"Can you tell what's wrong?" I said, trying to appear helpful while, in fact, I was noticing that Gregory's butt was a little on the flat side. His thighs, though, pressed against his jeans as he shifted his weight, broadcasting their strength.

"Not from here. If I could get to the top of this, maybe I could get a closer look." He rattled the handle of a door leading to an enclosed, two-story staircase that ran up the side of the building. "Where do these go to?"

Since high school, I had toyed with the idea of joining the

CIA. Tag always shot down my dream on the grounds that I couldn't keep a secret and that my powers of observation were non-existent. I rarely noticed a new haircut, a twenty-pound loss of weight, or a reupholstered couch, but I argued that these minutiae weren't important in cosmic, existential ways. I noticed important things.

The question confronting me now was: could a brand-new, locked, tunnel-like stairway on my property be considered important?

The few visits I'd made into the alley over the years had been kept as brief and myopic as possible—to show the fire inspector around when James was on vacation, to help the Caldwells retrieve a photograph that had blown out of their window—but still, I was certain I would have noticed a staircase. A whole staircase, enclosed in rough, unpainted plywood. A staircase that appeared to have a landing on the second floor and that ended on the third floor.

Except I wasn't certain. I cursed Tag as my dream of wearing a slinky dress at a cocktail party in the Uffizi and coaxing an international secret out of an Antonio Banderas look-alike with a five-o-clock shadow vanished. Had that staircase really always been there? How could it not have been? A staircase couldn't just be erected without anyone noticing. Without *me* noticing. Could it?

I took a turn at rattling the cheap, hollow knob, as if I could shake loose a missing memory.

"It goes to the third floor," I finally said.

"I can see that," Gregory replied. I pressed my lips together and threw pride to the winds.

"I've never seen this staircase before."

Gregory crossed his arms and looked me in the eye, but not the way I'd imagined fifteen minutes ago.

"I know that sounds retarded—"

"You're not allowed to say retarded," he interrupted.

"I refuse to be dictated to by the P.C. lexicon," I said shortly.

"My sister has learning disabilities," Gregory said warningly.

"Just like you're really from Iowa."

"Idaho."

I glared at him until he finally smiled. "Okay, not from Idaho, no sister, *mentally challenged* or otherwise. Are you telling me you've lived in this building—how long . . . ?"

"My whole life," I admitted.

"Your whole life, and you never noticed this stairwell?"

"No, I'm saying I think this stairwell is new." I think, I hope.

"You think?"

"No." I brushed away my doubt. "It's new. It's *new*."

"How new?"

"Since the last time I was back here."

"Which was?" He certainly *sounded* like an undercover cop.

To admit to Gregory how infrequently I ventured into the grotty parts of my family estate was to reveal how irresponsible, spoiled, and timid I was. This afternoon had officially lost all prospects of morphing into a date.

"About a year." As I studied the unimpressive structure, trying to atone for my earlier inattention, I suddenly realized what it was. "It's a fire escape!" I announced, impressed that James had had the concern and foresight to provide for the tenants' safety. I felt a stab of inadequacy, knowing I would never have taken such initiative as super.

Gregory frowned. "Then why wouldn't it go all the way to the roof? And why would it be made of wood?"

I shrugged.

"Well, if there's a door at the top of this thing, on the third floor, I could climb on top and get closer to the vent on the fourth floor. Let me have those keys Laurie labeled," he said, holding out his hand.

"You mean Lucy?"

"Lucy."

I felt a pang of pity for her. I handed over the key ring, which I'd run upstairs to retrieve after encountering the new lock that James had attached to the alley gate. For my trouble, I'd been rewarded with a snippet of argument between Roxana and Mini-Dolly on the landing above. I made enough noise to show I wasn't spying, but not so much that I couldn't hear them.

"What the fuck am I supposed to do? I need this," Mini-Dolly whined. Unsurprisingly, Mini-Dolly did not have Roxana's dulcet Franco tones.

"I am surry, but you are nut my prawblem enimore," Roxana told her quietly.

"You *are*. You *are* gonna be sorry," Mini-Dolly whispered melodramatically. A door slammed and I scurried out of the building, jumpy with curiosity. What could Mini-Dolly possibly need from Roxana? Why were they even breathing the same oxygen in the first place?

Now, back in the alley, none of the keys were working in the staircase lock, which made me hopeful. If I could get Gregory to forget about the dryer, we could get lattes and walk by the river and maybe just happen to catch the sunset over Hoboken. A sunset, even a Jersey sunset, was a surefire kiss catalyst.

"Let's see if we can get into the staircase through James's apartment." Gregory squinted up at the first landing. "It looks like it goes into his place." He headed for the gate.

It was bad enough that we were getting intimate with the alley, but the thought of picking around James's sty of an apartment was too much. What would Roxana do in my situation?

"Wait!"

Gregory turned to look at me.

"You called me last night for a . . ." *Date* was such a prissy word, I realized at that moment. "To get together. I didn't mean for you to spend the day on this," I gestured at the staircase.

Gregory crossed his arms. "But you did," he said, his eyes wide and innocent. "You said if I fixed your parents' dryer, you'd take me out to coffee."

Was he a wiseass or a dolt? Maybe he really did have a simple sister. Maybe slowness ran in the family. What would I do if faced with a conclusive genetic test?

"You've done enough for the dryer for today," I began carefully.

"I'm glad you think so," he said sarcastically.

And then, fueled by a clean blast of air scented by the apple tree in the front yard, I came to the end of my tolerance for Gregory. No one was worth this much trouble this early on. This wasn't heavy on the happy; this was saggy with snarky. Bloated with badinage. I'd flirt with Cliff, find a sexy tenant, date Dover Carter's ugly brother if he had one. I'd wasted enough time on Gregory Samson, Uppity Vermin Killer.

"You know what?" I said coldly, emboldened by Roxana's display of moxie with Mini-Dolly. "Enough. I've known you for less than a week and I'm already tired of you and your mixed signals and your weird, asocial way of talking, and your rude—"

"Asocial?" he asked. "I thought I was being straightforward."

"*This* is what I'm talking about," I said, pushing past him for the gate. "This little . . ."

"Repartee?"

"Yes, *repartee*," I said, exasperated. "I'm not interested in this!"

"What *are* you interested in?" he said quietly. It wasn't hostile or accusatory, but I wasn't going to be fooled.

"What?" I said, shaking my head and reaching for the latch on the gate. "You're doing it again—stop it! I'm *not* interested in being tired before I even begin."

He grabbed my hand, and I turned back, startled by his touch.

"So are we beginning something?" he asked hopefully.

"I don't know!" I yelled, and stomped my foot childishly. "Not at this rate!" I glared at him. I felt like Alice down the rabbit hole, if Alice had hit puberty in 21st-century Greenwich Village. Did that make Gregory the Mad Hatter? I wondered wildly. The Cheshire Cat?

And then Gregory did what he was supposed to do in the first place. He pushed me up against the gate gently but firmly, took my face in his hands, studied me for a moment, and then kissed me.

He softly kissed my lower lip. My upper lip. Then each corner of my mouth. I grabbed on to the bars of the gate to steady myself. For once, my entire body—all limbs and all brain matter—was perfectly focused, in unison, on one thing: where the next kiss was going to land.

Just as a moan of unbridled desire was about to escape me, Gregory softly covered my mouth with his. Not sloppy, not rushed. The most flawless kiss I have ever had the magnificent fortune to receive. A paragon of kisses. A kiss that convinced me that all my nerve endings were actually located in my mouth and that this man was able to trigger any extremity and any organ he wanted with a gentle flick of his tongue.

He touched his hips lightly to mine, with just enough pressure that I was obliged to grab his ass—it wasn't nearly as flat as it looked—and pull him to me so hard that his arm slipped and hit the gate behind me. He groaned in pain, jumping back to rub his elbow.

"Nooo!" I wailed, instantly mourning the premature end of our first kiss.

Gregory made a whooshing sound, inhaling through his teeth, trying to will a quick recovery. He looked at me and we chuckled at each other. Suddenly I had a terrible thought: how would I explain this to Lucy? Lucy, who was going to die. Someday.

Just yesterday, I'd assured her that Gregory was only interested in Mrs. Hannaham's mouse holes. If anything developed between him and me, it was supposed to have taken much longer than this. It was supposed to have happened because he was investigating James.

"Are you really an exterminator?" I blurted out.

He stopped rubbing his elbow and looked at me irritably. The best kiss I'd ever had was receding into the past at lightning speed.

"*Why?*" he said plaintively. "Why is it so hard to believe?"

"No," I began, "it's just that—" How do you explain to a man the intricacies of a female friendship? "This would all be easier if you were really an undercover cop."

Gregory stopped rubbing his elbow. His expression imparted so much doubt about my sanity that I knew for certain, and with a small whack of disappointment to my gut, that he was not a detective.

"Why in God's name would you ever think I was a cop?" he demanded.

"You don't believe in God, do you?" I said, worriedly.

"What? Wait." he pinched his brow between his thumb and forefinger, and it looked like he might now be the one to halt our inchoate relationship. "I'm a confirmed atheist. Why did you think I was a cop?"

"Because, because . . ." I stopped. I couldn't remember exactly how my brain had wound its way down that path.

"Because I don't look like an exterminator," he said wearily.

"Right!" I remembered. "And because you showed up right after James was arrested."

"I show up every month, whether or not James is arrested," Gregory reminded me.

I spread my arms in defeat and put on my best abashed face. Gregory looked at the sky and let out a small snort of laughter. I exhaled slowly.

"Tell you what," he said. "I like to finish what I start." He held up one finger. "I started to fix a dryer." He held up a second finger. "And I started kissing you."

I bit my lip, titillated by the mere acknowledgment of our intimacy.

"Let's finish dealing with the dryer. Then let's go for coffee and I'll tell you all about my exciting life as an exterminator. And then you can decide whether you want to finish that kiss."

TEN

IN TENTH GRADE, I HAD MY FIRST BOYFRIEND. HIS NAME WAS
Lance and he was a senior who had memorized every lyric
Stephen Sondheim ever penned. His heart was set on attending Carnegie Mellon and he hoped one day to become intimate
with the smell of Broadway greasepaint. Our three-month relationship consisted of a series of infrequent and awkward
make-out sessions on his mother's Upper West Side rooftop,
under the looming wooden water tower. I spent triple the time
of the actual relationship analyzing it with the Sterling Girls.

The best part of dating Lance occurred when he was onstage, playing the lead in Sterling's spring musical, or jazz-
handing his way around the Performing Arts Showcase, or
belting out his solo in Thursday afternoon glee club rehearsals.
His total absorption and consequent obliviousness to me, together with my knowledge that I got to do things with him (if
only of the PG-13 variety) no one else around me did, were
more of a turn-on than any of our inept encounters. It was my
first experience with the watch-and-want phenomenon of lust.

Now, being physically eager and legally permitted to do much more than swirl tongues, the watching was propelling the wanting into the stratosphere. Gregory tore down the sagging police tape in front of James's apartment and strode past my piles of paperwork with a determination that made Lance's fists-at-his-side rendition of "Not a Day Goes By" in the Sterling version of *Merrily We Roll Along* seem downright anemic.

As Gregory scrutinized James's toxic bedroom, I wondered whether watch-and-want could be sustained after decades of marriage. I'd have to remember to ask my parents.

"I think the first landing would come in right about here." Gregory knocked his fist lightly along the wall between the two closets.

Two weeks of inactivity had not improved the odor in the room. I realized that the pizza boxes were still beneath the bed. Did James deliberately set out to attract roaches? Maybe it was a ploy to see Gregory. Maybe James was in love with Gregory. Too bad, I thought triumphantly. He was mine. Well, I was pretty sure he would be mine soon.

Gregory had wanted to go directly to Roxana's apartment, where the exterior staircase appeared to end. I sorely wanted to help him get access so that he could examine the accursed vent and we could resume the kissing portion of our program. But despite the lust pounding in my ears, I wasn't eager to make Roxana invite us in. I had already intruded on her privacy too much in the past day.

Gregory reached for the closet door.

"You have to really yank it," I said knowledgeably, remembering my poor show of strength in front of Mercedes. "There's nothing in there. I already looked."

Gregory opened the door and pushed aside the clothes, squeaking hangers along the metal pole.

"Nothing," he concluded. *Now* could we kiss? I wondered. He headed for the other closet, which, I suddenly realized with a defeated shudder, I had forgotten to try to open last week. I had to face facts: the CIA almost definitely had no use for me.

The door swung open easily, of course. I peered over Gregory's shoulder, resisting the urge to rub my face along it, and saw a sparse array of clothes—the bomber jacket James wore throughout the winter and a couple of frayed raincoats. To one side of the clothes sat a torn cardboard box piled with paint-splattered, rust-encrusted tools.

On the other side of the coats, there lay not the stacks of bundled Benjamins I had briefly imagined I'd find, but to my prurient delight, boxes of condoms in a crowd-pleasing variety of colors and flavors. On the bottom shelf was a tangle of hand-cuffs, some fur-lined (for those cold days), and an array of dil-does that looked like parts of a dismembered Halloween costume. James apparently did not conduct privacy checks. Then again, he probably hadn't planned on calling Rikers Island home.

Gregory coughed.

"Two personalities *and* a sex addiction," I mused, feeling a touch of pride that our super had harbored such colorful dis-orders.

When Gregory pushed back the coats, we were rewarded with a door. It was raggedly set into a hole cut out of the three-brick-thick wall, with pink insulation escaping around the edges.

"I knew it!" He slapped the metal door, then tried the knob. "A fire escape? What kind of fire escape is locked from the inside?"

"James's fire escape," I said, handing over the keys before he asked. Gregory diligently tried all of them—even the ones that Lucy had labeled—though we both already sensed that none would work. I tapped my foot maniacally. This was some kind of appliance-driven morality battle: Gregory's unwavering resolution to fix the dryer versus our—or just my?—baser yearnings.

I leaned back against the doorjamb, then considered the kinds of upright acts that had been performed on that very spot and straightened up again with a shiver of revulsion. The biological atrocity of that apartment was the only thing keeping me from pushing Gregory to the floor and having my way with him.

"You want me to call a locksmith?" I offered halfheartedly.

"Do you really want some stranger to bust open a secret door in your home when you don't know what it's for or where it goes?" Gregory said, handing the key ring back to me.

A secret door? I stared at him.

I had a secret door in my home?

I did. I had a secret door! Mercedes had Dover Carter, but I had a secret door, something that, if I'd thought it was even a remote possibility, I would have longed for all my life.

Who could I tell? Tag was at the museum, having been forced by the director to charm a gaggle of potential donors. Lucy was semi-mad at me. Mercedes was giving free lessons in East Harlem. Abigail lived in a time zone scheduled to slide into the Pacific.

This would stay between Gregory and me. The intimacy of the thought shot a new prickle of longing through my body.

Wordlessly, I rummaged through the pile of tools and came up with a paint scraper. I crouched in front of the lock, which put my head just inches away from Gregory's crotch.

Ever the gentleman, he took a step back.

Channeling my frustration, I wedged the scraper into the flimsy lock and pulled back hard. The door popped open as though it were rooting for me. I jumped back, startled by my prowess, and found myself nestled against Gregory's chest. He tightened his arm around me for an instant, pressing me to him, the back of my thigh to the front of his. I swallowed hard.

Gregory nudged me forward and we stuck our faces through the doorway into cool, stagnant air. He craned his head and looked up and down.

"Pretty dark?" I said stupidly.

"Yeah, and really . . ." he felt around on the wall, "soft."

"What?" I put my hand near his and felt something like silk. And then a light switch. I allowed myself a brief image of triggering trapdoors or explosions, and then flipped it on.

Pink. Pink here, pink there, pink everywhere. Pink carpeting on the stairs, pink silk covering the walls, pink sconces lighting the pink banisters. This rabbit hole was cotton-candy-mates-with-Pepto pink. Barbie orgasm pink.

Gregory puffed out his cheeks in surprise and started to step inside.

"Wait!" I grabbed his arm. "What if it's unstable? Or booby-trapped?"

"Booby-trapped?" he repeated sarcastically. He was either fiercely brave or woefully unimaginative. He jumped hard on the pink-carpeted landing to prove his point.

I followed him onto the landing and looked down toward the door we'd discovered in the alley. Then we both looked up to where the staircase ended. Another pink door. This time, there wasn't much question about where it would lead.

My hesitation to intrude upon Roxana was pre-secret-pink-staircase. My discretion had evaporated as soon as I'd flipped the light switch. Plus, I'd been emboldened by the sight of Roxana leaving the building shortly after her tiff with Mini-Dolly.

Gregory followed me up the creaky stairs. I was walking

where I shouldn't be able to walk. These steps were not supposed to be here, and it felt as if any moment, the illusion would vanish and we'd be cartoonishly spinning our legs in midair.

At the top, I reached for the handle perfunctorily, assuming it would be locked like the other two. But it swung open easily and even Gregory inhaled sharply. My legs wobbled. Had I come in Roxana's front door, it would have been as her super. Coming in this way, through what seemed to be a closet, was probably breaking and entering. It should be entering and breaking, I thought. You enter illegally and then you . . . break things?

Gregory put one finger lightly in the middle of my back.

"Hello," I whispered quietly into the dark. I did a Mr. Magoo probe, tentatively waving my arms in front of me, afraid of what I'd find. My fingers brushed what felt like robes, exactly the kind I'd expect to find in Roxana Boureau's bedroom. Soft, feathery, filmy, but not cheap.

The door behind us swung shut and I felt Gregory start beside me. Ha, I thought and then wondered why I was bent on spotting the ways in which he was human, as if he were a myth that demanded debunking.

We stood still for a moment, our eyes adjusting to the dim shapes. Gregory reached past me and felt for a light switch, but I grabbed his arm.

"Are you crazy?" I hissed. "What if we're in her bedroom and you turn on the light and there she is!"

"Then she'll have already heard us, don't you think?" Gregory stage-whispered back. I pursed my lips: ha ha, very funny. But of course he couldn't see my face, so I jabbed him with my elbow.

"Ow!" he yelled out loud.

"Shhhhh!"

"You have bodily injured me twice in the last half hour," he grumbled.

"Bodily?" I whispered back.

"Bodily," he answered. But I felt him lower his arm.

We ducked through the robes and found that we were, in fact, in another closet. This wasn't Wonderland; it was Narnia with negligees. I stumbled over something and reached down to feel a jumble of furry mules that almost certainly matched the robes now brushing against my face.

I felt along the walls, but there was nothing else in the closet. Just as Gregory was about to turn the handle on the door that presumably did lead into Roxana's bedroom, light spilled across our feet from the other side and we jumped back through the robes. My throat closed up. Roxana was home!

With our backs literally to the wall, we listened in horror as Roxana paced around the room yelling in frenzied French. If my high school Spanish couldn't score me a meatball at the St. Regis, it certainly wasn't going to help me now. She was silent a moment, then started up again. So she was alone and on the phone, I concluded. Maybe the CIA would have me yet.

I watched helplessly as Roxana's movements made the light dance around the closet floor. What would I say if she caught us lurking in her closet? How could I possibly dissuade her from prosecuting me? This would ruin my father's reputation! My parents' disappointment over my premature adieus to two expensive professional schools would certainly be forgotten the first time they glimpsed me seated at the defense table. Were you supposed to look at the jury? The judge? Keep your eyes cast humbly downward? What happened if you had to pee in the middle of the trial?

I turned to Gregory to whisper my panic, but he took my

hand and pulled me down into a crouch, tightening his fingers around mine.

We stayed there, knee to knee, elbow to elbow, listening to Roxana alternately shout and then lapse into silence. As scared as I was, I was also entranced by the haughty French music coming out of her mouth. Crouching there in the dark, listening to Roxana tweet and growl, made me wish I were strolling along a tiny street in an ancient French town, a bottle of wine and some Brie in my backpack. I'd come across a sun-soaked field bordered by crumbling stone walls, the perfect spot for a picnic and a nap. I'd stretch out in the warmth, ready for anything. Anyone.

My fantasy was being fueled by the heat from Gregory's body. My sleeve was touching his, and though my arms and legs were growing stiff, I didn't want to break that meager contact. Every now and then he squeezed my hand, sending a pulse straight down my belly.

Here, in the dark of a strange apartment, with a strange man and no one in the world possibly imagining where I was at this moment, I was suddenly choking with lust, with the freedom from space and time. I didn't care about the crime I was committing or that I had no idea what I was doing with my life. I just wanted the man next to me, without thoughts of propriety or consequence. It struck me that we were no longer in James's infested apartment, but rather in a perfectly clean closet.

Ever so slightly, Gregory began rubbing one finger back and forth across my thumb. He might as well have been drawing one finger up the inside of my naked thigh. Did Hayden ever have this effect on me?

Gregory leaned over and kissed me, forcing the question from my mind as quickly as it had entered. Under cover of another outburst from Roxana, we pulled each other to the floor, brushing feathers and spiky heels out of our way as we went. Gregory stretched his lanky body on top of me, pulling my arms with his above our heads. I nearly groaned from the sheer pleasure of his weight, as if I'd been thirsting for it for years instead of a few hours. His mouth on mine was rougher this time, and I was glad for it. Anything gentler and I might have wept.

As if he knew how much I ached, he shifted his hips and drew one knee up until it was pressed firmly between my legs. I clamped his knee with my thighs and pulled his tongue into my mouth. He let go of my hands, sliding his down the length of my arms until they came to rest lightly on my breasts, his fingers and thumbs just far enough apart to give the suggestion of a squeeze. I wrapped my hands over his shoulders, then ran them up his smooth neck, to the top of his head. I tangled my fingers in his thick hair and gently tugged. Gregory pulled his mouth off mine and moaned quietly into my ear. The vibration of his voice, his breath on my face, his hands over my nipples, and his knee, which had more pinpoint accuracy than a heat-seeking missile, made me come right there, right on the plushly carpeted floor of Roxana's closet. I arched back, then thrust my face deep into the well of his shoulders to muffle my gasp.

Hayden had never done *that*, I couldn't help thinking. Not while we were both fully clothed and without the aid of a more precisely shaped appendage.

Just as I was about to release a sigh, we both realized no sound was coming from the other side of the door. We froze. Something small and round and sharp—a sequin?—was embedded on my cheek, but I didn't so much as lift a finger to remove it. My underwear was soaked, but I didn't dare move my leg. We heard Roxana moving around and muttering to herself, apparently having ended her conversation without us noticing.

From our new position flat out on the floor, we could see her slingbacked feet, not just the shadows they were casting. The feet headed toward us. My gut contracted with panic. I squeezed my eyes shut, dug my fingers into Gregory's scalp, and buried my face in his chest, this time out of abject fear.

Then the feet stopped just before the closet door and turned around again. And then turned around once more. What is she *doing*? I thought, impatience trumping fear for a nanosecond.

We heard some rustling, a few "*merde*"s, the sound of a bag being zipped, and then, to our surprise, the light went out. We remained still in the pitch black, Gregory hard against me, breathing softly near my ear. We listened to Roxana's curses grow fainter and then heard the distinctive creak and whump that all the apartment doors at 287 West 12th made. We lay motionless for another minute. And then another. I still couldn't see Gregory's face, just an inch from mine. I matched my breathing to his, deep, long breaths, and just when I was afraid he had fallen asleep, he put his hand on my cheek and stroked it lightly. He touched his nose to mine and then kissed me.

"I guess we should get out of here," I whispered, letting my hands travel down his back and come to rest with my fingers hooked inside the waist of his jeans.

"Uh-huh," he whispered back, and kissed me again, harder.

"This is insane," I murmured, finding the button over his fly.

"Completely."

"But we can't," I wailed quietly, clutching at his pants with both hands. "We don't have anything."

"Back pocket," he grunted. I felt around over his (definitely round) ass and almost laughed with relief when I pulled out a condom. And then I grew indignant.

"Wait," I said accusingly, "did you plan this?"

"Hoped. Only hoped."

"Since when?"

"Since fifteen minutes ago."

"This is James's condom," I hissed, dropping it as if James himself had just offered it to me.

"It's not *used*, Zephyr."

Why did the sound of my name crossing a man's lips do for me what it took roses and nights at the opera to do for other women? Shouldn't I have a higher threshold for swooning? I wondered as I hungrily pushed Gregory's jeans down over his narrow hips.

ELEVEN

"THEY MUST HAVE BEEN HAVING AN AFFAIR," TAG CONCLUDED as she stepped on and off the pink landing, studying the silky wallpaper in amazement.

I had kept the secret staircase a secret for nearly forty-eight hours, which I thought was a pretty respectable interval, and the Sterling Girls hadn't been able to come see it for another day, so it was almost as if I had kept it to myself for three days.

"Frenchie can really pick 'em," Mercedes commented lazily, her eyes closed, plucking at an imaginary viola. I wanted to pinch her. Everything she did reminded me that she was getting away with not telling us any details about her night with Dover Carter. I sincerely hoped it was as hard for her to withhold this information from us as it was for me to keep mum about Gregory. She certainly *looked* the picture of self-control. She was sprawled across James's bed, which we had stripped down to the mattress and scrubbed with Lysol at Lucy's direction. I had felt a small stab of guilt about showing Lucy the state of this room, as I correctly suspected that her cleaning compulsion would ignite at the sight of a cheese-encrusted fork nestled into a pair of tightie whities. But I was eager to make inroads on this garbage pit.

My need to kick-start my career as a minor Donald Trump had been stoked on Sunday night, a few hours after Gregory kissed me good-bye. I had returned to my apartment and was wandering around moonily, grinning at myself in mirrors, shivering at the memory of Gregory's warm face nuzzled into my neck, when my brother called to give me a piece of planet-realigning news.

Gideon, formerly the king of Steamboat Springs' double black diamonds, was calling to announce that his "film" was now a Film. No more quotes, no more rolled eyes, no more ex-aggerated sighs. His movie—about a ski bum who becomes a successful CEO by applying his slope credo to the board-room—was now viewable to people besides him and his room-mates. And. *And.* It had been accepted into the Tribeca Film Festival. Gideon was not only leaving me to fill his position as the least accomplished person in the Zuckerman nuclear fam-ily, but he was coming back to town. The prodigal son was to return home, redeemed, while the prodigal daughter remained prodigal.

I feigned delight in Gideon's news, but as soon as I hung up, I sank down on my kitchen footstool, my post-tryst glow evaporating as unbridled professional desperation set in. I stared at a rust stain on the cabinet beneath the sink and won-dered how fast I could get James's apartment cleaned out and rented. If I did that, then at the very least I could refer to my-self as "working in real estate" at my college reunion. Now *I'd* be the one with a job in quotes.

I'd give myself an hour to bask in the memory of Gregory and then, I swore, I'd take some garbage bags and rubber

gloves and go back across the hall to embark upon my new career. I headed into the bathroom to run a bath. I'd support myself—Gideon couldn't claim to do that yet—and I'd be able to
sustain a relationship with Gregory. I couldn't feel sexy for long
if I didn't have a job.

I didn't quite make it back over to James's that night—it
made more sense, since I was all clean and cozy after my bath,
to go to bed and get an early start the next day. But by the next
morning, my sexterminator had not yet called me, and I
couldn't complain to any of the Sterling Girls, because I didn't
yet want Lucy to know about Gregory. I was so upset by the
double whammy of his non-call and my inability to vent that I
knew I wouldn't be effective across the hall. I accepted a FedEx
package that arrived for Cliff and figured I'd done enough as
super for the day. I even shook the box and sniffed it—Cliff's
bass case and the late-night schedule were just too convenient
not to be a cover for at least a fake jewelry smuggling operation—but reluctantly concluded it might just contain a set of
spare bass strings, like the invoice on the front claimed.

By Tuesday, I knew I had to talk to somebody or I'd im-
plode. Gregory's continued silence, the arrival of my reality-
bearing bank statement, and the overwhelming prospect of
emptying James's apartment had all leveled me to a state of
cheese consumption and Olivia Goldsmith rereads not experi-
enced since I gave up Hayden. As a dog-eared page of *Flavor of
the Month* fluttered loose from the book's binding, I wondered
why I was working so hard to avoid telling Lucy about Gregory.
She was going to have to know sooner or later. It's just that
later was so much more preferable than sooner, I thought as I
unwrapped the block of cheddar I'd retrieved from the back of
the fridge.

The sight of teeth marks reminded me of my conversation
with Abigail and the seeds of a plan that were still bouncing

around in the back of my brain. Of course! I jumped up from the couch. I had a great reason to call the SGs. I grabbed the phone and left messages for three of them, enticing them with the promise of a secret staircase and the need to help our Left Coast friend.

They came on Wednesday night, even though it was pouring rain. As I waited for my friends, I peered past the apple tree branches scraping at my window and watched with satisfaction as the city was cleansed of dog piss, leaky garbage bag stains, and Saturday night vomit. It seemed appropriate that I was going to be performing my own indoor ablutions.

Inside James's apartment, Lucy made us put on rubber gloves and toss everything into trash bags. We got rid of the food items and saved the clothing, since I was still somewhat fuzzy on the subject of property law as it pertained to a convict's belongings. Lucy hadn't even let us put clean sheets on the bed, because she said she couldn't begin to imagine how James defined "clean."

Tag filled one bag before insisting on seeing the staircase. It was enormously gratifying to watch the expression on each of their faces as I silently opened the closet door and then, with an irresistible flourish, yanked open the door to the staircase.

"I don't think two consenting and unmarried adults, living alone, need to construct an entire staircase and decorate it in order to have an affair," I offered now in response to Tag's hypothesis.

"No, you're right, you're right," Tag muttered, unlocking a pair of furry blue handcuffs. She studied them, then snapped one of the rings around her left wrist.

"Tag!" Lucy and I shrieked as it clicked closed. Even Mercedes opened her eyes in surprise.

"I made sure they unlock," she said, waving the key in front of us mischievously. She clasped the ring of a sparkling gold pair of cuffs around her other wrist and let the two empty rings clang together. "This is what marriage felt like." She shuddered.

"I'm just curious," Mercedes murmured, closing her eyes again. "Would you rank marriage to Glen higher or lower than getting that carnivorous parasite in your scalp?"

"Oh, nasty." I grimaced, remembering Tag's trip to Costa Rica. "When you had to hold that slab of raw meat to your head to coax it out?"

"The botfly larvae." Tag smiled fondly at the memory, the way other people might have recalled a sunset in Hawaii. "I found thirteen new species on that trip. Marriage to Glen was way worse than some little endoparasite. Not technically carnivorous, by the way."

"Glen or the botfly?" I asked.

Lucy sighed and patted the laptop sitting between her and Mercedes.

"Are we doing this or not? I have to be at work early tomorrow."

Mercedes, Tag, and I exchanged glances. It was only six o'clock. Lucy was still unexpectedly prickly from Saturday night at Soho House, when Renee Ricardo had foreseen her undated demise. She was also not taking kindly to any mention of Mercedes's fairy-tale encounter with Dover Carter, which, I suspected, she felt should have happened to her as compensation for all her defaced ten-dollar bills and sodden Sundays on the Brooklyn Bridge. She was right, of course; it wasn't at all fair that a movie star should become besotted with Mercedes, who wasn't even looking for a relationship.

In reality, though, it made perfect sense. Mercedes was as self-assured, talented, and stunning as Tag—and looked ravishing in short-sleeved T-shirts over long-sleeved T-shirts, whereas I just looked bundled up—but also exuded a genuine warmth that Tag often didn't. Lucy, on the other hand, did not have a clear picture of herself or how she came across to others and therefore was never good at gauging men's responses to her. She was forever hoping for the wrong things to happen with the wrong people, and it was a topic of constant consternation among the rest of us as to how to handle her innate lack of perception. As the years passed, it became increasingly evident that she could not be taught. Should we guide her toward men who were not quite worthy of her, but would look up to her? Would she sense our condescension? Or should we fervently hope that some fabulous man would come along who would be able to see beyond the insecurities, the grating laugh, and the forced expressions she held on her face a moment too long, to the loyal, funny, up-for-anything Lucy behind those deficiencies?

At the moment, though, my concern for Lucy's fate was displaced by frustration that she was already too down in the dumps for me to reveal the agonies and ecstasies of my four-hour relationship with Gregory. It also meant that I couldn't grill Mercedes about her incipient Hollywood romance. All I could do was channel my pent-up irritation into the revenge plan I had dreamt up on Abigail's behalf, a scheme I had dubbed "JDate Jihad."

"We're doing it, we're doing it," Tag said soothingly to Lucy, plopping down on the bed beside her and Mercedes, her handcuffs clanking together. "Have you found him yet?"

"Here." Lucy turned her laptop around to show the rest of us the JDate website. She clicked and enlarged a photo of an underwhelming male specimen.

"You're sure?" Mercedes asked.

Lucy consulted the slip of paper I'd given her with the account information I'd set up and the screen name of Darren Schwartz printed on it.

"Maybe he's cuter in person," I suggested doubtfully. LinguaFrank, as Darren had named himself online, was pasty beneath his freckles, and his features looked as if they'd been pulled downward by a negative force. "He's some guy's stepson and he gave a great paper on something."

My friends glanced up at me dubiously. I shrugged.

"Okay, so what are we writing?" Tag asked.

"That we're a barely Jewish, stick-thin Asian woman who's looking for a nice Jewish man—"

"An ugly Jewish man," Mercedes muttered. Lucy started to make a little protest sound in defense of humankind, but then tiredly waved away her own generous impulse.

"Which of us is going to show up being Asian?" Tag said.

"I only got my stepfather's name," Mercedes said, and yawned exaggeratedly. I was again overcome with the desire to lock her in James's unwholesome closet until she spilled the details of her night with the movie star. She shot me an impish grin.

"We don't need to show up actually being Asian," I reminded them irritably. "We just need him to show up *hoping* to meet an Asian hottie, and then one of us goes in and tells him that she left because she took one look at him and decided he was too fat and Jewish-looking. Just like he said to Abigail."

This was not our maiden voyage to the land of revenge. In college, Tag had blazed the way with an arrogant legacy admit who'd passed off months of her research on the metazoan parasites of Indonesian sharks as his own. She responded to this trespass by using his Social Security number to un-enroll him from all his classes two semesters in a row, right around midterm, leaving him in a mysterious and hellish administrative quagmire that ultimately required him to spend an entire extra year in school.

I sat down beside Lucy and took over the keyboard.

"Dear LinguaFrank," I typed. "Your profile intrigues me—"

"*Intrigues?* Good Lord." Mercedes sat up and turned the computer to her, and pounded the delete key. "Dear Lingua-Frank, you look really hot—"

"Oh, for fuck sake!" Tag grabbed at the laptop, her manacles clanking. "I'm slim, I'm Asian, I've got a Ph.D." she typed, "and I think, at the very least, we should meet for coffee. I'm attaching a photo. Let me know if you like what you see."

"And what exactly is LinguaFrank going to see?" I demanded.

Tag Googled "photo Asian" and came up with the website for a company that sold stock photographs. She clicked on a wide-eyed model whose bee-stung lips were the plumpest part of her otherwise skeletal body. Tag looked up and we all nodded with awe. She dragged the image into the message and hit SEND with a flourish. She pushed the computer away from her, ready to return to business.

"Is it possible Roxana doesn't know about the staircase?" she asked.

"If she doesn't, don't tell her. Can you imagine?" Mercedes shuddered.

"Maybe you should call the cops," Tag suggested to me. "What if he was taping her secretly? Coming into her bedroom without her knowing? Extorting her? Keeping her as a sex slave?" Her eyes lit up.

"You sound like Zephyr," Lucy muttered.

"Hey," I said, "I don't revel in other people's misfortune! I just have an active imagination."

"I wasn't reveling," Tag said defensively. "I was wondering whether Roxana needs our help."

We looked at her in surprise.

"Wha-aat? How cold do you guys think I am?" Tag actually sounded hurt.

Mercedes changed the subject. "Zeph, how'd you find this thing in the first place?" She hauled herself off the bed and poked her head into the stairwell.

I hesitated. The truth would involve telling them about Gregory. A lie would probably also involve telling them about Gregory, because I was a lousy liar.

"I was in the alley cleaning up, and just, you know, saw this brand-new staircase," I hedged, licking my lips. "What was I gonna do, not check it out?" Tag and Mercedes shot me identical suspicious looks, but Lucy remained in her silent depression-fueled state. Just as Tag started to squint at me, the computer pinged and a message popped up from LinguaFrank. We all dove for the screen.

"I'd love to meet u. Where do u live?" it said.

"This man has a Ph.D. in linguistics," I griped, "and can't be bothered to type the 'y' and the 'o'?"

"Civilization is in the crapper," Mercedes said.

"Wait, he's online right now?" Lucy asked. "He's just sitting around waiting for women to e-mail him?" It was hard to tell whether she was deriding the practice or considering adopting it. I certainly wasn't going to be the one to highlight the relative advantages of sitting on your comfy couch scanning a website full of potential dates against the glaring disadvantages of trolling a bridge in inclement weather amidst a sea of pedestrians who could be married, gay, homicidal, or otherwise unsuitable candidates for romance.

"What do we say?" Mercedes asked, her mini dreds bobbing around her face as she bounced on the bed. Her enthusiasm—rarely ignited for anything other than Messieurs Schubert, Handel, and Mendelssohn—validated our mission. Even Tag and Lucy perked up.

Tag wiggled her fingers over the keyboard, frowning.

"Did Abigail say where he lives?"

I shook my head.

"He's an academic," Lucy reasoned. "Anywhere on the West Side should be fine with him."

"But not Starbucks," I cautioned. "He won't wanna go there."

"How about that place?" Mercedes said vaguely. "That place we went once where that woman had the weird coat?" she prompted.

"Yes!" Lucy shouted. "That's perfect! It's cozy, hip, a little dark. We could easily eavesdrop on their conversation." Lucy smiled for the first time in days.

"Luce," Tag began gently, then stopped. There wasn't any point in reminding her that there would be no conversation, because one half of this proposed tête-à-tête was imaginary. It would just be a tête.

"Okay, cozy, hip, dark, weird coats. Anyone remember the name?"

"It's on Perry, near Washington," I offered.

"A *name*, people." Tag tapped the laptop.

"It's not on Perry," Mercedes said, shaking her head. "Zeph, that was the other place, the one where Abigail found the bank deposit slip on the bathroom floor with six hundred thousand dollars in the checking account."

The thought crossed my mind that someone like a movie star, someone like, say, Dover Carter, might be bustling around town with over half a mil in his checking, but I said nothing.

Tag sighed loudly.

"Okay, okay," I said, "what about Grounded on Jane Street?" It's where I had hoped to take Gregory before we got sidetracked. I felt myself start to blush and tried to think of other things.

"How . . . about . . . Grounded . . . in . . . the . . . Vil . . . lage?" Tag dictated to herself as she typed. "This Saturday at 5 P.M. I'll be wearing—" She looked up at us.

"A lace teddy and stilettos," Mercedes said. "Carrying a whip and sucking on a banana."

"A tight red dress?" I suggested.

"My *favorite fitted* red dress," Tag typed.

"Sounds like an L.L. Bean catalog." I shook my head and turned the keyboard toward me, deleting the last bit. "You'll know me when you see me," I wrote. "*Believe* me."

"Perfect," Tag proclaimed, which apparently gave me the honor of hitting SEND. We all watched the screen in silence. In less than a minute, another message popped up.

"Looking forward," was all it said. I opened my mouth to protest LinguaFrank's lazy shorthand.

"Zeph, control yourself." Mercedes cut me off.

"Is this too mean?" Lucy said suddenly, sitting up on the bed.

"Oh, Jesus." Tag went back into the closet to rifle through dildoes and condoms.

"Abigail was heartbroken," I reminded her.

"C'mon, *heartbroken*?" Lucy said bitterly. "I know heartbroken and I know Abigail. She decides a few months ago it's time to get serious, and after one bad date, she's heartbroken?"

"You should have heard her," I said cautiously. This disagreement felt like a substitute for another conversation Lucy and I were not having. "Luce, she was hurt. He was cruel to her."

Lucy shrugged and I felt myself grow angry. Just because she couldn't land a date with a guy didn't mean she was allowed to pull everyone else down with her. I silently pushed the computer toward Lucy and followed Tag into the closet. Let Mercedes deal with the pity party.

Tag shook a box of batteries and whispered, "Cut her some slack. Mercedes snagged a movie star, and that guy, George or whatever, didn't call her. She's bummed out."

"Gregory," I blurted.

"What?"

"Not George," I said, wishing I'd kept my mouth shut, "Gregory."

Tag looked up from the box she was holding. "Oh, no. No, no."

"What?" I tried to look innocent.

"He called you, didn't he?" she hissed.

"It's not my fault!" I hissed back, relieved that she'd only guessed as far as a phone call.

"Did you go out with him?"

I hesitated for a split second before settling on the literal truth.

"No, I did not go *out* with him. Can we talk about this some other time?" I nodded toward the bed.

"Did you find the key, Tag?" Mercedes called out.

"To what?"

"Um, those pretty bracelets you're wearing?"

"Oh, it's around," Tag said dismissively.

"Around?" I said, alarmed. "You don't have it?"

"It's *around*," she repeated, though her forehead creased slightly. We emerged from the closet and started scouring the coarse gray carpet for a handcuff key, which Tag could only describe as a piece of metal that didn't really look like a key at all. Mercedes and Lucy peered under the bed.

"Girls?" came my mother's singsong voice from James's front door.

"Shit!" I hissed, and we all jumped up. Tag grabbed the various plastic penises that she'd used earlier to choreograph a shadow dance and threw them into the closet. I tossed in a few other unseemly items that had migrated out—a bag of feathers, a tube of glittery lubricant—and Mercedes slammed the door shut.

I hadn't mentioned the staircase to my parents. I told my-self it was because I didn't want them to tell Roxana, on the grounds that it might traumatize her forever if she didn't yet know about it. The truth was that I needed to have a secret right now. It made up for the fact that my brother was going to present a movie in Tribeca next month. It eased the reality of sitting on the floor of a convict's apartment sorting out water and sewer bills, contemplating the meaning of ten jars of Marmite, and reassuring a fractious widow that I was investi-gating her imaginary intruders.

I hadn't told the Sterling Girls that the staircase was un-known to Bella and Ollie, and I was pleased to see the parent radar that had served us so well in high school still fully func-tioning and able to kick into gear at the drop of a dildo.

"Making progress?" My mother's expectant face appeared at the door of the bedroom, glistening above the various Lycra contraptions encasing her lithe body. Sweat and rain streaked her French braids. We all stood around awkwardly, turgid little clouds of guilt filling the room.

Lucy, bless her tidy heart, grabbed a garbage bag and said, "Yep, we're getting there, but boy . . . !" And then she actually brought her arm to her forehead and said, "Whew!" which I thought was going a bit overboard, but Bella Zuckerman, no stranger to melodrama, didn't appear to notice this false ges-ture.

"It's disgusting in here, isn't it?" My mother wrinkled her nose. "Who would have thought? You know, with that cute British accent?" She raised her eyebrows and wiggled her head from side to side to suggest clipped Anglo tones.

"Thanks so much for helping Zephy," she chirped. "You know, the sooner it's cleaned up, the sooner she can get it rented out!"

"Mom," I said sharply. "We know. I know." My hackles went

up as my mother surveyed my friends, smiling. I knew she was wondering how she, one of *Newsweek*'s Fifty Women to Watch (seventeen years ago, I comforted myself), wound up with a daughter whom she couldn't even categorize as "opting out" because said daughter didn't actually have a career out of which to opt. Didn't she know I was doing everything I could to make that apartment profitable? I shifted my weight nervously and tried not to think about the past three days, during which I had not cleaned, had not called a broker, had not done anything, in fact, but moon over Gregory.

She put her hands on her hips and spun around to Mercedes, focusing her attention like a prison searchlight. "Mercedes, sweetie, I came down because Ollie and I have tickets for this Saturday—will you be onstage that night? We'd love to take you for a late dinner afterward."

Mercedes scanned the ceiling for a moment. "I-I'm not sure. If I am—I have to check—I'd love to. That's really sweet of you, Bella."

I glanced over at Mercedes at the same time Tag did. Mercedes was bald-faced lying. Unless she was on tour, she knew her Byzantine, erratic schedule down to the minute. She was a human Palm Pilot. I smelled Dover Carter.

"Merce, I'm pretty sure you told me you were on that night," Tag said evilly.

"Like I said," Mercedes enunciated stonily to Tag, "I'll have to check."

"But—"

"Tag," Mercedes interrupted, "I believe you're the one who's got some *constraints* right now, yes?"

Tag was holding her hands behind her back, assuming a ponderous pose to hide the handcuffs that, I now realized, were still encircling her wrists. A snort escaped me as I tried to keep from laughing. Lucy heard me and looked over. When she saw Tag trying to look innocent, she quickly turned away from my mother, her shoulders convulsing. Mercedes made a weird coughing sound. Tag just raised her eyebrows at us and smiled. My mother noticed nothing.

"A big trip lined up?" my mom asked eagerly. "South America? Asia?" I shot Tag a warning look in case she was suddenly struck with an urge to reveal her current state of bondage.

"Well," Tag said thoughtfully, "a conference in Spain and then Bora Bora this summer, but that's about it."

"Oh, how I envy you!" my mother trilled. "You know what I'm going to do for you girls? I'm going to whip up a batch of energy drink."

"No!" Mercedes cried out.

"Please don't," Tag said quickly.

Bella dismissed their protests with a wave of her hand and headed out of the room, a little bounce in her step at the thought of nourishing us. She paused and looked back.

"Oh, Zeph?"

"Hmm?" I said, looking up from my garbage bag with feigned distraction.

"Did you guys ever figure out the problem with the dryer? Can I use it?"

My breath caught.

"Didn't quite finish," I squeaked.

My mom nodded and shrugged. "Back in a minute."

I followed her to the front door. The moment I double-locked it behind her, I heard an explosion of laughter from the bedroom. I hurried back to find my friends in a tangle on the bare mattress, tears running down their faces, gasping for breath. I was just about to yell at them to pull it together before my mother returned, when I noticed a thin metal key sticking out of Tag's back pocket. I pointed at it and tried to tell them, but I was laughing so hard that all I could do was flop down next to them and try to catch my breath. The room stank of underpants, the closet was filled with a convict's trove of sex toys, and the heel of someone's clog was digging into my back, but it was, maybe because of all those things, a first-world moment.

Lucy, tag, and mercedes helped me fill up garbage bags and boxes for another three hours, energized not at all by my mother's viscous mauve drink (which we tossed down the sink, and which took an unnaturally long time to drain), but by the sheer delight of finding three packages of cookie dough in James's freezer. We worked our way through two of them—Tag and Mercedes washed theirs down with Brooklyn Lager—in the spirit of cleaning out the kitchen.

While we tossed condiments into the trash and condoms into storage boxes (it seemed wasteful to throw them out), four things happened. Tag discovered two keys hidden inside a picture frame. Mercedes confessed that she had a date with Dover Carter next week. I came clean about Gregory. And Lucy decided to throw a death party for herself.

My mother, when she returned with the energy drink, had pressed Mercedes again about her plans for Saturday night, as if Mercedes had had the inclination to check her schedule in the intervening ten minutes. Mercedes, knowing she wouldn't be able to fend off my mother for very long, admitted she already had a post-performance date. My mother accepted that with minimal disappointment, but after she left, Tag slipped over to Mercedes and quietly snapped handcuffs on her.

"What the fu-freak!" Mercedes yelled. She looked so panicked, I almost felt sorry for her. "My wrists, don't hurt my wrists!"

"Then don't wriggle."

"Take these off me!"

The three of us looked at her calmly.

"Okay, okay." She spoke in a quiet rush. "Dover spent the rest of Saturday night with me, but all we did was kiss."

"C'mon!" I said, feeling whorish by comparison.

"Swear to God. Take these off me, please?" she begged.

"We'll need a little more, Ms. Kim," Tag said with fake nonchalance, pretending to examine her fingernails.

Mercedes hurried to admit that in the past three days, Dover Carter had sent her two bouquets of orchids and three of his favorite recordings of Bach cantatas, which we all agreed was commendably understated for a movie star who could have sent her a new car as a token of his affection. And Gregory couldn't even pick up the phone for me? I fought off a wave of self-pity.

Tag nodded, satisfied, and unlocked the cuffs. Mercedes rubbed her wrists dramatically. Lucy started to distribute rubber gloves from a box that, both disturbingly and reassuringly, had been in the closet next to the lubricants. Finally, I couldn't keep my sad state to myself any longer.

"I slept with the exterminator!" I blurted out. We stood in James's gray and black and stainless-steel kitchen as I poured out my woeful tale about the broken dryer and the alley and the staircase and Roxana's closet and Gregory's non-calling. I feared chastisement (Mercedes), mockery (Tag), and angry jealousy cloaked in false sympathy (Lucy), but they weren't judgmental at all. In fact, it seemed I had overestimated their opinion of me. Mostly, they were relieved I hadn't hooked up with Hayden again. How weak did they think I was? I tried to impress upon them that I was the victim of a hump-and-dump, that I deserved some sympathy, but they were unimpressed.

"He'll call," Tag said, turning back to James's pantry shelves, tossing an open box of crackers and a dusty bag of flour into the trash.

Mercedes nodded and flipped on the vacuum cleaner. I flipped it off.

"Why don't you just call him?" she said, and switched it on again. Frustrated, I followed Lucy into the bathroom. She pulled on a second pair of gloves over her first and sprinkled some Comet into the toilet bowl. A part of me was glad I could report to her that I'd been used; it made up for the fact that Gregory had called me and not her. But even Lucy seemed unaffected by my news.

"You know," she said, swirling a toilet brush around the bowl, and I figured she was about to launch into an over-generalized characterization of the male species' insipient mating behaviors, "I've decided to throw a party for myself."

"Okay." I picked up a sponge and waited for her to explain the non sequitur.

"A death party."

"Lu-uce—" I protested.

"Do you even know what a death party is?"

"Do you?"

"I'm inventing it," she said, "so of course I know what it is."

"What is it?" I asked with measured patience.

She sat back on her heels, holding the dripping wand over the toilet. "It's when you have the good fortune—see, I'm referring to Renee's prediction as good fortune—to get advance notice of your death, but you're in good enough health to throw a party that you can enjoy."

"Lucy," I tried again.

"People can give the eulogies they'd give at my funeral, but this way I can actually hear them. Isn't that what everyone wishes for a dead person? That they could hear all the great things people are saying about them?"

She brushed the back of her wrist across her face, trying to push a damp lock of blond hair off her cheek. I reached over and tucked the strands behind her ear. This close up, I noticed how tired her eyes looked on her angular face, and a lump formed in my throat.

"Whatever you want, sweets," I said lightly, trying not to let her hear the pity I knew she'd resent.

"People are going to have to fly in," she continued, "like for a wedding. Or a funeral. It's going to be just as important."

"But then," I reasoned, "will they have to come back for the funeral itself? Or is this instead of a funeral?"

Lucy frowned. "I can't ask Abigail to fly in twice. She doesn't have that kind of money." She shook her head resolutely. "No, if they can only come to one, it has to be this."

Just as I was trying to figure out whether I needed to expend energy trying to dissuade her from this plan, Tag yelled out, "Hey, can I put away these creepy photos?"

"Which creepy photos?" I shouted back, heading out of the bathroom.

"The double whammy over the fireplace!"

Tag was in the living room, standing in front of James's shrine to himself. For kicks, she'd turned off the lights and lit the candles beside the picture frames. The candlelight flickering across James's grinning mug, together with the rain pounding at the dark windows, transformed the room from a mildly creepy place to a downright sinister one.

"Tag!" I shrieked, and Mercedes and Lucy came running.

"Oh, gross!" Lucy yelled, flipping on the lights.

"I just wanted to see what James saw when he worshipped himself," Tag cackled.

"So what do you see, Granger?" Mercedes asked crisply.

"Dust," Tag concluded, and blew out the candles. She picked up one of the photos and chucked it to me.

"Adios," I said, catching it and putting it in a box with some of James's towels. Tag threw me the second one and something rattled as I caught it. We looked at one another. I groaned, suddenly exhausted by James and his pink staircase and his icky mysteries and his multiple personalities, which were becoming less exciting by the minute. I turned the frame over in my hands and pried off the back.

Two keys stared up at me. Two more damned keys that opened who knew what. Another staircase? Another closet? James must have been best friends with a locksmith. I didn't care what these keys opened. I wanted to be done with James. I wanted Gregory to call. I wanted this apartment cleaned up and rented out so I could be done with it, too.

I handed the keys to Lucy, who happily trotted off to find her color-coded labels. As long as they were categorized in some way, she would not be bothered by them. Neither, I decided, for the moment, would I.

TWELVE

On thursday morning, i woke to a stale, acrid odor. Gas? Smoke? Helium? I jumped out of bed and frantically sniffed around my apartment. I looked outside for fire trucks, utility trucks, smoking telephone wires. Nothing except an oil truck parked outside. I opened my apartment door and the smell hit me harder. I began to whimper, panic fanning out from my heart to my fingers and toes. Calm, Zephyr, calm. I threw on some jeans, grabbed my keys, and headed for the basement.

I liked our basement about as much as I liked our alley. It was dark and low-ceilinged, crowded with the moldy detritus of past and current tenants. Pipes and wires were exposed in an acrobatic tangle that looked, to my untrained eye, to be up to the safety codes of centuries past.

I flipped the light on and was rewarded with the sight of a cluster of roaches scurrying for the walls. What the hell were we paying Gregory's company for? I gulped back the bile that rose in my throat and made my way gingerly along the narrow corridor, toward the front of the building. The smell grew stronger, and as I threw open the door to the boiler room, my eyes started to sting. The entire floor was covered in thick black oil, which was quickly spreading toward me and the door. Did I think to throw sand from the red fire buckets in the path of the encroaching goo? Did I throw down an old mattress to stanch the flow? No. I turned and ran.

My heart was pounding. Could the building catch on fire? Should I call the . . . the police? A plumber? The oil company that James had been getting kickbacks from? Were we allowed to keep using them? Why hadn't I thought about this sooner? Because it was April and the oil tank had stayed full enough. Until now.

I hurried out the front door and down the stoop. An unshaven guy who I was pretty sure shouldn't have been smoking a cigarette while he pumped oil through our sidewalk fuel line looked up.

"Stop!" I screamed. His eyebrows lifted imperceptibly, which infuriated me. He should have dropped his hose and matched my panic.

"There's oil all over my basement floor!" I shrieked. He let the lever on the hose snap free.

"Aw, shit." He actually smacked his cigarette-gripping hand against his head in a gesture that had been abandoned in a Hollywood studio lot decades ago. "You guys got the broken gauge."

I just stared. He stepped over to his truck and hit a button, which made an enormous wheel retract the hose.

"You guys got the broken gauge, right?" he repeated.

"I have no idea," I said in a hoarse whisper.

"Yeah, it's you guys, cuz James usually hangs out downstairs and then comes up to tell us when it's gettin' full. Right. But he's not here, right? Cuza the money shit, yeah?" All I could do was look at him, my shoulders sagging, my jaw hanging slack. "Yeah, right, so it probably overflowed, huh?"

"You could say that. I have gallons of oil all over my basement floor," I told him, waiting for him to offer to clean it up as part of what was surely our comprehensive service plan.

He grabbed a rag off the driver's seat and wiped his hands. "Eh, it's probably not gallons. Just seems like it cuza the properties of liquid."

A physics lesson from James's former colleague at seven in the morning? I would have preferred ten phone calls from Mrs. Hannaham.

"What do I do?" I pleaded, my voice dangerously close to tears.

"Kitty litter," he said, yanking up some levers on the back of the truck.

"Kitty litter."

"Kitty litter soaks it up and then you just throw it out. Any old cheap brand, but not the organic crap. That don't work."

"Maybe you could have warned me that my gauge was broken," I told him incredulously.

He shrugged. "It's your building, lady."

"Can you help me?" I said in a small voice.

He jumped into the truck and lit another cigarette. "Sorry, sweetheart. Other deliveries." He looked at me, closing one eye against a curl of smoke. "You the new super?"

I nodded.

"A lady super. Cute. Feminism and shit, that's good stuff." He started the truck. "A piece of advice?"

I waited, hoping for some secret brotherhood knowledge, a tenet known only to supers.

"Get the gauge fixed." He drove off.

My dad went to work late that morning, having helped me haul fifteen jumbo bags of Tidy Cats Long-Lasting Odor

Control Scooping Multi Cat Litter from Artie's Hardware on Fourteenth Street, in a handcart the owner lent us. He tried to keep me from thinking about what a loser I was by shoving the purported bright side in my face.

First, there was: "We don't have to go to the gym today!" and then: "Kitty litter! Brilliant!" and finally, my least favorite: "Darling daught, think of everything you're learning. How many women your age get this kind of practical education? I think this is great! You'll be glad this happened."

In fact, the only bright side was that the whole incident had proved Mrs. Hannaham to be an olfactory liar. If she hadn't called this morning, of all mornings, to complain about the worst smell to hit 287 West 12th Street since before the days of closed sewers, then clearly the helium and the gas and the smoke she claimed she smelled were all lies, designed to get attention or just to torture me. Had I not stunk of fuel-grade petroleum and a chemical simulacrum of springtime, I might have felt a tinge of pity. Instead, the little singed devil perched on my shoulder clapped with glee at having found her out.

I trudged upstairs in a cloud of self-disgust, eager for a scalding shower. I had just pushed back the curtain when the phone rang. Unable to stomach Mrs. H.'s complaint du jour, I let the machine screen—I very purposely did not have voice mail, for situations such as this. But instead of Mrs. H., it was a message from a broker who'd heard about James's apartment from a "friend," and wanted to come see "the listing." I grabbed the phone and answered breathlessly, pretending I'd just walked in.

I figured he was a colleague of my mom's friend Eva Lowell. But when I pressed him, it turned out that Officer Varlam, who'd been assigned to James's case, liked to help his

brother-in-law by alerting him to the vacancies that often re-
sulted from the collars he made. Freddy Givitch and I made an
appointment for that afternoon. I was so excited about having
a listing that I surprised my workout clothes by putting them
on and taking them Rollerblading along the river. I figured
since I was already sweaty, I might as well purge the oil fumes
from my skin and the black thoughts from my tired head.

Outside, branches littered the street, and soggy circulars
from Rite Aid clung to every step of our stoop in mushy lumps,
but the air was crisp and clean and dry. I crab-walked down
the steps, strapped on my helmet, and took off along Twelfth
Street. I whizzed over the jagged sidewalk, past the neighbors
waiting for their parking spots to become legal. They were
making the best of their bi-weekly, car-bound ninety minutes.
There was the hefty woman who leaned out her door, rolled up
her jeans, and applied depilatory to her legs (only in warm
weather). There was the frazzled pale woman in a tracksuit
who pounded on her laptop, shouted into her headset, and
guzzled caffeine from two Murray's Bagels coffee cups on her
dashboard. There were the three guys in a row—a pickup
truck, a dented blue van, and another pickup truck—who
slept, mouths open, radios blaring.

I turned twice and continued along Thirteenth Street, past
the yoga center, past the drunks who reigned over the triangu-
lar patch of ragged green struggling to be a park, and past
Aqua Kids, the clothing boutique that sold ninety-five-dollar
shirts for toddlers and that the Sterling Girls had deemed the
embodiment of everything wrong with the world.

I had crossed the highway and was about to take off down
the riverside path when I noticed two policemen and two tall
women in snug, sequined clothing tottering on high heels, arguing in front of the public bathroom. I made my way over as

casually as I could, trying to commit the scene to memory in case I needed to serve as a future witness. What does a witness wear to court? I knelt down and pretended to tighten my laces.

"I know my rights!" the taller woman, dressed in a glittering, zebra-striped pantsuit, yelled at the cops. She swayed back, hands on her hips, chest forward. "I have a human right to relieve myself in a dignified fashion!"

"That is her *right*!" emphasized her rainbow-hued friend, jutting her finger in front of the shorter cop's face.

"Ma'am," the taller, redheaded cop said loudly, with exaggerated patience, "no one is denying you—"

" 'Ma'am,' you said 'ma'am'!" shouted Zebra Stripes. "So you concur that I am *indeed* a woman! Now, Officer, you let me into this bathroom!" She crossed her arms in front of her ample chest.

The short cop shook his head and groaned. "O'Ryan, man, why you gotta go and say that?"

"Now, you listena me," said O'Ryan quickly to Zebra. "I am calling you 'ma'am' out of respect for your choice, but you cannot inflict your choice on other persons, who may want to utilize this public restroom that they paid for with their tax dollars."

"Are you accusing me of tax evasion?" Zebra shrieked. "I am being falsely accused!" She looked around wildly. "You tell me who I'm inflicting on? Who? *Her?*" She pointed at me and my stomach clenched. Oh, God, why had I stopped? The four of them looked at me crouching over my laces, and I smiled wanly.

"You," Zebra yelled at me, her eyes blazing. "Do you have a problem with me using this ladies' restroom? Do you reject me because I was not as fortunate as you to be born into the body that I was meant to be born into?"

"Amen!" bellowed Rainbow in a baritone voice.

"Okay, enough," said the short cop. "We don't gotta take a survey. I tell you what. If the bathroom's empty, you can use it."

"What? I . . . I . . . !" stuttered Zebra in a crescendoing falsetto.

"Take it or leave it," he said, resting his hand casually on his nightstick.

No, no, no, I thought. I wanted excitement, but not this. I didn't want to be involved in a brawl. I didn't want to witness police brutality. I liked cops, I liked trannies, and I didn't want to be in a situation where I'd regret dropping out of med school.

Zebra crossed her arms haughtily and Rainbow followed suit.

"Miss," the cop said.

"Me?" I said, pointing to my chest and standing up.

"Yeah, you. Would you please enter the ladies' room and ascertain for us whether it's vacant?"

"Her he calls 'miss,' " Zebra muttered, her voice suddenly dropping two octaves. "How come I get 'ma'am'?"

I was going to be part of the solution! My confidence returning, I rolled past them, contemplating a career in mediation and also noticing that all four squabblers had stubble on their cheeks. I pushed open the door and peered inside.

"Anybody in here?" I called out. I skated in and looked under both doors. Just as I spotted a pair of feet, a nervous voice answered, "Yeah?"

What would a mediator do?

"Well," I said, choosing my words carefully, "there are two . . . women . . . outside who would like to use this bathroom, but I believe that they are, perhaps, in possession of . . ." How did I get here? I suddenly thought. Just before I burst out laughing, I said in a rush, "I think they have male genitalia. Does it bother you if they use this bathroom?"

I heard some grunting, shifting, then a snapping sound like a rubber band, and the owner of the feet let out a loud, relaxed sigh.

"Not. At. All. Nothing bothers me. Chicks with dicks. Dicks with chicks. Wha-ever. Tha . . . as cooool." The voice faded away.

I listened for a moment more, then left the bathroom. The quartet looked at me expectantly. I couldn't deny that I was getting a small thrill out of being in the middle of this situation, rather than making it up to amuse myself at some wingding for the ambassador from Venezuela.

"The person in there does not seem to mind anything. In fact," I turned to the Eves with Adam's apples, "you may want to let these nice officers go in there first and make sure it's safe, because I suspect that whoever is in there is beginning her morning with a needle in her arm."

Zebra and Rainbow gasped dramatically, while the cops cursed under their breath.

"Drugs, honey?" Zebra reached out to me as though she felt faint, her enormous biceps rippling against her sequins. She closed her eyes, placed her other hand on her chest, fingers splayed, and went through the motions of regaining her composure.

"I do not want to be around anyone messing with drugs. Evian, let's go. We'll relieve ourselves somewhere respectable."

Evian made an "mmm, mmm, mmm" sound of disapproval and tottered off beside Zebra.

The cops shook their heads at me like it was my fault they had to go deal with a junkie on a clear, sun-drenched Thursday morning.

I adjusted my wrist guards and took off down the path, my arms spread, hugging the breeze as I rolled along beside the Hudson River.

*   *   *

WHEN I GOT BACK, MY BUTT AND THIGHS WERE CRAMPING, but my day kept looking up. Gerard, the chipper Vietnam vet who wore pith helmets in summertime and a Ruskie top hat of the variety favored by Hasidic Jews in wintertime, was in our foyer, chucking mail bundles into metal slots. Gerard and I had become buddies during my various professional-school forays. He had presented me with every application, every test score, and every acceptance and rejection letter, proffering predictions with each one.

"You scored high," he would say, weighing my LSAT results in his open palm.

"I don't think you should apply here," he'd warn, handing me an application for a medical school that was far from home, making me wonder whether he was secretly in the employ of my parents.

"I don't think you got into this one." He'd wink, handing me a thick envelope.

"Bad news," he said now, handing me my mail. A bright orange envelope peeked out from under a Sierra Trading Post catalog.

"Jury duty," he said gravely, as though he were a doctor diagnosing cancer.

I froze.

"It's okay," he said. "You can get out of it. Just tell 'em you got a crack on your ceiling you gotta watch. That's what my cousin did." He jabbed a thumb over his shoulder to indicate his cousin's dismissal from service.

"Jury duty?" I repeated. *"Seriously?"*

I tore open the envelope and there, in my hands, was my call to civic duty. My ticket to a front-row seat at the best show in town. My personalized pass to the most crucial of American

responsibilities. My guarantee that I would be expected somewhere every day for at least a week. Best of all, the notice had
been delayed by misdelivery and redelivery, so I was expected
downtown in just four days. I turned to Gerard and puffed up
with self-importance.

"Gerard!" I chastised. "You put your life on the line for this
nation. You lost friends, brothers, countrymen, and you're
telling me to evade jury duty?"

Gerard had the good grace to look sheepish.

"Do you know how *great* jury duty is?" I asked him, already
picturing myself, inexplicably sepia-toned, in a high-ceilinged
courtroom, savoring the weight of responsibility. I would be
the fairest juror that ever was, I solemnly promised both parties.

The last time I was summoned, I'd been dismissed after
two days, not having set foot in a courtroom. I was horribly disappointed, especially because my dad had prepped me for an
hour on how to be picked. I was to say as little as possible about
myself without actually evading the lawyers' questions. I was
to appear detached without crossing the line into dim-witted.

It was a tricky dance, but I was ready. This time, I would
land a seat in that wooden box. I tore off my Rollerblades and
ran upstairs to shower, trying not to let my mood plummet at
the sight of my non-blinking answering machine broadcasting
my non-messages. Forget Gregory, I reprimanded myself. I
would meet the love of my life on jury duty. On our first day of
deliberations (we'd tell our kids), we would vehemently dis-
agree, practically spitting venom across the copper-colored
water pitchers. In the ensuing days, though, I'd be so articulate
that he'd come to see my point of view and be in such awe of my
verbal acrobatics that he would fall madly, helplessly in love
with me. We'd be like Katharine Hepburn and Spencer Tracy

in *Adam's Rib,* but jurors instead of lawyers. Was there a paying position whose requirements included exceptional execution of jury service?

Just as I was about to step under the hot spray, there was a pounding on my apartment door. I grumbled as I wrapped a towel around myself, wondering whether it was Gerard coming to apologize for his un-American attitude. I padded down the hall and cracked open the door.

Gregory.

I wanted to drop my towel, grab him, and throw him to the floor. I also wanted to smack him—left cheek, right cheek, left cheek, like a slapstick routine—until he begged forgiveness. I opened my mouth to demand reasons for his radio silence.

"Why didn't you call me?" he asked me hotly, his eyes blazing, arms folded tightly across his chest.

I stared at him, furious and light-headed, suddenly aware that I had been bracing myself for the possibility of never seeing him again. The physical reality of his lanky body and warm scent and long eyelashes was such a relief that, to my complete mortification, I burst into tears. Angry at both of us, I started to slam the door in his face. To my relief, he shot one hand out to keep it from closing.

"Why didn't *you* call *me*?" I wailed, throwing what remained of my pride to the winds. If pride weighed anything, I'd have the upper-body strength to pitch an entire season in the major leagues.

"*Why?* I've never had—" He raised his eyebrows to convey fornication and all its attendant complexities, "so early on in a relationship or in, you know, that *way.* I figured you had used me and I was waiting for an apology."

A confused grunt stuttered up out of my throat as I tried to make sense of this insult.

"You think I make a habit of seducing men in my secret pink closet?" I asked incredulously, clutching my towel around me.

"We don't know that the *closet* was pink. Too dark." He waited, as if this were an adequate response. It wasn't, so I remained silent. He shrugged. "Are you planning to apologize?"

"Hell, no," I told him. "Are you?"

"Nope."

"Bye, Zephyr!" Gerard yelled up the stairs. I closed my eyes and mashed my lips together.

"Good-bye, Gerard!" I singsonged, accepting this final icing of embarrassment. We listened to him turn the lock and jangle his way outside.

"Can I come in?" Gregory sounded annoyed, which annoyed *me*.

"Be my guest." I waved him in and slammed the door behind him. I briefly wondered whether there couldn't be a whole new field of therapy based on door-slamming. Kind of like primal screaming for the new millennium.

Gregory sat down hard on the couch, hunched over so that his elbows dug against his thighs. He glared at the floor.

"I think our problem—" he started.

"We already have problems?"

"Our *problem* is that we need to start over with a proper date. Have the coffee we didn't have. Talk."

I wondered what he would do if I suddenly dropped my towel.

"Okay," I said.

"Okay," he said, looking up at me expectantly. I mirrored his expression. He straightened up suddenly, almost violently, startling me.

"Has the feminist movement completely passed you by?"

he growled. "*You* can ask *me* out, you know, just like *you* can call *me*."

"Is that what you think the feminist movement is all about?" I asked archly, as if I were well versed in the ins and outs of Gloria Steinem's rhetoric. I was buying time.

"Why didn't you call me?" he asked again, this time in the same plaintive voice that had undone me in the alley four days earlier. Was he for real or could he just turn on the earnest puppy dog act at will?

I shook my head and shrugged. It was unbearable to me that we weren't naked and wrapped around each other.

As if he could read my mind, he said gently, "Let's go out to dinner Saturday night."

It hurt that he could resist me, standing before him wearing nothing but a drape of woven cotton purchased from the discount table at the Astor Place K-Mart. But I was flattered that he cared enough to go backward, to get to know me apart from secret staircases and faulty dryers.

"Fine," I said as lightly as I could muster. "When and where?"

"Six o'clock," he said, suddenly cheerful and apparently oblivious to my fragile emotional state. He seemed callous in his certainty that our reset button could be pressed so easily. "I'll come by here."

He rose and I followed him to the door.

"Wait!" I said, remembering the JDate Jihad I had planned for five o'clock. "Let's do seven."

"Seven what?" he asked.

"Seven o'clock," I enunciated slowly, wondering whether he had Asperger's.

"Why?" Now he looked hurt, perhaps insulted, by the thought that I could hold out an extra hour. I felt vaguely, childishly triumphant. What a sick and dysfunctional four-day-old relationship this was.

"I have something at five with my friends. Seven, okay?" I said gently, opening the door. He studied me, trying to decide whether I was telling the truth or playing a game.

"I swear," I assured him, softening. "Meet me here at seven. Or," I amended, thinking of his earlier accusations that I had betrayed the sisterhood, "I can come pick you up. Where do you live?"

At that moment, one floor above us, Roxana's door flew open, and she came racing down the stairs, uncharacteristically clad in jeans and a man's plaid shirt. She looked wan and tired, but still sexier than I could have looked in a ball gown after a week at a spa.

"I'm comeen, I'm comeen," she yelled sullenly. She stopped short, her eyebrows traveling ever so slightly north when she spotted me in my towel, ushering the exterminator out of my apartment in the middle of a Thursday afternoon. I felt our score become slightly more even. I also felt a small thrill poking through my embarrassment that for once it was I, the vanilla, plasma-screen American, who was cloaked—or uncloaked—in mystery and intrigue.

"Someone dooble-lucked zuh door," she explained, regaining her regular dulcet tones. She started to slip past Gregory, when he suddenly straightened his shoulders and said in a booming voice completely unsuited to his proximity to Roxana,

"Ma'am, aren't you the resident in 3B?"

Roxana looked at him like a frightened puppy. She nodded, and I wondered why he was sounding like he'd stepped off the set of *Dragnet*.

"There were two rooms in your apartment I couldn't access when I sprayed the building last Monday. They were locked." This was news to me. A qualified landord, I thought morosely, would have kept an eagle eye on the stranger she let into her tenants' homes instead of engaging in petty rivalries out on the landing. Another black mark on my quickly darkening record.

"James knoss zey are never spread," she said quickly. "I am very sensitive to zuh poison." She started down the stairs again, her tiny back rigid.

"Uh-huh, uh-huh," Gregory continued tenaciously. "Right, he's told me that, but is there any way we could schedule a time when, say, you'll be out of town, that we could do it? It's just that it makes spraying the rest of the building nearly ineffectual if we have to skip a spot. The vermin congregate where the poison isn't."

I shuddered, and Roxana's eyes grew wide. "Zere are no vehrmin in my apartment," she said defensively, as someone started pounding on the outside door. "I keep eet vere clean. Everysing ees vere, vere clean!" She twisted away, down the stairs.

"Why didn't you tell me there were locked rooms in her apartment?" I whispered accusingly.

"You didn't ask."

I couldn't let go of my towel to strangle him so I stamped my foot, which conferred upon me all the dignity of a child having a tantrum.

"How could I know to ask that?" I hissed. "Is it the room we were . . . in?"

Gregory looked at me, his lips twitching slightly at the corners, then reached across the threshold, pulled me tight against him and planted his warm, soft mouth over mine. His tongue teased its way inside for a liquid second and then it was over.

"You should get back inside," he said, pulling away, leaving me limp and damp. He nodded down the stairs, to where Roxana was greeting her visitor in hushed, tense murmurs, then bounded off in their direction.

Dizzy, I started to shut the door, but not before glimpsing Senator Smith's hoary head close behind Roxana's. She glanced up and our eyes met briefly, just long enough for me to register the cloud of fear enveloping her delicate face. Helplessly, I let the door click shut and stood frozen inside my bright apartment. I strained to hear their fading footsteps, and when Roxana's own door closed with a quiet thud, it was like a muffled gunshot triggering the worst my imagination had to offer.

FREDDY GIVITCH WAS A PORTRAIT IN PATHETIC. I PULLED OPEN the door later that afternoon to reveal the saddest sack I'd ever seen taking up space on my stoop. Droopy eyes and a belly to match; moist, blubbery lips; coarsely shaven jowls; fingers worrying the loops around his belt buckle. His checked shirt was two decades late, his pants on the muddy side of brown, and he bottomed out the outfit with a pair of dingy, scuffed sneakers. Of course he was bald. He could have been twenty-five or fifty-five; I couldn't tell and it didn't really matter anyway. He sucked sympathy to him like a pile of sand drinking up salt water. He looked at me through thick glasses, and I could see why Officer Varlam tried to help his brother-in-law any way he could. I decided at first glance to give him the listing.

"Come in, come in," I said quietly, as though ushering him into shelter after a natural disaster, which, I supposed, was what his entire life was.

"Thank you, thank you," he croaked, his gaze darting quickly to meet mine, then resting somewhere in the vicinity of my forehead. I wondered whether we'd say everything twice for the remainder of his visit.

He followed me upstairs, making little grunts as he went.

"Here it is." I led him into James's apartment, wondering

whether Freddy had ever successfully rented a place in his life or if I was tossing away my only potential source of income because a man's floppy, overly long shoelaces made me want to weep.

Freddy crossed his short arms, an effort that elicited another soft grunt. He glanced at the living room, trudged into the kitchen, opened the refrigerator, one cabinet, and one drawer.

"I threw out most of—" I began, but Freddy was off again, darting his eggplant-shaped head quickly into the bathroom, then galumphing into the bedroom at a surprising speed.

"You should have seen this room before. It was disgusting," I told him proudly. The Sterling Girls and I had effected a Mary Poppins–like transformation, so complete that I had briefly entertained the idea of starting a world-class, white-glove cleaning service. I had made it as far as our *Good Morning America* segment before I remembered that my friends were already gainfully and contentedly employed in careers that did not require squeeze mops.

Freddy nodded and headed back to the front door. The entire tour had taken under a minute. I wondered how he planned to attract future renters to a property he had only given a glance.

He said to the door, "You still got a buncha cans of film or something in the fridge. Get ridda those." He paused, keeping his back to me and the rest of the apartment. "Fireplace work?"

I started to nod, then said, "Yes."

"Under the winda seats—any storage under there?"

"I have no idea," I said, surprised. I walked over to the benches that James had installed, and squatted down. I lifted one cushion and ran my hand along the solid, polished oak surface. I let the cushion drop and picked up the next one, to find a set of hinges gleaming back at me. I wondered how much value the apartment had just gained with the discovery of this precious storage space. Five dollars? A hundred? I hoped Freddy knew.

When I tried to lift the seat, though, it resisted. Looking closer, I found a small lock built into the base. I sighed and wondered whether James wasn't actually happier in jail, where locks and keys constituted most of the landscape.

"There's storage space under here," I announced to Freddy, standing up, "but it's locked."

"Clean it out and then we can rent you."

"Sooo," I said hesitantly to the folds at the back of Freddy's neck. "Any idea, I mean, do you think—well, what do you think is the least I could—"

"Four thou. I'll get you four thou," Freddy told the door abruptly, before he opened it and left.

I froze in my tracks, afraid that if I moved I'd distort the words still bouncing through the air. I darted my eyes over to the fireplace, as if to ask the grate, Did you hear what I heard?

"A month? Four thousand dollars a *month*?" I asked aloud, and waited to see whether Freddy would burst back in, pointing at me, his doughy gut jiggling with laughter.

I hurried to the closet in search of the box that held the framed photos of James. I suspected or hoped—the line between the two was blurry—that one of the keys rattling around inside one of those pictures would open the window seat.

Lucy had carefully wrapped the photos in stained linen placemats. I shook each, unfurling the one that rattled and holding it gingerly by its edges as though it was contaminated. If ever there were a boy with cooties, it was James.

I palmed the two keys and started out of the closet. I stopped abruptly and spun around, suddenly inspired. I stuck one of the keys into the lock of the staircase door, the door I'd pried open with Gregory. The lock turned easily and I felt a short-lived flash of triumph. I'd figured out something—Agent Zuckerman reporting. But I didn't know what it was I'd figured out—back to Chambermaid Zephyr here for mopping.

I glanced up the staircase, allowing myself a brief, delicious replay of my sweaty, bizarre encounter with Gregory—had I really done that?—then closed the staircase door and hurried back to the window seat, the other key already slick with palm sweat. I lifted up the cushion and turned the key in the lock. Agent Zuckerman! Carefully, afraid of finding a bomb, a snake collection, or locks of my hair, I lifted the seat.

Inside was a blue plastic cooler, the ten-dollar kind you grab at the drugstore when you realize you don't have enough room in your fridge to hold drinks for a party. Gingerly, I lifted the grimy white lid and peeked inside, squinting with anticipated revulsion.

Ten test tubes (one for each jar of Marmite? Did James also have OCD?) with red stoppers were jabbed crudely into ten overturned Styrofoam cups to keep them upright. The cups were surrounded by wet, flaccid ice packs that had long since lost their cool. A stale, synthetic smell wafted up. I reached for one of the tubes, then stopped and grabbed a pair of rubber gloves off James's counter.

I held each tube up to the sunlight spilling through the window. Inside all of them was a tiny amount of viscous fluid; it looked like whatever had been in them had mostly evaporated. I tilted the tubes in different directions, letting the fluid ooze around the glass like the contents of a lava lamp. Drugs? Explosives? Medicine? Semen? I shuddered and replaced the tube I was holding in its cup.

I closed the cooler, locked the window seat, and washed my hands for a long time under scalding hot water, wondering whether I should call someone. Gregory popped into my mind and I chastised myself. Why would I want to tell him something before I told the Sterling Girls? I'd known him less than two weeks—he wasn't qualified to be my go-to person. I felt like a traitor.

Officer Varlam, I reminded myself, pumping out gobs of soap. If there was anyone I should call, it was the law enforcement official in charge of James's case. But I didn't want the cops back here, rooting around my building. Delaying my income.

Was I an accomplice to something by not reporting the cooler? The secret staircase? As the hot water ran through my fingers, I tried to reason through the facts as my father might.

Fact: James had been arrested for embezzling money from the oil delivery company.

Fact: James either had a personality disorder or was an international double agent or was excessively narcissistic or was some combination of all three.

Fact: James had an unusually large collection of sex paraphernalia (though that was a judgment, a qualitative and subjective observation, I reminded myself).

Fact: James may or may not have built a pink staircase with access only to his apartment and to Roxana's, the key to which he kept inside one of two identical pictures of himself.

Fact: James had a hidden, locked cooler under his window seat, with tubes of unidentified fluid inside it.

Fact: For ten years, James had been a responsible, cheerful super.

I turned off the water. Except for the embezzlement he'd already been arrested for, James's other behaviors weren't necessarily illegal. In fact, they probably weren't any odder than those you'd find if you randomly sampled forty-year-old bachelors living alone anywhere in the country, and possibly even common if you narrowed your survey down to those living in New York City.

Still. The prospect of four thousand dollars a month in income had instilled in me, in the past seven minutes, a new sense of self-importance and responsibility. The sugar in my NASA lemonade. It was like my mother preached in her seminars: Ladies, you want your menstrual flow light and your cash flow heavy! The higher the dollar amount, the taller you stand! I had previously accused her of spouting specious maxims, but now I saw a glimmer of truth to them. Now I felt it was incumbent upon me to preserve this strange collection of behaviors and artifacts until time united those facts into a cohesive story, one that would transform those artifacts into evidence.

It was in this new role as evidence protectress that I crossed the hall to my apartment and returned with some cold ice packs to arrange carefully around the test tubes. I thought back to the third grade, when my class had waited for baby chicks to hatch out of the seemingly lifeless shells that had been FedExed into our care from a farm in Utah. We'd had to keep those fragile ovals at 99.5 degrees or they would have sat there forever, as lifeless as their cousins on supermarket shelves. If I kept the test tubes cool, maybe whatever potential they possessed would be maintained.

I put the warm ice packs in James's freezer, grabbed the film out of his fridge, and closed the door to his apartment. As the latch clicked, a swell of satisfaction rose up inside me and I felt a few millimeters closer to being a grown-up.

And then I was blindsided: by a vivid, pulsing memory of Hayden's languorous gaze admiring the length of our naked bodies sealed together with sweat. I smacked the wall, trying to make the image disperse, as though it were a rat. A new relationship inevitably brings up old ones, I comforted myself right before I started wondering where Hayden was at this very moment. Stop! What would he think of me earning as much money as he did? Damn it. Was that why we hadn't worked out? Because I wasn't his earning equal? Was I going to start thinking about him again now that I was? Did I have no control over my anarchic brain?

I stomped into my apartment and slammed the door—twice in one day. I sat down at the desk in my bedroom and tried to distract myself with a pile of heating bills that needed deciphering. The words "just an exterminator" rose to the surface from wherever I'd been keeping them tamped down. Tears of self-disgust and hypocrisy welled in my eyes and I dropped my head into my hands, exhausted by the hopelessness of ever completely getting over Hayden.

THIRTEEN

Saturday afternoon, after I strolled through the frenzied Union Square farmers' market, and just before I went to execute the richly deserved humbling of LinguaFrank at Grounded, I dropped off James's film, wondering whether it was the British or the Brooklyn side of him that had preferred film to digital. I'd briefly weighed the legal and moral implications of developing the photos and tried to convince myself I was doing him a favor—they might be pictures he'd like to have with him—but really, I just wanted to know what a convicted con artist felt compelled to photograph.

Did he have a soft side that inspired him to capture close-ups of urban flora dotted with ice drops? Puppies frolicking in a basket lined with red velvet? Or would there be pictures of guys in stained coveralls delivering fuel oil? Maybe, I thought as I let the door to Fast Foto bang shut behind me—if they'd bothered with the "Ph," I might have closed it gently—James's dual personality made it hard for him to remember people and he needed head shots to keep his deals straight.

I stumbled as I left the store (I'd broken with my "comfort first" rule and was wearing shoes not designed for walking). But even as my calves ached and I had to downshift my stride so I didn't overcompensate and do that weird forward hip scoop—the hunchbutt—that cancels out any sex appeal imbued by the shoes in the first place, I was feeling my place in the city. I had a job, I had friends, I had a lover, I had very bearable parents. And I'm a native, I added smugly to two willowy transplants opening the door to Equinox to shed pounds they couldn't spare. My hair was behaving, my mid-section felt flattish, and the spring air teased my pale green sundress around my freshly shaved legs. The blue cloudless sky, the late-blooming hyacinths, the light green leaves with their false promise of an endless summer—the city itself was urging me to overlook my Hayden hiccups.

After Gregory and I went on our real date tonight and got going full force, I'd be rid of the Briggs pig forever. It would speed things along just a tiny bit, I couldn't help thinking as I maneuvered my way across Greenwich Avenue against a red light, if I could see Hayden in person just once, to exorcise him. And it would help a big bit, I added, darting past a conveyor belt swallowing barrels of texturized vegetable protein into the basement of Soy Luck Club, if I saw him right at this moment, while I was feeling very catalog-sexy and suffused with the appeal of a full Saturday night agenda ahead of me: vengeance followed by romance. I looked around hopefully, on the off chance that in this city of eight million people, Hayden would be walking toward me at exactly that moment, preferably looking bereft, having just been fired, and able to tell just from my expression that I'd be on my back with another man just hours from now.

As I rounded Jane Street, my hands flew to my thighs to keep my dress from flying up (on Marilyn, sexy; on me, like wrestling a parachute). As the fabric threatened to slip through my fingers, a barrel-shaped guy with a thin ponytail came blasting by on a skateboard, pounding his straightened, pumping leg into the blacktop like a metronome.

"Hey!" I yelped as he whizzed by, just inches from my exposed toes.

Without looking back, he held up his middle finger to me.

"Fucking . . ." I spat, my man-eater mood dissipating into thin air. I looked around indignantly to see if anyone else had witnessed his random act of spite. I should start a kindness movement. I'd lobby the state, then Congress. I'd write a charter and guidelines and usher in the Century of Goodwill.

The guy got off his skateboard, flipped it into his hand, and headed into Grounded. There was no mistaking the freckles or the pasty face beneath them.

LinguaFrank.

My ire bloomed. He was a hypocritical, arrogant, arguably misogynist, and definitely anti-Semitic boor. And he was even uglier in person than he'd been on his JDate profile. Was Abigail's bad taste caused by poor judgment, or by desperation? Either way, LinguaFrank deserved no leniency. I felt like a warrior. The justice of what we were about to do made my heart begin to race and I choked back a demonic cackle.

He cased the tables and, seeing no Asian females, sat down near the front, facing the open double doors. He crossed his leg, ankle on knee—the arrogant, space-hogging leg cross, I noted bitterly—and started picking at his teeth with the corner of an Equal packet. I uttered a quiet gurgle of disgust.

He squinted out at the street and I ducked behind a ginkgo tree. As I did, I spotted Lucy hiding behind a large planter next door to the café. She was watching the front door and taking notes on a small steno pad, which instantly irritated me. We didn't need a written record of this. At the most, we were going to snap a photo of the moment we told the great scholar Darren Schwartz, aka LinguaFrank, that his would-be Asian dream girl, who happened to be our friend, had seen him from afar and decided he was too fat. And too Jewish. And she had left.

I wanted to shout to Lucy to stop playing Nancy Drew and go inside, but I couldn't without drawing Lingua's attention. I left my post and resumed walking west on Jane Street. As soon as I was out of his line of vision, I crossed the street, doubled back, and poked Lucy hard from behind.

She shrieked.

"Shhh!" I whacked her gently.

"What do you mean *shhh*?" she hissed at me. "You hit me!"

"I didn't hit you."

"What do you call this?" She jabbed me.

"A poke."

"*Hey*. No fighting." Tag sneaked up behind us, making us both jump. She rubbed her hands together and raised her perfect eyebrows. "It's time to go slit 'im."

"He's not a shark," Lucy reminded her nervously.

"You mean we can't disembowel him, toss his entrails overboard, and send his head to the Midwest for further research?"

"Down, girl." I patted her arm. But I was remembering how adeptly she'd handled herself in front of the King of Spain. I felt a rush of gratitude for Tag's steely constitution, which in turn inflated a small balloon of generosity toward Lucy. "This is gonna be good," I reassured both of them.

Lucy boldly led the way inside.

Even though none of us had discussed attire beforehand, my friends had also dressed up for the occasion. Lucy was wearing a short, flouncy skirt; Tag was showing cleavage; and both were navigating on high heels. If we were going to make LinguaFrank feel deep, abiding regret and repentance, and we were representing the hot woman he couldn't get, we had to be ambassadors of hot in her place.

As I followed them to the vacant table, skirting other customers' legs, ducking the stale Valentine's Day decorations still hanging campily from the ceiling and trying not to snag my dress on potted cacti, I felt the first prickle of doubt since concocting the plan.

Lingua openly checked us out as we walked by his table. He smiled a self-knowing smile, which made his Wonder Bread face even less attractive. My nerves recovered a little.

Lucy and I sat down. Tag remained standing.

"What can I get you?" she asked us.

"No foam double latte," Lingua piped up behind her in a surprisingly solid and sexy voice. Maybe that explained Abigail's attraction: she'd gotten to know him on the phone. A face for radio, I thought.

Tag turned slowly to him, and I nudged her foot with mine to remind her not to blow it. It worked. She forced a thin-lipped smile and turned back to us.

"Cocoa," Lucy said.

"Small coffee," I said.

Tag shook her head, disappointed in our predictably low octane tastes, and headed for the counter.

For the first time in the fourteen years we'd known each other, Lucy and I could think of nothing to say to each other, hyperaware that Lingua was listening. A few awkward moments passed.

"I have this new client," Lucy finally blurted out. "He left his wife for someone thinner and he's just hating himself now."

I glared at her. She looked at me helplessly.

"I'm seeing Gregory tonight," I rebutted as Tag returned to the table. "Retroactive first date."

Lucy was confused. In one meaningful look, I tried to convey that we ought to be presenting ourselves as active-duty hotties, not offering Lingua abstract morality tales that he couldn't absorb.

"So you're gonna do what besides hop into bed with him?" Tag asked, following my lead. We all felt Lingua's attention bearing down on us. I thought Tag didn't need to reveal quite so much information about me.

"Bed?" Lucy picked up on the tactic. "That would be progress if they could make it to a bed this time." The two of them cackled and in my peripheral vision I saw Lingua shift in his seat.

"Tag, did you ever talk to that guy again, the one you slept with in Madagascar?" I had no intention of being the sacrificial lamb.

"I never slept with anyone in Madagascar," she said coolly. Damn my wretched geography. M . . . M . . . It was in some M place she had had a one-night stand with another parasitologist. Mexico? No, I'd remember that. Malawi?

"Do you think Mercedes will sleep with Dover Carter tonight?" I said, sacrificing the friend who wasn't there to defend herself. It occurred to me, though, that if Lingua was as much an ivory tower prisoner as Abigail, the name Dover Carter might not mean much.

Lucy and Tag looked at each other, trying to decide whether to let me off the hook.

"Oh, I bet they won't," Tag conceded. "Mercedes has that prudish side that comes out when she really likes someone."

"Wait," I said, forgetting the eavesdropper for a moment. "Do you think she'll actually fall for him? He's a movie star. He won't commit!" I felt myself getting upset at the thought of Dover's future transgressions.

"First of all, calm down," Tag admonished.

"And second of all," Lucy added, "he's a real person, too. He probably wants a meaningful relationship as much as the next guy."

Now Tag and I looked at Lucy dubiously. She remembered where we were and whom we were sitting next to and shrugged.

"Well, some guys really do want meaningful relationships," she amended. "And Dover could be one of them. He's had a successful career, he's never been married, never had a kid. Maybe he's ready."

Tag shuddered her shoulders like a horse keeping a fly at bay. I knew that she was also trying to picture, and not for the first time, pale little Lucy sitting in her dark basement in Bed-Stuy with not much more than a Rolodex of phone numbers to assist her, offering real comfort to a desperate, unemployed, abused single mother of three. But as I looked at Lucy's open face, shot through with apparent innocence, I wondered whether we hadn't all been mistaking hard-fought conviction for naiveté. If a social worker couldn't have some faith in everyone from the street to the screen, then there wasn't much point in her doing the work she did. Maybe this same trust in Dover Carter's good intentions, informed by nothing more than a few issues of *People* magazine, served Lucy's clientele far better than we ever gave her credit for.

I looked at Lucy with new admiration. She returned my glance with one of suspicion.

"What?"

"Nothing," I said, giving her arm a brisk, affectionate rub. "Maybe you're right about Dover."

Tag hung her head in defeat, as though she'd lost another friend in her ongoing personal crusade against the Warm Fuzzies. She looked at her watch.

"Okay, it's been ten minutes. Let's do it," she hissed.

"I think we should let him sweat it out another five," I said in a low voice, growing nervous again.

"But look at him. He's not sweating. He's as cocky as he was when he came in here." We glanced over. He was lounging in his chair now, elbows back, surveying his kingdom.

"He's too interested in our conversation to notice he's being stood up," Lucy suggested.

"Don't flatter yourself," Tag told her. "Unless either of you want to do the honors, I'm itching to do the deed."

"Wait," I said, "we haven't gotten our drinks!"

"So? We'll tell him, then have our drinks, then go."

"That doesn't make for much of an exit," Lucy said, and I silently agreed.

So we waited another minute until the barista called out Tag's name. Tag brought back our drinks and we blew on them and sipped them in silence.

"Are we taking a picture?" I whispered.

Lucy held up her cell phone.

"I'm nervous," I finally admitted.

Tag and Lucy nodded their heads.

"Wait, you? You're nervous?" I said to Tag accusingly. She was shattering my world order. Nothing made Tag nervous.

"Well, not nervous exactly . . ." she corrected me unconvincingly.

"We don't have to do this," Lucy suggested. "Even if we do nothing, he'll still have been stood up."

The thought of not following through made me feel like I'd failed Abigail, who back in Palo Alto was eagerly awaiting our phone call. Tag had the same thought.

"No," she said, gulping the rest of her espresso, "let's do it."

She surreptitiously dialed my cell phone. I took a deep breath and answered. She hung up, but I pretended to have a conversation.

"Oh, hi!" I began too brightly. Tag and Lucy shook their heads at me. I brought it down a notch. "Uh-huh. Uh-huh." I was stalling, giving my unrealized acting career a moment to dust itself off. "Ohhhhh," I said knowingly, glancing over at LinguaFrank, who was openly watching and listening.

I brazenly caught his eye. "Yeah, I see what you mean." It was a pleasure to watch his narrow eyes grow even closer together with concern. "Yeah. Yeah. No, don't waste your time. We'll handle it."

I snapped shut my phone and shook my head dramatically at my friends. With the safety of numbers behind me, I turned abruptly to Lingua.

"You're waiting for someone, yes?" He looked startled. "Asian? Thin?"

"Red dress," Lucy piped up.

Lingua just looked at us, surprised.

"She's not coming," I told him cheerfully.

"Who are *you*?" he asked.

"Her friends. Her good friends."

"And she's too cowardly to come in here and tell me herself?" he demanded.

I hadn't thought of it that way. Tag jumped in.

"She's busy. She doesn't have time for men like you."

"Like me?" he said, leaning forward menacingly. But Tag leaned right back at him.

"Fat. Jewish," she said, enunciating evilly. He sat back as if she'd slapped him, and even I felt my heart race. Then his eyes narrowed again.

"But we met," he said through gritted teeth, "on *J*Date."

"Ironic, isn't it?" I was happy to interject with fake thoughtfulness. "What kind of person would say that to someone they met on JDate?"

"What kind of person," Lucy said, warming up, "would say

that to anyone at all? What kind of thing is that to say to *any-one*?"

The three of us watched him, waiting for the light to dawn, waiting for him to look ashamed or beaten. But instead, the scholar just sneered at us impatiently.

"What kind of people have nothing better to do on a Saturday afternoon than be their friend's lackey?" He sat back and crossed his arms, scowling.

"Why are you surfing JDate if you don't want a Jewish woman?" I blurted out.

He considered me for a moment, and a lewd smile crept across his face.

"Because plenty of shiksas wanna screw a good Jewish man. I only aim to please, ma'am." He tipped an imaginary hat. Tag fake-lunged at him and he flinched. She snorted with disdain.

"In what world are you a *good* man?" I demanded.

"Zephyr!" I was off-script and making Lucy nervous.

"Well, *Zephyr*," Lingua smirked at his discovery of my name, "good, in this case, can be a means of describing someone's abilities in bed, and not necessarily an overall character assessment."

"Well, *Darren*, it's good you've got that linguistics degree," Tag snapped at him. His face darkened.

"How the hell do you know my name? Or what I do?" Suddenly, it seemed we had the upper hand. Or, at the very least, it seemed like a good time to end this party, especially as our conversation was starting to attract the attention of other patrons. The three of us stood up, prepared to make a haughty exit.

"Where do you think you're going?" Darren stood up too, cementing our position at center stage. Lucy and I looked to Tag for backup, but she looked just as surprised as we were.

"We're done with you," she said quietly, trying to project authority. She started to thread her way out, and we followed her. Darren Schwartz followed us.

"What do you mean 'done with' me? What did you come here to do? Why doesn't your friend come and tell me to my face that I'm too fat? Too Jewish?" His voice rose to a whine but he still didn't seem to recognize his own epithets.

By now, the four of us were out on the sidewalk, but the wide-open doors only framed us so that no one inside could do anything but watch the free entertainment. I wondered why I had ever thought this plan could come to any kind of satisfying or remotely dignified conclusion.

"Mature, very mature." He was warming up now, his arms gesturing wildly around his torso. "Your friend stands me up and you watch and report back? Oh, that's brilliant. A brilliant plan. Great use of your time." He tried to cackle, but he had the wild look of a leashed dog confronted by a predator.

The fact that he actually thought his fantasy woman was out there in the Village at this moment, wearing a tight red dress and rejecting him, made us realize we'd succeeded.

Tag, Lucy, and I all burst out laughing at the same time.

"Why are you laughing?" he demanded, which only made us laugh harder.

The three of us ignored him and started strolling toward Greenwich Avenue, our arms linked. I didn't want to turn around and ruin the effect of our dramatic, triumphant leave-taking, but I could practically see him staring after us, open-mouthed, frustrated, duly punished.

Nobody messes with my friends and gets away with it, I thought, as the breeze rushed at us and tossed the front of my dress up over my face.

*   *   *

Tag and lucy peeled off at the corner of twelfth and Seventh to go buy Beard Papa cream puffs and catch the second night of the Weighty Eighties film retrospective at the IFC. For a moment, I felt a tug of longing, wanting to be sitting with them in the dark, gorging on sweets and John Hughes movies, exchanging whispered trivia about Molly Ringwald. I wanted to be in the comfort of their safe, familiar company instead of mustering the energy required to launch a new relationship with a testy and unpredictable man. Spinsterhood seemed to have its benefits.

I made my way along Twelfth Street but stopped mid-stride when I spotted a figure sitting on our stoop, hunched over, appearing to study his feet. A drunk I was going to have to ask to move along? A New School student needing to be reminded to take his cigarette butt with him? A construction worker who would leave McDonald's ketchup packets behind him? I tensed with the anticipation of confrontation.

My anxiety turned to irritation when I saw it was Gregory. An hour early. Again. What was *with* him? Didn't he understand anything about a standard social protocol that had been in place (or so I assumed from reading Jane Austen novels) for centuries? Yet, I was flattered and impressed. He was eager to see me and wasn't going to hide it for fear of seeming vulnerable. Either that or he'd forgotten what time we'd agreed on.

A piece of newspaper blew along the sidewalk and wrapped itself around my aching calf. I plucked it off, wondering if he'd even notice my legs, when he suddenly raised his head, looked straight at me, and smiled a soft, knowing, lopsided smile. The sunlight filtering through the apple tree in the front yard made his thick brown hair shine golden, and his cheeks looked warm and pink. I wanted to race up the stairs and dive headlong into his embrace.

I waved and smiled coyly, trying to pick up my pace without succumbing to hunchbutt.

"Hi," I said, hoping to infuse the single syllable with multiple meanings.

"Hi," he returned, still smiling. This was the furthest we'd ever gotten without a misunderstanding. He turned and picked up a flimsy plastic-coated box sitting beside him on the step. Cream puffs. Beard Papa cream puffs. The fortune-teller's prediction that Gregory and I would spend our lives together flashed through my mind. I stared at him, wondering how he knew that Beard Papa was the way to my heart.

"It's so nice out, I thought we could maybe sit here for a while and have dinner a little later. You know, the whole thing about life being uncertain, so eat dessert first?" He actually looked nervous.

I sat down as gracefully as I could and tried not to yell over the thumping of my heart.

"Actually," I said lightly, "I put that saying on my senior yearbook page in high school. I think being able to eat dessert whenever you want is one of the unsung benefits of being an adult." Even as I said it, I was surprised to hear myself describing myself as an adult.

He nodded seriously. He was making a concerted effort to make this date go smoothly, without sarcasm or squabbling. I was touched, but the moment felt as precarious as if we were playing catch with a soap bubble. It made me acutely aware of the fact that we were complete strangers.

"So," I began awkwardly, "I know virtually nothing about you." I quickly bit into a cream puff.

He raised his eyebrows at me, started to smirk, then caught himself.

"I grew up in Alabama—"

"Seriously?" I interrupted, my mouth full of custard. I swallowed. "I don't think I've ever met anyone who grew up there who wasn't—" I hesitated, looking for the right words.

"Baptist or black?" he offered. "There are more Jews down south than you'd think, but no, it's no New York."

"Is that why you moved here?" I asked with trepidation. Too observant or too tribally constrained and we'd never make it as a couple.

"God, no," he grimaced. "I moved here for graduate school."

"Ha!" I shouted. My first impression of him had been right. Ridofem jumpsuit and all, I'd pegged him for an academic. I smiled triumphantly.

"Ha, what?" he said suspiciously.

"Nothing, nothing." I waved my hand, eager for more. "Where? To study what?" I prompted.

"NYU. Shakespeare." He dug around for a second cream puff just as I was debating what to do with the last corner of mine that had no custard touching it. The dry corner.

"So, what happened? Are you still there?" I discreetly laid the unappetizing remnant on the step and helped myself to a second puff. I hoped he would notice I was a good eater and not a girly salad type.

He shook his head. "You ever heard of Harvey Blane?"

I nodded, surprised, and mentally thanked Abigail. Blane was a Shakespeare scholar legendary for his prolific writing, his insatiable appetite for female grad students, and his vulgar, unpredictable temperament, all of which he robustly maintained despite being blind since birth. Abigail had told me one infamous story about a woman who was sitting beside Blane in a seminar when he suddenly wrinkled his nose, turned to her, and said, "I can tell you're menstruating." He had single-handedly spurred the creation of NYU's sexual harassment policy.

"Don't tell me he hit on you, too?" I laughed, glad I could hold my own.

"I might have had more fun, at least." Gregory licked custard off his fingers and I suddenly had an image of what he had looked like as a little boy. "No, I made it to my orals and afterward he told me that even though I'd passed, I just didn't have that extra something that makes a truly gifted scholar. So I asked him if I should start coercing my undergrads into sleeping with me, if that would do the trick, and, well, after that," Gregory shrugged, "things became very unpleasant between us. On top of which, I basically realized he was right. I just wasn't cut out for academia. So I left."

"To become an exterminator?" I asked doubtfully. As someone who had less of a right than most to pass judgment on anyone quitting professional school, I was surprised to feel a pang of disappointment in Gregory.

He looked at me sharply. "Is that a problem?"

"No," I said quickly, then grew angry at the implication that I was a snob even if it was a little bit true. "But you have to agree it's a big change. I mean, do you find spraying for roaches as gratifying as parsing *King Lear*?" I asked.

Gregory looked me straight in the eye, and I watched him decide not to fight.

"No, it's not," he said quietly. "It's what I'm doing now, until I figure out what I want to do. Kind of like you, I'm guessing."

I nodded, trying to ignore the sinking feeling in my stomach. Both of us floundering? Both of us taking too long to grow up? I needed someone more certain of himself than I was, someone who could give me a boost up into adulthood, not someone who needed that from me. But even as I had that ungenerous thought, I still sensed a groundedness in Gregory.

While he continued to watch me with his baby-owl eyes, I tried to shake off these premature thoughts. Enjoy the moment,

Zephyr. The cream puffs, the warm breeze, his long legs brushing against mine on the cool, hard stone, the promise of having
him inside me that night.

I leaned forward and kissed him.

"What was that for?" he asked quietly.

"Cream puffs," I said. Two squirrels tussling in the branches
above our heads set off a shower of twigs and leaves. Gregory
pulled a leaf off my lap. The nearness of his hand to my thighs
triggered a shudder that wove its way up my ribs and settled in
the back of my throat.

We sat there and talked for a long, long time, the growing
certainty of where the evening was headed giving us the stam-
ina to draw out our stationary mating dance. As he painted his
past for me, Gregory's surly shell softened before my eyes. If I
stripped away the matzoh ball gumbo at Passover and the bar-
becued brisket during Rosh Hashanah, we had a lot in common. We both agreed that we'd give anything to spend a night
aboard one of the houseboats docked at the 79th Street Boat
Basin, that friends were as important as family, that Gatorade
tasted like Jell-O before it gelled, that future generations
would label George W. Bush a criminal, and that Bleecker
Street Pizza was far superior to its famous neighbor, John's
Pizza.

"So," I said tentatively, twirling a twig between my fingers,
afraid of disturbing the groundwork we'd laid, but unable to
keep my curiosity at bay. "How do your parents feel about your,
uh, change in professional direction?"

To my relief, Gregory laughed.

"Let's put it this way," he said, studying the sky for a moment. "My brother teaches math to inner-city kids in
Montgomery and they're disappointed that he's not teaching at
Harvard, where of course he'd win a Nobel. So my choice,
well . . ." His voice trailed off.

My blood heated at the prospect of defending my children from their unreasonable grandparents. I also felt a rush of gratitude for my own parents, who saved their disillusionment for truly deserving situations, like when their daughter turned tuition deposits into unintended charitable donations.

I was halfway to imagining a face-off with his ogre parents on a bridge in Alabama—possibly borrowing from news footage of Selma in the sixties—when Gregory shrugged and added, "But it's the parents' responsibility to distinguish their hopes from their expectations for their kids. This is their failure, not mine."

If he had whisked me off to Paris on a private jet at that moment, he couldn't have swept me off my feet more completely. It was the most enlightening declaration I'd heard in a long time, delivered so plainly and coming at such an unexpected moment—when was the last time a date had improved my understanding of my attitude toward my parents? It was my first glimpse of how a relationship with a man could have elements of best-friendship in it. Perhaps a boyfriend could fortify me in some of the ways that my Sterling Girls did.

Gregory and I kept talking as the sun sent long streaks of red down the side streets, taking breaks to help the Caldwells unload their carful of Fairway groceries, to hold the door open for Cliff and his suspicious bass case, to assure Mrs. Hannaham that we would not catch cold sitting on the steps for one hour and forty-five minutes on a balmy April evening. I didn't even care that she'd been spying on us the whole time and watching the clock as though someone else might be waiting to use the stoop. I couldn't remember why I'd ever been attracted to Cliff and I felt sorry for the Caldwells, who, with their separate beds, were pitiful compared to the young couple falling in love right there on the steps of 287 West 12th Street.

Because I was almost positive Gregory and I were falling in

love. I'd only felt this way twice before, first with a summer camp boyfriend who turned out to be site-specific and then with Hayden, who turned out to be a piece of old gum on the heel of humanity. But I was ready to dive in again, wear my heart on my sleeve, risk my pride, go out on a limb, walk the plank. My parents had always reminded me, grinning stupidly at each other, that by definition only one relationship could ever be The One That Worked. In order to find the real thing, you had to keep investing yourself in other people, making bad choices, breaking your heart, and imagining you had found the real thing even when you hadn't.

I heard the skateboard before I saw it.

I was regaling Gregory with a dependably funny story about backpacking through Greece with Tag. It involved a fight between me and some Gypsy children over floor space on the ferry from Patras to Brindisi, and it was one of the few times in my life when I had been as bold as Tag. I relished the memory, though not half as much as I was relishing the pleasure of making Gregory laugh in the retelling. But the familiar clatter of wheels over cracked pavement stopped me mid-sentence and reduced me to the paralyzed state of a rabbit facing a fatal fender.

"YOU WHORE!" Darren Schwartz bellowed before I could grab Gregory by the collar and drag him inside.

I vainly pretended I hadn't heard anything. "So then the youngest Gypsy kid just flung himself onto my sleeping bag—" I continued in a high, shaky voice.

"You can't even wait long enough to make it to a bed!" Darren, aka LinguaFrank, aka The Devil, had squealed to a stop at the bottom of the stoop. He flipped his skateboard to a vertical position and glared up at us. From this angle, he looked like a red-faced gnome. I had a powerful urge to step on him.

My mouth fell open. "Did you *follow* me?"

"You know this guy?" Gregory looked at me with a mixture of horror and betrayal.

"No," I said emphatically, "I mean, he went on a date with—"

"Oh, you know me, *Zephyr*," Darren drawled, "you know me really, really well. But then, you know a lot of guys, don't you?"

I looked at Gregory pleadingly, but he crossed his arms and frowned, waiting for clarification.

"She and her friends," Darren spat, "they don't stay with any one guy for long. We were just chatting about it over some java at Grounded. They sleep with everyone, all over the world."

One corner of my brain was masochistically impressed by Darren's powers of hearing and retention, but mostly I was consumed by the drowning sensation I felt as I watched Gregory's face. It was like watching time-lapse footage of a tender bud of trust withering under a late frost. And there was something else there, too, something I wouldn't understand until much later. Gregory put his head in his hands, as if he were disappointed in himself as much as he was in me.

"Gregory," I said with a harsh laugh, trying to convey how absurd this was. "You're not going to listen to this guy, are you? Hey, look at me. Let me explain." I tried to pull his hand away from his face but he jerked away from my touch so abruptly that my hand hit the step. I stared at him.

"Is that what you use the staircase for?" he whispered.

"Wha—" I didn't understand what he was talking about, but LinguaFrank caught on like a shark to bloody chum.

"Oh, yeah," he crooned, "she likes it on the staircase. She luuuuvs it on the staircase. And in hallways. Elevators. Fire escapes. I'd watch out if I were you. She's toxic."

I sprang up.

"Shut up!" I screamed. "Shut up, you sick, perverted, nasty piece of shit! Go crawl back under your rock!" As I cursed him, I cursed myself for not coming up with something more original, and for sounding as petulant as he had sounded outside Grounded. But I was desperate to make this stop, desperate to make him climb back on his skateboard and roll away from me before any chance of a future with Gregory was snuffed out.

"I want to meet the Asian slut," Darren said calmly, flipping his stringy ponytail from one shoulder to the other in a gesture that was decidedly unmanly. "You tell your friend she'd better show up next time."

I let out a crazy laugh and saw Gregory flinch. "You moron," I spat, "there is no Asian, or anyone else! No one stood you up. We set you up because you were such a pig to Abigail Greenfield. You don't remember? You don't remember calling her fat? Too Jewish? Telling her you liked thin, Asian women?"

I couldn't believe I was having to spell it out—it significantly detracted from a revenge fantasy when you had to point out to your target exactly why you were getting revenge. I glanced over at Gregory, who was edging away from me.

"No, wait," I shrieked at him. "Darren, you shit, you tell him what you did. You tell him that I've never seen you before today."

"You're Abigail's friend?" Darren said disbelievingly.

"Who's Abigail?" Gregory asked.

"The fifth friend. Remember, I told you about my high school friends?" I said pleadingly. "The one in California?"

"Why would . . . *he*," Gregory didn't even look at Darren, "be on a date with someone in California?" He studied me carefully.

"What does that have to do with—? Gregory, this guy is *ly-*

ing." I paused. "Do you think I would ever, ever, in a million years go near someone like him?"

I glared at Gregory, my need to be vindicated momentarily overshadowing my fear of losing him.

"Zephy? Is everything okay?" I whirled around to find my father standing in the doorway. I felt the blood rush to my face. My parents and I had what most people would call an open relationship, but there was still a limit to what I wanted them to know. The fact that I'd had sex with the exterminator on a secret staircase they didn't know about, presumably built by our convicted super, wasn't something I was eager to share. I was also in no hurry to introduce LinguaFrank to my father.

But Lingua's world had apparently righted itself.

"Abigail's friend!" he chortled to himself, morphing into an avuncular figure, shaking his head in an "Oh, those crazy kids" way. "Got it. Okay, then." He gave the rest of us a cheerful grin. "I think my work here is done. Later, dudes."

He tossed his skateboard to the ground and pushed off, his dingy khakis straining against his wide ass. I glanced at Gregory, who was now standing as far from me as possible, arms crossed, his angry gaze fixed on his scuffed oxfords.

"It was just, uh, well, the decibel level was on the high end," my dad pointed upward, apologetically, to his open windows, then noticed Gregory. "Hey, it's the exterminator! Gregory, how are you, lad?" He looked as if he'd found his long-lost son.

"*Dad.*" I widened my eyes at him.

"Were you yelling about staircases?" he persisted. I chewed my lip. "You know the dryer is working beeeeautifully!" he told Gregory, snapping his fingers as though he'd just walked out of the 1950s. "Did you and Zephy fix the pipe?"

"Yes," I lied, just as Gregory said, "No, we never got around to it." We exchanged mutual looks of disgust.

"Well, whatever magic we worked together really, uh, worked. Hey, cream puffs! Any extras for a guy with hollow legs?" Without waiting for an answer, my giraffe of a father bent down and helped himself to a chocolate pastry. He made cooing sounds as he bit into it.

"Is there anything we can't get in this town? Don't you think about how lucky we are when you taste something like this?"

"Dad!" I repeated sharply.

"Have the rest." Gregory reached down and grabbed his backpack.

"Are you leaving?" I asked in disbelief.

"I really think I should." He wouldn't look at me.

My father finally sensed the lava flow about to envelop his daughter and her exterminator.

"Oh, don't let me interrupt! You kids keep talking, yelling, staircases, what have you. Mom and I have to get going, we're seeing the great Mercedes Kim shake out some Shostakovich, ba-da-da, ba-da-DAH." He headed inside, taking another bite of his cream puff. "I should quit law and become a baker . . ." The door closed behind him.

"Gregory," I said firmly, reminding myself that none of Lingua's slander was true, "we are supposed to go out tonight." And then go *in* tonight, I added silently. "Are you really gonna let some insane stranger end what seems like the beginning of something pretty great?" My voice trembled with the courage it took to be honest.

"I need to think," Gregory said quietly. "I need to know you are who you say you are."

"And you're going to do that by leaving?" I said as coldly as I could. And before he could abandon me, I turned and ran inside so he wouldn't see the tears beginning to stream down my face.

FOURTEEN

I'M SMELLING IT AGAIN," MRS. HANNAHAM SAID WHEN I PICKED up the phone Monday morning. I glanced at the clock. Six-thirty. A new low. I had grabbed the receiver before the end of the first ring, hoping it would be Gregory apologizing for his behavior on Saturday night. Instead, I heard Barry Manilow crooning "Copacabana" in the background.

"The helium?" I said impatiently.

"Don't get yourself in a swivet, missy," she croaked at me. "And don't take it out on me just because you had a fight with your new man friend," she added.

I pulled the comforter over my head, but that only made the crone's voice more intimate, so I flung it off again.

"My Compton and I never had a single fight in all our years. We were blessed," she bragged.

Yeah. You, Compton, and the secretary. The holy trinity.

"I'll go into Roxana's apartment again," I promised, neglecting to tell her I'd still never been in there.

"When?"

"Today."

"When today?"

I sighed loudly, a huff full of self-pity. "I have jury duty, so after that. Okay? Mrs. Hannaham, is there something else about Roxana that's bothering you? Something I could actually help you with?"

"Jury duty!" she said excitedly. "Maybe you'll meet Lennie Briscoe."

I opened my mouth but didn't know where to begin. Did she know that *Law & Order* was fictional? That Jerry Orbach was dead? Was Mrs. Hannaham fit to take care of herself, or should I be consulting social service agencies about her welfare? Maybe I should call Lucy for advice. I bet it would help her flagging self-esteem if her friend called her for her professional opinion—

"As for Mrs. Boureau," Mrs. Hannaham continued haughtily, "I've urged you to keep an eye on her visitors."

I made a "Yeah, and?" gesture to my ceiling.

"You got it," I said. "Will do. Done."

"Don't tell them you read the *New York Times*."

"Excuse me?"

"They'll think you're too liberal. But not the *Post* either. The defense will knock you off. If you want to get picked for jury duty, you say you read the *Daily News*."

"Thanks for the tip." Did scanning the occasional left-behind copy of the *Post* for Hayden's byline count as reading?

Mrs. Hannaham hung up.

I lay in bed and considered the fact that Mrs. Hannaham and I shared an apparently rare passion for jury service. I had a choice. I could either let that thought depress me and accelerate the downward spiral triggered by Gregory on Saturday night, or I could ignore it and focus on my immediate future as a star juror.

I swung my feet to the floor and studied the contents of my closet. Maybe I'd get to be foreman. I'd stand before the entire courtroom, visibly bearing the weight of the jury's decision, and solemnly reveal the long-awaited verdict. And before that, I thought, thumbing through yards of non-professional clothing accumulated over half a decade of being a staunch non-professional, I'd be in the jury pool. I'd meet businessmen and ballerinas, immigrants and heiresses. There would be drama in the courtroom, in the jury room, in the hallways, and maybe even in a hotel room, if we were sequestered.

I'd have to remember not to lie about myself. No tales of roping cows on my Australian uncle's Outback ranch or going mountaineering with my Chilean cousins while under oath. I selected a gray turtleneck sweater and black pants—neutral colors for the impartial juror. I replayed the scenario in which I met the love of my life in the jury room, but now, as I recounted the story to my children, I built on the drama: I had trudged to the courthouse *thinking* I was nursing a broken heart, but the idiot I was crying over—funny, I can't remember his name now, George? Geoffrey?—was just a hotheaded, judgmental grad school dropout who couldn't hold a candle to your father, the man who'd halted global warming. As I zipped up my leather boots (a post-Hayden consolation purchase), I felt my excitement recovering.

If I had known just what the next two days had in store for me, I might have opted to tell the judge I read the *Times* and the *Post* whenever I wasn't studying the crack on my ceiling, and hurried back to Mrs. Hannaham and her helium odors as fast as I could.

By eleven o'clock that morning, I had read most of a *Wall Street Journal* left behind by a CFO who had thoroughly

bored me with a lengthy monologue on why he was too important for jury duty. I was pleased to watch his face pinch up as
his name was called, but it wasn't enough to relieve the tedium
of sitting in an enormous gray room for nearly three hours. I
had also watched the video on how to be a good juror, read
thirty pages of my new Ian McEwan novel, and taken a couple
of laps around the room to see what other people were doing,
which yielded no entertainment: knitting, reading, staring
into space, sleeping.

I stood up, stretched, and looked hopefully over at the
clerk, the guardian of the phone line over which demands for
potential jurors came. He was slowly thumbing through the
Post, so I embarked on another tour of the trenches. This time
I decided to explore the little workroom adjacent to the main
holding pen.

In here, the more industrious members of society could
plug their laptops into individual carrels. This crowd was
younger, chic, and equipped with portable electronics. The
quiet clack of keyboards sent a wave of collegiate nostalgia
through me and I paused, awash in an unexpected memory
from my first winter at college. I'd been toiling away in the
warm library, a little too conscious of being engaged in the no-
ble pursuit of Higher Learning, when word quickly spread that
a snowball fight of massive proportions was unfolding on the
central campus. I abandoned my paper, had the time of my life,
and wound up with pneumonia and my first D.

The halt in my stroll caused a short, curly-haired man in
his thirties to look up at me sharply. He was geeky cute, as if he
worked in tech support: collared shirt half-buttoned over a
T-shirt bearing a logo of a fish-fry joint, wire-frame glasses
slipping down his nose, a nervous energy vibrating around
him. He was using the top of his closed iBook to organize his
cash, laying it out according to denomination, putting all the

bills faceup in the same direction. He had already attended to the rest of his wallet, because next to the computer was a neat pile of receipts and business cards. I had almost passed him, thinking how Lucy would appreciate this use of time, when I caught sight of his ten-dollar-bill pile. I halted mid-stride and backed up.

There, on top, in no-smudge Sharpie, was "3 Lives Books, Sun, noon."

"Oh my God," I said quietly, but in a room that was library silent, it made heads turn.

The techie looked up at me with real alarm and put his arm over the bills.

"No," I said, reaching out my hand, which scared him more. He gathered up the money and shoved it in his wallet.

"Wait," I whispered, while he looked around for a court officer. "That ten-dollar bill, the one that was on top, look at it."

He narrowed his eyes at me. I drew my shoulders down and tilted my head at him: do I *look* like a criminal?

"Take it out and look at it," I insisted.

Reluctantly, he opened his wallet again, keeping one eye on me. He pulled out the ten, glanced at Lucy's handwriting, then looked at me blankly.

I hesitated, wanting to strike a balance between honoring Lucy's trust in fate and giving fate a little leg up.

"Do you know what that means? What's written on there?"

He squinted at the bill again.

"The bookstore in the Village?" His voice was a touch nasal for my taste, but this wasn't about me.

"It is, it is! You know it?" I said excitedly.

He shrugged.

"See the rest? Day and time?" I prodded. "Say you had noticed it yourself. What do you think you might have done?"

Other prospective jurors were looking at us now, trying to

figure out whether we knew each other or whether I was hitting on him. I grabbed a chair and sat down.

"What would you have done?" I repeated with more irritation than I'd intended. Cupid's assistants should probably use
a more tender tone.

"Done?" he whispered. "Nothing. I don't take orders from
graffiti scrawled on currency."

Smart man.

"Okay, look." I pointed at the bill. "That was written by a
really good friend of mine. She's a romantic. She believes that
the right man out there will see this and meet her at the bookstore and they'll love each other forever." I spread my hands as
if to say, I'm just the messenger.

"And it wound up in my wallet?" The techie looked prop-
erly awed. I opened my mouth to explain that there were
dozens of Hamiltons out there, not just this one, but then
changed my mind and just nodded.

"Huh." He squinted at it. "So, what, does she go there every
Sunday at noon just waiting for some guy to show up?"

I wondered if Lucy had ever gotten this far in her scenario,
to the point where she had to admit that she did, in fact, do just
that.

"She's a romantic," I repeated helplessly. "And a bibliophile.
She loves to be around books anyway, so she figured . . ." I
couldn't tell if this was a good route. "She's pretty and smart
and has a fabulous sense of humor and she's loyal." I was getting angry, as if he'd already rejected her.

"Okay, okay, don't get worked up," he said, starting to
smile. He pushed his glasses up on his nose and did a funny little flick of his earlobe. "Why not? Even if she's a serial killer,
she can't hurt me in a bookstore, right?"

It wasn't the most stouthearted comment I'd ever heard
from a man, but it was reasonable.

"How will I know who she is?"

I thought for a moment, then pulled out my cell phone and surreptitiously turned it on.

"You're not supposed to have that on in here," he whispered urgently. Ah, he and Lucy would have a beautiful life together, living by the letter of the law.

I scrolled through my pictures until I found one of the four of us at the party at Soho House. I held it up to him. "The blonde in the blue dress."

His jaw fell open. "Seriously? What's her name?"

I shook my head. "Pretend you saw the note yourself. But you'll go this Sunday, yes?"

He nodded vigorously, twisting his neck to follow the image as I put my phone away. I stood up and put my chair back, satisfied that even if the clerk never called my name, I had performed a great service this morning.

HALF AN HOUR LATER, WE WERE MERCIFULLY RELEASED FOR an early lunch. The first thing I did when I stepped out of the building was call Lucy.

"You still go to the bookstore on Sundays, right?" I said when she answered.

"Zephyr?"

"Because I want to make absolutely sure that you'll go this Sunday."

"Why?" she said suspiciously. I heard a man screaming in the background.

"Are you okay?" I said, thinking that Lucy and I should have a safety code. If she was ever being held at knifepoint by one of her clients and I happened to call, she could say, "Wow, wasn't Sterling a great school?" and then I'd know something was wrong and could call the police. I'd make a fascinating career out of lecturing all over the country, advising social service agencies on effective and innovative security measures.

"I think the janitor stubbed his toe," she said, her voice momentarily distant as she leaned away from the phone to confirm. "Sometimes I still stop by the bookstore," she admitted. "Why should I go this Sunday?"

I chose my words carefully. "I'm downtown on jury duty—"

"Oh, yeah, how's that *going*?" she interrupted in a concerned voice, reassuring herself that she was tuned in to even the most mundane details of her friends' lives.

"Fine," I said impatiently. "I mean, totally boring and I haven't been called in, but fine. Listen, I saw a guy there with one of your ten-dollar bills."

I heard her suck in her breath and my heart ached for her hopefulness.

"He's cute, Luce, and I think he'll be there."

"What did you say to him?" she said accusingly.

"Nothing!"

"Liar."

"All I did was notice it and joke that he should stop by," I lied.

"And?"

"And he kind of laughed and said, 'Hey, yeah, you never know!'"

"Cute?"

"Totally," I said without hesitation, on the grounds that people had wildly different definitions of "cute." "So you'll go?"

"Sure."

"You don't sound excited."

"I am, it's just, you know," she said forlornly.

"I know," I said sympathetically, "but this time might be different." I was bolstering my own broken heart as much as I was hers.

"How's Gregory?"

"Over," I said curtly.

"Oh, Zeph, what happened?" There was genuine dismay in her voice.

I shook my head, suddenly afraid I'd start crying right there among the defendants' wives and landlord-tenant lawyers, all smoking in one indiscriminate mass in front of the building.

"Long story. I'll tell you guys when I see you. Are we all on for TV night tomorrow at Mercy's?"

"Yeah, unless she ditches us for Dover, in which case it's just the two of us." Crap. In my self-pity slump on Sunday, I'd forgotten to call Tag to say good-bye. She had left for a week-long conference in Senegal. Or Saudi Arabia? No, Senegal.

"Mercedes would never do that," I said with little conviction. Mercedes had never been in love with any man but Mozart. Who the hell knew how she'd behave? I immediately chastised myself for my bitterness. I could not let Gregory win. If I hadn't let Hayden get the best of me, I certainly wasn't going to let some gangly, barbecuing Shakespeare-shirker trample my optimism.

"Have you talked to her since Saturday night?" Lucy asked suggestively.

"Did she sleep with him?" I yelped a little too loudly, eliciting some guffaws from a coterie of passing detectives wearing identical trench coats—perhaps to protect them from the bright sunlight.

"You'll have to ask her yourself," she said lightly. The prospect of meeting the love of her life the following Sunday had already put Lucy in a playful mood, which irrationally irritated me.

After lunch, I returned to purgatory. The boring CFO had been dumped back in among us mere mortals, but his brief foray had made him an instant critic.

"I'm a big believer in getting things done," I heard him proclaim. I turned to see who his new victim was, and found an artificially tanned, face-lifted ambassador of Park Avenue listening raptly. I glanced at her left hand: ring finger naked. I stood up and changed seats. Where was the popping, sparkling melting pot that was supposed to be my city?

"Okay, listen up, people!" the clerk boomed, his voice a defibrillator on our collective asystolic body. "If you hear your name, line up, and Officer Pendleton'll take you upstairs." He gave the ancient, rusty cylinder on his desk a spin, and began calling out names.

"Sean O'Malley. Jennifer Smith. Astrid Heffenfigger. Concita Buenavista," he said, mangling all the names except for Smith. Though in this town it was always possible that their names actually *were* Seen, Astride, and Consitta.

Ohpleaseohpleaseohplease. I knew it was pathetic to depend on jury duty for excitement, but I needed something to take my mind off Gregory. Off the fact that I was twenty-seven and lived downstairs from my parents. Off the fact that my friend was dating a movie star. Off the fact that my little brother was about to be outed as the next Scorsese. I needed a little boost of something, just a tiny swirl of chocolate through my pound cake.

"Ebony Leonard. Tamara Weinstein. Marguerite DuBois," he droned, pronouncing the silent "s." "Zephyr Zuckerman."

Adrenaline surged through me, but I tried to look nonchalant as I gathered up my things and made my way over to join the chosen ones. I felt like I was in grade school again, remaining silent as we were escorted through a gray-tiled corridor that reeked of ammonia. We piled into an elevator, rode up to the eleventh floor, and lined up outside a set of double doors. I glanced at my fellow jurors, but couldn't spot anyone who might be feeling as thrilled as I was. Officer Pendleton, who brought to mind Nurse Ratched with a gun holster, held up her hand and opened one door, leaning in to confer with someone. She turned back to us.

"You will sit in the back two rows of the courtroom," she instructed. "No talkin', no gum chewin', no eatin', no cell phones, no readin', no hats. This judge, she don't put up with *nuthin'*." She glared at us to convey her approval of the judge's standards.

I figured I knew what to expect better than most. I'd been visiting the courthouse since I was seven, proudly watching my father in action. I already knew it was nothing like on TV. The paint peeled, the windows stuck, court officers sat around reading the paper, there was usually no one in the audience, it was dead quiet, and the action was very, very slow. That someone's life might be hanging in the balance was rarely reflected at any given moment. Even my father's line of questioning was often a dull litany, designed to clarify over the course of an hour exactly how many steps it was from an elevator to a drug dealer's front door.

So I was surprised to find a packed courtroom thrumming with an energy I'd never felt during any of my father's cases. Except for the rows reserved for us, every seat was filled. A line of court officers, holding their arms akimbo to accommodate their sagging weapon belts, stood behind the defense table, which was also packed. I couldn't distinguish the accused from their lawyers—they were all wearing equally spiffy suits. As we entered, everyone turned to look at us.

I took my seat beside a mouth-breathing meathead with ropy tendons in his neck who'd been in front of me on the way up from the jury-pool room. A personal trainer. On my right sat an elderly black woman with thick glasses. She smelled of coconut, wore a pillbox hat with a hatpin through it, and kept her hands tightly folded over her stiff purse. I felt an urge to put a protective arm around her, and mentally heard Mercedes accusing me of reverse racism.

The judge smiled at us coolly, casting a professional eye over the motley crew before her.

"Welcome to Part Seventy-two, and thank you for fulfilling your civic duty."

I sat up a little taller in my seat.

"I'm going to give all of you a brief background of this case, after which we'll seat you in the jury box and question you individually as part of the formal voir dire."

The tedious CFO from the jury pool, who'd been three names ahead of me, raised his hand. The judge narrowed her eyes and continued speaking to all of us, while looking directly at him.

"After you are seated and addressed, you may tell the court any reasons you may have for not being able to serve. While I understand that for many of you a long case, which this promises to be, is difficult to commit to for a variety of reasons, I will *not* excuse anyone because she or he has a business deal pending or a trip planned to the Bahamas." The suit put his hand down and pressed his lips together so hard they turned white.

"While we generally prefer that jurors have no familiarity with the details of a case," she continued, "there is little chance that you have not heard of this one, unless you've been living under a rock for the past year." I liked this judge and, in the same pathetic way that I wanted to be Jill Amos's new best friend, I wanted her to like me. I tried to look smart.

"The four defendants are accused of conspiring to steal a piece of artwork from a museum here in Manhattan, replace it with a forgery, and sell the original. In addition, two of them are charged with the murder of the guard who attempted to stop them. They are all charged with felonies."

Oh my God. This was the "Adios Pelarose" case. I inhaled

sharply and started jiggling my foot, trying to reroute my excitement. The mob case had been all over every paper for the last twelve months. The "piece of artwork" was nothing less than a Picasso, the museum was the Met, and the media had been acting like it was Christmas morning. The story was that Luis Pelarose, one of the dirtiest mob capos of all time, had lost his head and heart to a size DDD girlfriend named Maria Anna Mariza. She had wanted him to prove his love with something bigger and better than a Harry Winston bauble, and soon it was rumored that she had a Van Gogh gracing the gas-fueled fireplace in her Sheepshead Bay apartment. When Pelarose's wife found out, she was so humiliated that she threatened to go to the cops and inform on his lifetime of murders and thefts if he didn't top that gift with a better one for her. Hence the attempted Picasso heist, and now here we were, all together, in one room.

I *had* to get on this jury.

The judge kept talking and I strained forward to see if I could tell which one was Pelarose. I scanned the courtroom for big blond heads and was rewarded with a glimpse of Maria Anna herself, wearing bright pink Chanel and matching lipstick. She leaned over and whispered to the man next to her. He looked as familiar as she did, and I racked my brain trying to remember which family member he was.

"Zephyr Zuckerman."

I jumped an inch in my seat, startling the personal trainer next to me. The old woman patted my hand and smiled reassuringly.

I made my way to the front and a court officer escorted me into the well and up into the jury box. With all eyes on me, I felt like a minor celebrity. I took a shallow gulp of air and exhaled in ratchety breaths. When the officer sat me in the first seat, my legs nearly buckled. He handed me a laminated sheet of paper with a list of perfunctory questions on it, which I glanced at and then laid in my lap.

As I waited for my fellow jurors to be seated, I grew nervous. Where should I look? I didn't want to make eye contact with the defendants or their lawyers. Would I need protection if I voted to convict? Would I find a suitcase full of money in my apartment as an invitation to acquit? Would they hurt my family or my friends? No way Dover Carter would stick around if his girlfriend started receiving death threats from the mob. I decided to keep my eyes firmly on the judge. As the last juror was seated, she glanced at her watch.

"All right, ladies and gentlemen," she said sternly to the lawyers, "because of the morning's mishaps"—What mishaps? Gunplay in the courtroom? Unruly outbursts of undying love?—"you only have time to question one, perhaps two potential jurors before we break for the day. We'll begin with," she glanced down at her desk, "Ms. Zuckerman. Ms. Zuckerman, please use the questions you've been given to provide the court with some information about yourself."

I looked down and found the stiff plastic sheet trembling in my hand.

"My full name is Zephyr Anne Zuckerman," I croaked.

"Please relax and speak up so that everyone can hear," the judge instructed.

"Zephyr Anne Zuckerman," I repeated in a stronger voice. "I live in Greenwich Village, where I've lived my whole life." I glanced down at the questions. "I'm single, twenty-seven, and . . ." *How many adults are in your household?* "I live alone." It was true, I reminded myself.

A small commotion in the second row caught my eye and I glanced over. I was dismayed to see a couple of buzz-cut guys in Gap sweatshirts and baggy jeans whispering to each other and squinting at me.

"Ms. Zuckerman, please continue," the judge said firmly.

"Education. Uh, I have a bachelor's and I've completed some graduate work in medicine." *Where are you currently employed?* I swallowed hard. "I . . . I manage my parents' apartment building in the Village." No gasps of disappointment. No explosions of laughter and finger pointing. I relaxed a little and continued, running my eye down the list.

"I don't know anyone involved in this case, and . . ." I paused over the next question. "My father is an attorney, but no one else in my family is in law or law enforcement." I hoped we could glide past that issue.

"Thank you," the judge said. "Mr. Suarez?"

One of the lawyers jumped up from the defense table, nearly knocking over his chair. He looked like he was my age.

"Your father is an attorney, Ms. Zuckerman?" he said too eagerly. I took a deep breath.

"Yes."

"What kind of law does he practice?"

"He's an assistant U.S. attorney."

"In other words, a prosecutor."

"Yes," I said, looking Suarez straight in the eye.

"And where does he work?"

"In Brooklyn."

"I see," he said suggestively. "And you don't think having a father who is a prosecutor would compromise your impartiality in this case?"

"Not at all," I said calmly.

"A father who has successfully prosecuted people with alleged mob ties?"

I was going to find a horse's head in my bed tonight.

"My father's profession would have no influence on me as far as this case is concerned," I told him, thinking how proud my dad would be of this well-crafted answer.

"Do you see your father often?"

Who the hell was on trial here?

"I am close to him, but we rarely discuss his work." Not until after a trial ends, I added silently.

"Where does he live in relation to you?"

I paused.

"Ms. Zuckerman?"

"Upstairs," I practically whispered.

Mr. Suarez grinned.

"Would you please repeat that so the court reporter can hear it?"

"Upstairs," I said, and the whole room laughed. Even the judge smiled. My face was burning.

"And you wouldn't discuss this case with your father, the mob prosecutor who lives upstairs from you?" More laughter. I licked my lips and met his arrogant gaze again. His cheeks were pocked with post-acne craters.

"No. I wouldn't." I hoped I sounded assertive, not petulant.

"Uh-huh, uh-huh." Suarez the Cocky strutted away from the jury box and I exhaled, thinking he was through. Suddenly he whirled around, feigning a jolt of sudden memory.

"Didn't your father write a book about the history of racketeering in this country and the far-reaching adverse effects it has on local economies?"

The Book. The stupid, goddamned book. My dad had coughed it out twenty years ago, as part of an attempt to see whether he'd prefer the Life of a Writer. It had sold about ten copies and no one but the other A.U.S.A.s in my dad's bureau had ever read it—except, apparently, for this guy. I was tempted to ask Suarez whether he was admitting that his clients were mobsters, but he looked triumphant, as if he'd already won the case.

I waited until the laughter died down again, then said, "I

think he wrote that when I was seven. I don't know much about it." That was unfortunately true. My father, who had sat through countless dreary school plays, read reams of lifeless poetry, and proofread dozens of sophomoric term papers, had an ungrateful daughter who had never cracked the cover of the only book he would ever write. But at the moment, it seemed my selfishness was coming in handy.

"No further questions, Your Honor," Suarez said, grinning. I gripped the edges of what could be my chair, the forewoman's chair. The chair of Juror Number One. It was still within my reach.

"Ms. Langley?" The judge raised her eyebrows at the prosecutor, a tiny wisp of a woman. Langley smiled broadly, spread her arms, and replied, "That's all I need to know," sending the room into another round of tension-breaking chuckling. Great. I was the comic relief.

I sat stewing while Suarez began questioning the personal trainer. He'd been seated next to me in the jury box and now turned out to be an orthodontist. No one laughed while *he* was questioned, and Suarez sat down after the guy said his main source of news was Animal Planet.

"That's all we have time for today," the judge said, with a final reproachful glance at the lawyers. "Ladies and gentlemen," she said, turning to us. "I remind you that, as potential jurors, you are under oath and must refrain from discussing this case with *anyone*. That includes all involved parties as well as members of the press. Please return to this courtroom tomorrow at nine-thirty. You'll take the same seats and we'll continue the voir dire then. Officer Pendleton?"

The court officer who'd read us the riot act stepped forward to lead us out. As I followed her, I noticed again the group of men in the second row studying me intently. I was thinking of a way to ask Pendleton whether I might be able to get protection for the evening without sounding hysterical, when something else—some*one* else—caught my eye.

There he was, sitting behind my sweatshirted admirers, grinning the same self-satisfied grin that had cost me two years of sanity.

Hayden.

Out in the poorly lit corridor, surrounded by the excited jabberings of my formerly tight-lipped comrades, I grabbed for a wall as tunnel vision set in. Hayden would pile out of the courtroom with the rest of the press in just a few seconds, and I had to decide whether to face him or run for the stalls.

But in the time that it took to persuade my body not to pass out, Hayden had sidled up to me and thrown a casual arm over my shoulder, as if we saw each other every week. He was apparently unconcerned about the judge's injunction against jurors consorting with members of the press.

"Hey, you," he whispered into my ear. His voice vibrated straight down my spine and landed between my legs. I cursed him, me, and Luis Pelarose as I caught a whiff of the musk and soap scent that had done me in the first eight times and now promised to level me again, right there in the over-sanitized halls of justice.

"Hey," was all I could muster as I tried to collect my thoughts and my hormones soared to prom night heights. A few new laugh lines only made his eyes sexier, and his thick reddish hair still begged to be raked by my fingers. Despite myself, I checked out the rest of him, most of which I'd groped, stroked, or clung to at one time or another.

"Let's go get a drink," he purred, catching me in the act.

I opened my mouth to express shock, but all that came out was a stuttering grunt.

"Ooh, I remember that sound." His eyes flashed with mischief.

"Wait. Just fucking wait," I growled. He had the good grace to look surprised, and I was about to recover the power of speech when the group of sweatshirts emerged, deep in conversation with the prosecutors.

"Come on." I grabbed his arm and pulled him around a corner, toward the elevators. When I looked at him, he was grinning again.

"Still eager," he commented.

"Eager to get away from the *lawyers*," I said pointedly.

"If you're so nervous about being seen by the lawyers, let's go to your place," he said, not missing a beat.

I emitted a slightly hysterical, disbelieving snort that was supposed to be a laugh. "You haven't changed."

"Only gotten better," he promised.

"No. You're as bad as ever." I was stalling, and in the process, seemed to be flirting. "Aren't you supposed to be somewhere, filing a story or something?" He had never been this available when we'd been together.

He shrugged, not taking his eyes off mine. "There's no story yet. Come on, Zephyr." He lowered his chin and dipped his head to one side. "We'll just talk."

FIFTEEN

So you're the super?" Hayden said, opening my refrigerator later that afternoon as easily as if we lived together. "Hey, you have alcohol. *That's* newsworthy."

"It belonged to the other super," I said as he popped open one of James's Brooklyn Lagers and slunk toward me, grinning impudently.

What are you doing, Zephyr? What the *hell* are you doing? "I'm just going to run to the bathroom," I squeaked, and left the kitchen to get a grip.

I headed past the discarded clothes on my bedroom floor, unzipping my boots and kicking them off as I went. It had been light years since I'd left my apartment that morning. That had been the part of my life in which I still looked for Hayden in every corner of the city. This afternoon, I had crossed into the next part, the uncharted territory where I finally found him.

But, I realized as I eyed my un-privacy-checked home, I'd never scripted anything beyond the very first moment of our reunion. I'd imagined being in a restaurant, on a date with

someone else, looking fabulous. Our eyes would meet as
Hayden passed my table. I would smile victoriously and it
would be clear from both his face and his pug-nosed, bespecta-
cled date that he was devastated by his loss and would be
plagued with regret for the rest of his life.

That's where the fantasy had ended. I never imagined him
crossing my threshold again, and I certainly never imagined
him swilling beer in my kitchen. If I had, I would have cut the
teeth marks out of the cheddar and stashed the reeking workout clothes airing out on bookshelves and chairs.

I slipped into the bathroom and locked the door. In here,
at least, I could hide the plaque rinse and the tampons. Hating
myself, I propped the condoms on the back of the toilet. Then I
hid them again. Then I put them out again.

I sat down on the toilet and pressed my palms into my
eyes. We were alone together in my apartment. No one in the
world knew where we were. If anything happened, it would almost be like it didn't really happen. There would be no record.
What was I planning to do with this secret freedom?

I started to pee and immediately the bathroom filled with
the stench of the asparagus salad I'd had for lunch. Oh, God,
what if Hayden came in the bathroom after me and smelled it?

Screw what he thought! Why would I want to be with
someone who made me feel embarrassed about natural body
functions? I opened the cabinet again and exchanged the condoms for the tampons. I wasn't going to sleep with him anyway. I didn't care if he smelled my asparagus pee.

Damn it. I did care. I frantically looked around the bathroom for something to cover up the smell. I looked at the bottle of mouthwash. Would Hayden think I had brushed my
teeth for him? Was that better or worse than him smelling my
asparagus pee?

I cursed him again, and the thought crossed my mind that

even though I'd only known Gregory for two weeks, I would never have been this self-conscious around him. He was real. Hayden was fake.

I splashed some Scope into the toilet bowl and swirled the brush. Now if I flushed again, would he think I was pooping and couldn't get it all down in one flush? Oh, my God, I was going crazy. I looked at myself in the mirror to see if I looked crazy. I did, I looked crazy.

Deep breaths. Remember his breakup note. The cockroach lowercase letters. All those times I ate sushi alone. Clearing empty beer bottles from under the bed. This is not the right man for you, Zephyr. Get him out of here.

But I don't have anyone else right now, crowed the little devil homunculus on my shoulder. Gregory dumped me because he'd rather believe a lunatic on a skateboard than give me a fair chance. And the rest of the available men *were* the lunatics on the skateboards. Maybe I could just sleep with Hayden but not get emotionally attached.

Yeah, that should work.

Still undecided, I flung open the door and found Hayden standing there barefoot, shirtsleeves rolled up, freckled arms braced on the doorframe, waiting for me. His mouth was exactly where mine needed to be, and it seemed easiest to postpone any further decisions until after I'd kissed him.

Hayden's kisses contradicted his arrogance and selfishness. His kisses caressed, lingered, explored. They were thoughtful and patient and generous. He bit gently at my lips, then let his tongue take a slow tour of my mouth, while the rest of me quivered helplessly. I let him lead us to my bed and pulled him on top of me, grabbing his hips, grabbing at another chance, blissfully succumbing to bad judgment. He felt better in my arms than I'd remembered, warmer and more solid, and my whole body nearly wept with the release of years of squelched desire.

Hayden started working his way under my shirt, letting his fingers trail up and down my belly, until I was nothing more than a sack of goose bumps. I groaned softly as he released the clasp of my bra. The only thing that mattered at that moment was having his hands reach my breasts, but he was going to make me wait. I persuaded my own hands to leave his firm, round butt and go hunting for even better territory. Just as I was poised to release his straining zipper, the phone rang.

"Let it go," he murmured, planting a line of kisses from my waist to my chest. I grabbed his head and pulled him up to me so that I could taste his mouth again. The phone stopped ringing and I relaxed, letting my fingers work their way back down to his jeans.

"I've missed you," he whispered. "I've missed your skin and your hair and your ass and your gorgeous gray eyes."

He called them blue in his breakup letter, I thought as the phone started up again.

"Damn it!" I yelled. I lunged across him and grabbed it off the cradle.

"Zephyr, he bought me hemorrhoid cream."

I panted into the phone, the wires of my addled brain completely crossed.

"Zeph, are you okay? It's Mercedes."

"I . . . what? Hemorrhoid cream?" Hayden rolled me back on the pillow and started tracing the outline of my ribs with his tongue. I suppressed a groan.

"Dover," Mercedes said. "I was in agony after the concert on Saturday night—your parents started the standing O; they're so sweet, even if they are bizarre—and we were already at my place and he went around the corner to the all-night

Duane Reade and bought me Preparation H. Zephyr, I'm in love. I totally get it. I get the fuss. I love him."

This was the closest I'd ever heard Mercedes come to raving. In fact, for her, this *was* raving. I pushed Hayden off me, holding up a finger.

"One second," I whispered.

"Is that Gregory?" Mercedes asked.

"No, just a delivery guy." Hayden climbed back on me and started tracing his finger around the top of my jeans. I choked back my lust and wondered if there was any good way to hang up on my friend.

"Mercedes," I croaked with as much false enthusiasm as I could summon, "I want all the details, but I want them in person. Phone isn't good enough. Tomorrow, right? You, me, Lucy, okay?" I hoped I sounded persuasive.

"Both his parents died when he was ten. He was raised by his sister," Mercedes said dreamily.

"Merce, the whole world knows that," I said as Hayden bent over and darted his tongue in and out of my belly button.

The intercom buzzed, which at least permitted me to groan out loud.

"I'll get it," Hayden drawled. I covered the phone up as fast as I could and glared at him.

"Zeph, who's with you?" Mercedes demanded. Hayden jumped off me and headed for the intercom, smirking at me.

"Don't you dare answer that," I hissed, jumping off the bed. He put one finger on the lever and I had to take my hand off the phone to bat it away.

"Hayden, cut it out!"

"Hayden's there? *Hayden?*" Mercedes shrieked through the phone. "Zephyr, goddamn it, don't make me come over there. I'll wring his scrawny little dick. I swear to God! And then I'll fucking kill you. *Kill* you. Do you hear me?"

Hearing Mercedes curse—and with Tag-like vigor—stopped me in my tracks. Hayden abruptly removed his teasing finger. For the first time since I'd known him, he actually looked something other than completely confident.

"Who *is* that?" he said, a worried frown creasing his brow.

"Yes?" I shouted into the intercom, choosing to ignore him and Mercedes.

"It's me." Gregory's sweet, cracking voice wound its way up the wires, into my apartment, and through my heart.

Fuck. Fuckfuck *fuck*.

"Zephyr," Mercedes said threateningly.

I opened my eyes and found Hayden crossing his arms and smiling, looking immensely entertained. The threat of dedicking had passed.

"I have to go. I'll see you tomorrow," I said to Mercedes, then added, "I'm not doing anything stupid."

"Yes, you are," she said with resignation.

"Yes, I am," I agreed, and hung up. The intercom buzzed again, a giant angry wasp.

"Coming!" I let go of the lever and looked at Hayden, wishing I could vaporize him or at least stuff him in a closet.

"You were about to," he growled, putting both his hands around my waist.

"Stay right here," I instructed, hoping to strike a tone both menacing and seductive.

I bounded down the stairs, trying to rehook my bra and figure out how to get Gregory to leave as fast as the physical world would permit, while also being receptive to any olive branches he might be proffering.

I flung open the door and found not only Gregory standing there, but also Freddy Givitch with his gray face and a woman who was a dead ringer for Sandra Oh. For a second, I wondered whether in some perversely roundabout way to win me back, Gregory had conjured up a hot Asian woman for Darren Schwartz.

"The apartment," Freddy muttered to my feet. "She's interested." Sandra Oh's clone smiled tightly from above her perfectly tailored suit, indicating that we had already wasted too much of her time on introductions. She gave a little shake of her black mane and looked behind me up the stairs. I stood aside and gestured for them to go in.

"I can answer any questions you might have . . ." I said to their receding backs in a tardy effort to appear professional. At least I was still wearing my responsible, impartial juror's outfit.

I turned back to Gregory and said nothing, not trusting my voice. The pain of his rejection on that very stoop just two days earlier made it hard for me to do more than glance at him every few seconds, like a Tourettic mouse.

"Zephyr," he said, spreading his arms pleadingly. My throat tightened. "I need to explain something to you. Can I come up? Can we talk inside?" I wanted to throw my arms around him, nuzzle his neck, and feel his palms press into my back, but instead I had to shake my head.

Gregory looked stricken.

"Zephyr," Hayden crooned from somewhere above us, "I'm wai-aiting!"

I ran both hands through my hair, pulling at it as if I could trigger a trapdoor to fall through. My breathing grew shallow and I realized that, for the second time that day, I was at risk of passing out. Then my eyelid started twitching, the way it had when Tag and I got caught at the St. Regis. I had to get Gregory out of here.

"Who was that?" Gregory asked.

"The broker," I gulped.

"Him?" Gregory said doubtfully.

I looked up and there was Freddy following Sandra down

the stairs, with something vaguely related to a smile plastered on his face.

"I'll take it," she said breezily, waving her hand in the general vicinity of the building and starting down the stoop.

"It's not ready to be rented," Gregory said suddenly.

I looked at him, surprised. Sandra froze on the step, one gym-toned calf in mid-plunge. She turned her head slowly and fixed Freddy with a deadly glare.

"Make it ready," she intoned.

Perhaps there was more to consider in a potential tenant than the size of her Marc Jacobs purse.

"Who is this guy?" Freddy muttered in Gregory's direction, as Sandra marched toward the corner in full taxi-hail stance.

"Yeah, Zephyr, who are these guys?" Hayden cheerfully padded down the stairs and leaned against the wall of the vestibule, nursing another beer.

Gregory looked back and forth between Hayden's shoeless feet and mine, then turned to me, betrayal flashing in his eyes.

"It's not ready to be rented," he repeated slowly, but of course what he meant was, You whore.

"Zephyr?" Freddy whined.

"There are still some things that need to be fixed," Gregory said pointedly to me.

The staircase. Was he holding on to the chance that we could have another escapade within its rosy confines? Did I mean that much to him? Did he mean as much to me as four thousand dollars a month?

"Anyone want a beer?" Hayden offered.

"Oh my God!" I exploded. "Hayden, you have to leave. Now."

Hayden didn't budge.

"Freddy, the apartment *is* ready to rent," I said, looking at Gregory. It was a stupid staircase, and whatever runty relationship Gregory and I might have been starting was already over.

He was sullen, judgmental, unpredictable, interfering, and unsocialized. I'd wall over the door or solder it shut, and if Sandra Oh or some variation of her rented the place and asked about it, I'd tell them it was a relic from another age, that it went nowhere. Not unlike my life at that moment, which felt as if it might actually be moving backward.

"It's ready," I said firmly. "When does she want to move in?"

Gregory roughly cupped the back of his neck with both hands and pulled, as though he was displacing a desire to strangle me.

"Is this your boyfriend?" Hayden asked nonchalantly, slugging back the rest of his lager.

Freddy looked up, possibly for the first time in his life.

"Not you. Him." Hayden gestured to Gregory with his bottle.

"No," Gregory spat. "I'm just the exterminator."

Without giving me another glance, Gregory turned and left. I braced myself against the smooth oak door. How could I be dumped by the same man twice in the space of two days? And how could it hurt just as much? Wasn't there some law of physics that prevailed here?

"The exterminator?" Freddy said, his gaze having returned to its comfort zone near my knees. "Is there a pest problem in this building?"

"Yeah," I said, looking at Hayden, who smiled and did a Charlie Chaplin eyebrow dance.

"Fix it," Freddy muttered, and galumphed down the steps to the street.

Wordlessly, Hayden slipped past me, letting his chest graze mine, and locked the door behind Freddy. He took my hands and pulled me to him.

"Hey, you," he whispered, his lips fluttering against my ear.

"What's my name?" I couldn't resist whispering back to him.

He leaned back and regarded me with amused confusion. "What?"

I shook my head and looked into his green eyes. I waited for my lust to overpower me again, but all I could think of was Gregory. Gregory on the front steps, licking custard off his fingers. Gregory's sweet breath on my cheek in the dark of Roxana's closet. Gregory teaching me more about myself in an hour than Hayden could in a lifetime.

I squeezed Hayden's hands, willing myself to go back upstairs and pick up where we left off. The Zephyr of the past two years demanded it. God knows I *wanted* to keep wanting Hayden. Gregory was gone—again—and here was the man I'd been obsessing about, offering himself to me.

Hayden started up the stairs, pulling me behind him. I walked slowly up the steps, counting them while I hashed it out with the devil homunculus.

I came to my decision with two steps left to go.

"Hayden," I said, stopping short.

He turned and looked at me, giving me a soft smile.

"That *was* your boyfriend, wasn't it?" he said almost wistfully, exhibiting more insight in that one question than he had in nearly five months of dating. I wavered.

"I don't know what he is," I told Hayden apologetically, feeling like I was jumping off a cliff, "but he's . . . he's on my mind," I finished lamely.

"So should I go?" He encircled my wrist with his thumb and forefinger. My knees almost buckled, but I clenched my jaw and nodded.

He nodded back, with a hint of self-pity, and dropped my wrist. I sucked in my breath. Oh, God, I was never going to see him again. I'd been given my second chance and I was chucking it away, as if I were a rich woman tossing pennies. It took all my willpower not to push him inside the apartment and tell him I was just kidding. I studied him hard. This was it.

"Okay, just gotta get my shoes," he said, suddenly jovial again. He winked at me and pushed open the apartment door.

I shook my head, pitying him. Poor deluded guy. This is really it, Hayden, I told both of us silently. It's Over.

I watched him slip his shoes on and sling his red Manhattan Portage over his shoulder.

"See you in court tomorrow!" He kissed me on the nose and bounced down the stairs.

He read my book, Zephy? Really?"

I lay on my parents' couch that night with one arm flung over my eyes, slumped against my father. It had started to rain right after Hayden left, and the sound of the water splattering on the skylight perfectly matched the drowning sensation I'd labored under all day.

My dad was supposed to be giving me a neck rub, but he couldn't resist tugging at my ears as he thought aloud.

"Ow! Dad, no ears."

"Sorry. What did he say? Did he like it?" my dad persisted, pulling at one lobe again.

"Daddy, ow, I don't *know*. He was out to get me. He used it as a weapon against me." I knew I was being melodramatic, but I didn't care. My heart was broken and my dad only cared about what some over-zealous defense lawyer thought of his book.

"What do you think of Anne?" he said, referring to Langley, the blond prosecutor. "She's a superstar. Did you like her? What did she ask you?"

"Dad," I muttered somewhere toward my armpit. "This is why I'm never going to get picked for a jury. Stop asking!"

I heard ice rattling and peered out from under my arm to see my mother conveying their nightly sherry and whitefish salad ritual out on a small brushed aluminum tray.

My dad took a sip of sherry and smacked his lips.

"Ah, Zephy, it's too bad you don't like to drink. Times like this, it would do you good."

I groaned and closed my eyes again.

I felt my mother sit down beside me. She started stroking my hair and I squirmed away from my father and closer to her. I intended to soak up every ounce of coddling before my brother the auteur arrived the following week.

"Zephy, honey, I'm not sure I understand," she said gently. "You've only known this boy—"

"He's a *man*," I said grumpily. "I date *men*."

"This *man* for two weeks, and you're already fighting? Maybe he's not worth the trouble."

"You're just saying that because you don't want me to date an exterminator," I said accusingly, knowing even as I said it that I was getting myself in trouble. Her hands stopped moving and she tapped one nail lightly on my scalp.

"Zephyr," she said sternly.

"Sorry," I muttered, pushing myself up into a sitting position.

"Why are *you* having trouble with the idea of dating an exterminator?" she asked.

"I'm not," I said, trying to figure out whether that was true. "I mean, do I wish he had a more exciting career, like, say, I don't know, a . . . a homicide reporter for a major newspaper? Yeah, I guess I do."

My parents looked at me quizzically—I'd successfully kept Hayden a secret from them.

"You're the ones with these important, successful careers," I whined, hating the sound of my own voice, but unable to resist the tantalizing allure of regression. "*You've* sent me subliminal messages about who's right for me to date and who isn't. *You're* afraid I'm never going to succeed at anything."

"Whoa," my dad said, raising his eyebrows.

"Two different things," my mom said.

"You can date whomever you want, as long as he's kind and good to you."

"That's different from what we hope you'll make of your life."

Hope. She said "hope." Gregory had said a parent's responsibility was to distinguish between their hopes and their expectations for their kids. Mine actually knew the difference. A sob sprang up from my throat. I tried to gulp it back, but it exploded and I flung myself against my mother's shoulder.

I felt her hand her drink to my dad and then wrap both arms around me. I watched the footprints on their Greek dancing instructions bounce up and down as I shook. I cried because I didn't want to be a super; because I was trying to make cosmic lemonade out of lemons and it wasn't working; because I couldn't understand how I could be so ambitious and so lazy at the same time; because Gregory knew I thought he wasn't good enough for me and I hated myself for that. I couldn't blame LinguaFrank for Gregory's desertion. Gregory kept trying to come back and I kept sending the message that I had better options. I hated myself for the way I'd treated him.

My dad patted my ankle. "You know, Zephy," he began gently, "what so many people don't understand is that true love, if you're lucky, means in-laws, mortgages, and diapers. If you look for constant excitement, you're going to wind up alone. Either because you won't find it, or because your true love will run out of oxygen climbing Everest." He gave a half-hearted chortle.

I sat up and my mother wiped my tears away with the length of her thumb. "I'm not looking for constant excitement," I whimpered. "I just want . . ."

My parents looked at me expectantly, as if they were on the brink of hearing an answer to a question they'd asked themselves repeatedly. Perhaps they wanted to hear that I was ready to resume law school, or pick up a stethoscope again, or sit for the Foreign Service exam. I still didn't know what I wanted to be when I grew up, but at least now I knew who I wanted to be with.

"I want the exterminator," I said plaintively. "And I missed my chance."

SIXTEEN

THE NEXT DAY, I SLUMPED IN MY SEAT BESIDE THE BEEFY orthodontist and bided my time until I was kicked back into the jury pool with the rest of the untouchables. I wound and unwound a loose thread on my black sweater—the only item of Tag's I'd ever successfully fit into—hoping that the next case wouldn't have such industrious attorneys. While Commando Suarez interrogated the doggie spa owner behind me, I tried to keep my gaze from straying to the mop of red hair in the audience. The energy it took not to look toward the fourth seat of the third row made my neck ache, and I wondered, statistically, how many times per minute I'd otherwise be inclined to look there.

The room was packed again, but now the sight of Maria Anna Mariza in an electric blue suit, whispering to her seatmate—I still couldn't remember which Pelarose underling he was—only depressed me. Sitting in the jury box just made me wish I was back on Twelfth Street sweeping cigarette butts out of the alley.

A court officer who'd been conferring with two of the thick-necked buzz-cuts—today they had squeezed themselves into pigeon-gray suits—straightened up and pushed his way through the swinging door into the well. He whispered to the clerk, who stood up, tottering on heels that looked like engineering impossibilities. She slipped a note to the poker-faced assistant sitting in the box adjacent to the judge's bench. He read it and whispered to the judge, who looked, I swear, straight at me. I sat up in my seat, resisting a nervous urge to rearrange my hair.

"Mr. Suarez, excuse me," the judge said, interrupting Clarence Darrow mid-spittle-spray. "Gentlemen, is this really necessary right now?" She addressed the buzz-cuts, who stood up from their seats in the audience to answer her.

"Yer Ahna," the rounder one said in heavy Bronxese, "we apologize for the disruption, but we do feel that it is necessary at this time."

Out of the corner of my eye, I saw Hayden's head swivel between the men and the judge.

"In the future, I suggest you do your job while the court is in recess instead of disrupting my jury selection." She looked at them sternly.

"Yes, Your Honor," the taller one said respectfully. "We don't foresee that we'll need to do this again anytime soon."

The judge sighed and looked at me again.

"Ms. Zuckerman, would you please follow these two gentlemen? I apologize to all parties for the disruption."

I swallowed hard and felt my ears grow hot. I'd never heard of anything like this happening. Had they decided I'd lied on the stand about my living situation? But I really did live alone! Were they going to take me downtown and book me for perjury? They can't take me downtown, I already *am* downtown, I thought wildly, gathering up my backpack.

I caught a glimpse of Suarez, his eyebrows raised in surprise. The blond prosecutor frowned and scribbled something on her notepad. She had wanted me. I knew it! Oh, it would have been a beautiful trial.

I trembled slightly as I made my way past the knees of my former fellow jurors. The entire courtroom was silent except for the sound of my footsteps and the rustle of the buzz-cuts' suits. I kept my head down as I followed them toward a side door, but at the last moment, I glanced up. Hayden was looking right at me. Instead of his usual sexy, mischievous, infuriating grin, he looked genuinely curious. Intrigued. So this is what he looked like on the job, picking up the scent of a story.

This, I defended myself to my demons, this is why I fell for him. In fact, Hayden looked more interested in me at that moment than he ever had when we were alone together in bed. The thought was tantalizing—*finally*, I had his attention—but mostly, it was breathtakingly depressing.

Goon Number One held the door for me and Goon Number Two gestured for me to go first. The tops of their heads might have looked like freshly mowed lawns, but they were gentlemen.

"Am I in trouble?" I blurted out the moment the door shut behind us. We stood in a narrow, fluorescently lit hallway with tiles peeling from the ceiling.

"Not at awl," said Number One, the rounder one. Number Two said nothing. Good cop, bad cop. My fingers were white against the strap of my backpack, where I clutched it to my shoulder. I relaxed my hand and wiped the palm on my pant leg.

"I'm Agent Mulrooney, and this is Agent Underhill. Just come this way," Mulrooney continued soothingly. "We got a few questions."

Agents? FBI? They really were going to get me for fudging

on "Do you live alone?" I felt a new quiver in my right eyelid. We turned a corner and started along an identical hallway.

But what if they weren't who they said they were? I thought frantically. What if they were tied to the Pelarose family, but *posing* as law enforcement, and they had fooled the judge and everyone else and now they were going to dump me in the East River? Maybe, I thought, my heart pounding in time with my eyelid, the Pelarose family and the Sanchez family were allies, and they were all out to avenge my father's prosecution of Tommy "The Manhole" Sanchez.

"Good thing that rain let up, huh?" said Mulrooney.

"Yeah, I got tickets at Shea tonight," said Underhill.

At least I knew they weren't planning to keep me all night. Or it meant they were going to dispose of my body somewhere in Queens in time to fortify themselves with knishes before the first pitch.

We turned another corner and passed a door with a sign announcing: "Jury Deliberating. Do Not Enter." A court officer of bouncer-like proportions was tilting back in his overtaxed chair, holding a dented phone to his ear, and squinting at a scrap of paper.

"Take duh casserole outta duh fridge. Turn duh oven tuh tree-fifty. Stickitina oven." He paused and listened for a moment. "I dunno, half ow-ah? What am I, some kine uhva chef?" He hung up, letting the legs of his chair thunk forward, and rolled his eyes at us.

"It ain't enough I gotta run all around fuh dem?" He jerked his head toward the citizens carrying out justice behind the closed door. "I gotta tell their fuckin' husbands howda cook?"

It didn't look to me like he did much running.

Mulrooney made sympathetic clucking noises and opened the door next to the one the chef was putatively guarding.

A jury room. The single window was cracked and the

table's cheap veneer had been decimated by ballpoint-wielding jurors unable to make their fellow citizens see things their way. A government-issue water pitcher sat sweating in the middle of the table, surrounded by a dozen glasses. I was growing more terrified by the minute. Why couldn't they have just excused me? Why had I been escorted through a rabbit's maze to a room where no one could hear me scream?

Underhill pulled out a chair and gestured for me to sit down.

"I really do live alone," I blurted, clutching my backpack as if it were my only friend in the world. "The apartment has its own entrance, its own kitchen. I even have a washer and dryer," I said, my voice cracking.

Mulrooney raised his eyebrows at Underhill. "Just relax," he said. "I'm sure you have a lovely apartment." He poured a glass of water and pushed it across the table.

Underhill pulled out another chair and straddled it backwards. Oh, come on, guys, I couldn't help thinking. This isn't an audition for *SVU*. I took a sip of water.

"A few weeks ago, Saturday, the fourth of April, to be exact," Underhill said, looking me straight in the eye, "you were seen fleeing the St. Regis Hotel."

The wheels of my brain screeched to a halt. Crash test dummies flew into a brick wall.

"Excuse me?"

"The St. Regis."

"We have it on tape," Mulrooney said with a pitying smile.

I shook my head quickly, wondering if I was dreaming. Were we still in a courthouse? Was it still Tuesday?

"Have *what* on tape?" I demanded.

"You fleeing the St. Regis," Underhill repeated slowly.

"I wasn't fleeing," I said, trying to get up to speed. "I was leaving."

"You left real fast, wouldn't you say?" Mulrooney amended.

Underhill leaned forward and spread his elbows on the table.

"You ran out of a party attended by the defendants and their colleagues."

The crash-test dummies shimmied out of my mind, abandoning me in an alternate universe.

I licked my lips and tried to pick my words carefully. "What?"

"You were at a party with members of the Pelarose family three weeks ago, and now here you are, about to be seated on a jury that will decide whether they go to jail for the rest of their lives. Or go free," Underhill said, emphasizing the last three words. "You're telling me that's a coincidence?"

"Wait," I said, holding my face with my hands, feeling my entire life swerve horribly off course. "That party was for Spain. For Spanish people," I said stupidly.

"The Pelarose family is Spanish," Mulrooney said, as if to a sanatorium resident.

"I thought the mob was Italian."

"So why were you there?" Underhill pressed, impatient with my limited knowledge of the underworld's apparent Benetton-like breadth.

"I was just crashing a party," I said in a strained voice. I never thought I'd be in a situation where confessing to crashing was my best option. "With my friend Tag. We do that sometimes. Crash parties." Used to. Used to crash parties. I wanted to kill Tag. This was her fault.

"So you're claiming it was just a coincidence?"

I nodded vigorously. "Not just claiming. Telling you the absolute truth."

"Why do the cameras show you running for the stairs?"

I blushed. "Well, you know, like I said, we were . . . crashing." Maybe Underhill hadn't been much of a party boy in his day. "We weren't invited. We had to leave in a hurry."

Underhill put his chin in his hand as if he had all day to extract the truth.

"Jury-rigging is a felony."

"I wasn't jury-rigged!" I yelped, a sob rising in my throat. "I mean, nobody planted me. No rigging. Nothing. I never saw any of those people before that party, and I never saw any of the defendants while I was there," I pleaded, just as I realized that the guy Maria Anna had been whispering to in the courtroom was the hottie who'd been manning the door of the Cavendish ballroom. I groaned to myself.

"Where can we reach your friend?" Mulrooney said, peering at me with big eyes. "It would help if we could back up your story."

"She's at a conference."

"Where?"

I bit my lip as my malfunctioning geography gene chose that moment to right itself. She wasn't in Senegal *or* Saudi Arabia.

"Spain," I whispered.

"Could you speak up?"

"Spain." I began to see spots.

The pair exchanged triumphant glances.

"Why do you suppose she went to Spain, honey?" Mulrooney said. I resisted correcting his mode of address.

"She's a parasitologist. She studies tapeworms in sharks," I said, thinking how ridiculous the truth sounded. Why couldn't Tag have just become a lawyer? What the hell kind of person mucks around in shark stomachs, I thought angrily.

One of the lights overhead sputtered and died.

"Tell us a little more about what you do. You manage your parents' building?"

I nodded, nervously working the zipper on my backpack.

"You don't look like a super. How did you wind up doing *that*?"

So this was how I made Gregory feel. No wonder he hated me. I shook my head, trying to focus on one earthquake at a time.

"The previous super left. My parents needed me."

"Why did he leave?" Underhill asked.

My shoulders dropped and I rubbed my eyes as hard as I could stand.

"Arrested."

"Arrested?" Mulrooney said, surprised. "For what?"

"Kickbacks," I told them, wishing I could put my head down on the table.

"And you didn't think that was worth mentioning?" said my buddy Underhill.

No, I didn't, but I wondered now if perhaps I should be telling them about the secret staircase James had built.

"I want a lawyer!" I yelped, suddenly remembering I was a prosecutor's daughter and should have known better than to sit there for ten minutes like some yo-yo without demanding representation.

"You've got one at home, I hear."

I looked sharply at Underhill. He was actually cracking a joke. At my expense.

"You're free to go," he said, spreading his arms, as if to persuade me I wasn't there against my will. I looked to Mulrooney for confirmation. He smiled and nodded. Apparently, we were all buddies now.

"Should I come back tomorrow?" I said, pushing back my chair.

Underhill's stony face cracked into a smile. "Uh, no," he chortled, sliding his business card toward me, "consider yourself relieved of jury duty."

*   *   *

I TOOK THE STAIRS OUT OF THE UNION SQUARE SUBWAY station two at a time—surely that would make up for a shortage of visits to the Y in recent weeks—and gulped deep breaths of the sun-warmed air. As I dodged kamikaze skateboarders and Falun Gong protesters, I embarked on a campaign to be grateful for my current state of affairs. Wasn't there a Chinese blessing that wished the beneficiary a dull life?

So I had missed an opportunity to serve on the Pelarose jury. That was a huge disappointment. But I had also missed being prosecuted myself. That was a very good thing. So good that it made the prospect of going home to pay bills seem soothing. As long as I didn't think about paying the exterminator's bill.

I shook my head, clearing away the thought. I would do my job, get the apartment rented, go to Lucy's tonight to hear about Mercedes's smooth sail to the isle of love, be a supportive and dependable friend. I'd even prepare to be a proud sister to my Spielbergian brother. Love would come in its own time. If I didn't look too hard, it would find me. I just had to figure out how to stop looking.

I turned onto University Place and spotted the dingy yellow awning hanging crookedly over the door to Fast Foto. I considered abandoning James's prints there instead of forking over my own cash to pay for them. All I planned to do was stick them in the basement with the rest of his stuff anyway.

Closure. Closure and responsibility. I sighed. They were his property. Reluctantly, I pushed open the door.

I handed my claim stubs to the gangly teen attempting to hide his pimples behind sprouts of wiry facial hair. The effect was that of an adolescent Osama bin Laden. I tried not to grimace.

The boy silently disappeared into the back, but when he returned, he brought with him two similarly unappealing teenage specimens. The three of them moved toward the counter in a huddle, guffawing and watching me with wide eyes. I shifted uneasily.

"Are these yours?" Baby Osama squeaked.

I glanced down at the envelope, which had my name on it, and looked up at the trio impatiently.

"Okaaaay," he said gleefully, punching numbers into the cash register. "That'll be fifty-two seventy-five."

"What!" This was going to come out of the building's account, damn it. I handed over my credit card, glaring at the ugly boys as if they had forced me to develop the photos.

"Some people pay a lot more than that for . . . pictures," said the one wearing a tattered Sex Pistols T-shirt. The third casualty of adolescence elbowed him and snorted.

I grabbed the fat envelope and wrenched open the door. I made it as far as the corner before I stopped under the shade of a birch tree and unsealed the package. Pulling out the first envelope, I prayed for photos of kindly old relatives. Rocking chairs on a porch covered in peeling white paint. An old sheepdog curled at their feet. Please.

As I flipped through the first three photos, I was indignant. Why should I have had to pay for poorly developed film? I could barely make out faces. But at the fourth, I froze. It was grotesquely clear, as if the photographer—as if James—had perfected his technique. A wave of nausea rose in my throat.

The pictures—about seventy of them—were of Roxana. Roxana pale and naked and having sex with lots and lots of different people. Or wearing the lingerie I had brushed up against in her closet, having sex with lots and lots of different people. And then there were photos of other women having sex with lots and lots of different people. One of the women looked like it might be Mini-Dolly. One of the men was definitely Senator Smith; I recognized the gray helmet of hair.

I opened the next pack, and the next one, terrified that I would find pictures of myself. In some, Roxana wore expressions of ecstasy, but the worst were the ones in which all that was visible was a man's face, contorted with pleasure over a naked breast or bare ass.

I shoved the photos back into the envelope, sending a couple of negative strips fluttering through the air in my haste. I whipped around, trying to catch them. A woman with a newborn strapped to her chest stopped to help, and an elderly doorman limped out of his building to capture the flyaway celluloid.

"Thanks, no, really, thanks, you don't have to . . ." I grabbed the negatives from them, trying to sound grateful instead of panicked. I wondered how many other New Yorkers at that very moment were carrying dark secrets inside something as innocuous as a photo lab envelope stamped with a cartoon smiling sun wearing sunglasses.

I hightailed it across Twelfth Street, eager to return to the safety of my apartment and unload my illicit haul. I barely managed a smile for the bald guy toting his pet macaw on his bare shoulders, as sure a sign of spring's arrival in the neighborhood as daffodils might be elsewhere. As disturbed as I was by this new image of Roxana as a whorish sex addict—no judgments, I chastised myself, no judgments—I knew I had to tell her about these photos. I was more certain than ever that she didn't know about James's staircase. He had been using it to spy on her, to take pictures of her titillating sex life.

I clucked with disgust at this rapacious side of James, and absently stepped into the crosswalk against the light. A Harley farting its way down Fifth Avenue swerved to avoid me and I gasped, more terrified at the thought of the photos being found on me by an ER attending than by my brush with death. I hopped back onto the curb. A rail-thin, tattooed dog-walker being pulled along by a dozen mutts staggered to a halt beside me, and the fourteen of us waited for the light to change.

After I showed Roxana, then what? I crossed Fifth Avenue with the dog-walker, who managed to light a cigarette as her canine charges surged toward Washington Square Park.

I was going to have to give the photos to the police. Or, more specifically, to the FBI. To Underhill and Mulrooney, who, just hours ago, had accused me of having mob ties. What if James was spying on women and then selling unauthorized porn? Someone was going to find out—I shuddered, thinking of the pubescent counter help at Fast Foto—and I needed to get to the cops before they did. But it was only fair to break the news to Roxana first.

I finally crossed Seventh Avenue, dodged a phalanx of Trinidadian nannies pushing orange Bugaboos, and broke into a jog. I raced up my front steps, ignoring Mrs. Hannaham, who was puttering around her garden looking like a holy terror in an oversized sailor's uniform, her garland of white paper clips drooping low over one ear.

"Zephyr, I need—"

"In a sec," I said, knowing I'd pay for my brush-off with a dozen pre-dawn phone calls the following week.

Upstairs, the door to James's apartment was open, and the Sandra Oh clone was marching around, measuring every stretch of wall and calling out numbers to a young woman who was wearing the exact same outfit as Sandra, right down to the thin-lipped expression of concentration.

"Uh . . ." I said.

Sandra snapped shut her measuring tape. She and her doppelgänger whipped around, fixing me with identical glares.

"Who let you in?" I asked, wondering whether I had definitively told her she could have the apartment and had just forgotten.

Sandra put one hand on her hip and cocked her head as if to say, Please, is there anything I'm not capable of? The assistant put her hand on her hip, too.

I rubbed my forehead hard, trying to triage. Sandra could wait, I decided, and turned to go.

"Is she always this loud?" Sandra barked. I stopped and caught the strains of an argument between Roxana and a deep male voice above our heads. "If she is, I'm going to require some kind of soundproofing."

The toady assistant echoed "soundproofing" a moment after Sandra said it, as if to prove her allegiance to her boss.

"I've never heard her before," I said firmly. "I'll go check."

I dumped my backpack in my apartment and listened to the row upstairs. It wasn't in English or French, and every now and then an exchange was punctuated with a thump, like a palm on a wall. I remembered the naked fear I'd seen in Roxana's eyes as Senator Smith followed her up the stairs, and her hushed argument with Mini-Dolly on the landing, and I wondered if I should get someone to go with me to her apartment.

No. There was no Hayden, there was no Gregory, and my father was at work. I was no fairy-tale bimbo awaiting male assistance. I was going to do this myself. I donned my super's cloak of responsibility, girding myself with thoughts of all the organized files now neatly lined up under my bed, and how I knew what tax forms to file and what grade oil we used. Clutching the photos, I made my way upstairs.

The voices grew louder. They were speaking Spanish, not with the usual Mexican lilt I was accustomed to hearing from the kitchen of every restaurant in the city, but a lisping, mother-country Spanish. More slamming. More yelling. Roxana was sobbing.

I nervously flicked the packs of photos against my hand,

hesitating. This was a test. If I could stop the fight, go to the cops with the photos, and get a nice, fat deposit out of Sandra—to whom I had apparently rented an apartment—then I would have finally completed something. I would have proved to my parents and myself that I was an adult. I didn't know what would come next in my life, but whatever it was, I'd be coming at it like a cheetah charging through the jungle instead of an alley cat skulking along the top of a Dumpster.

I took a deep breath and knocked. We were in a town house in the middle of Greenwich Village on a Tuesday afternoon.

I mean, really, what was the worst that could happen?

SEVENTEEN

THE YELLING INSIDE ROXANA'S APARTMENT WAS DROWNING out my knocking, so I pounded on the door. Silence, and then a low, angry rumble of voices. I banged a third time, my determination building.

"It's Zephyr. Roxana, open the door right now!" I shouted, thrilled by my own authority.

Roxana flung open the door. Her eyes were puffy and damp, her topknot was unraveling, and her lip was bleeding. Behind her, the apartment was a wreck. Moving boxes were everywhere, stuffed chaotically with unmatching items—fringed pillows and a lamp sticking out of one, books and pots sticking out of another, as though the boxes weren't going to be closed, just thrown away. Shards of a vase littered the floor in front of me.

I carefully stepped over the broken pottery, toward her. When I looked up, I was face-to-face with the presumed vase tosser. It took a second to place the sharp jaw, the black eyes, and the even blacker hair.

Ferdinand.

Ferdinand, the shrimp-eating Spaniard I'd elbowed up to at the St. Regis. Ferdinand, who, just four hours earlier, I might have been thrilled to reencounter so serendipitously. I might have picked up my fantasies where I'd left off—imagining us touring the world together in his private jet, my dad dandling our dark-haired babies, our lives perpetually framed by Mediterranean sunsets, our thirst ever slaked by cold, slushy drinks.

But that was this morning, before the party at the St. Regis had ballooned into an event that seemed destined to cause me no end of regret. As I cursed Tag yet again, I watched the rage in Ferdinand's face flicker to confusion and settle on—could it be?—fear.

"What *you* doing here?" he rasped in heavily accented English. Just as well he'd kept silent during our first meeting.

"What the hell are *you* doing here?" I retorted, panicked by the thought that he'd been tailing me since the St. Regis. Maybe Underhill and Mulrooney had seen him following me and assumed that he and I—

"*Carajo!*" he bellowed, echoing my own sentiments. "*Caaa-raaaa-joooo!*" Ferdinand fixed me with a searing stare of such loathing that I stopped in my tracks, my foot crunching a shard into smithereens. Roxana slumped down on the couch and began weeping.

"*Silencio!*" Ferdinand raged, whirling around. I jumped between them, afraid he was going to strike her. It was as useless a move as a driver whipping a hand in front of her passenger as she slams on the brakes.

Ferdinand pulled a gun from his leather jacket and pointed it at me.

Over the years, especially while toiling over the cancerous guts of my med school cadaver, or listening to Abigail gripe about the pressures of being a highly sought-after academic superstar, I had found myself fantasizing about changing the course of my life in a single, unplanned moment—imagining a shortcut, really, to figuring out who I was: I happened to be near City Hall just as the mayor's toddler son raced into the street. I would grab him and roll us to safety, rending my garments and sustaining a slight but camera-pleasing cut on my face. I became a hero, touted on the front page of all the dailies for my quick wits and bravery. Sometimes, I even broke a bone or two during the rescue.

Other times, I chased down muggers and sat on them until help came, or I wrestled back a despondent subway-track jumper, thereby saving a life *and* preventing thousands of New Yorkers from being late to work.

But when the moment actually arrived, I discovered as I looked into the nostril of Ferdinand's gun, it turned out that I was utterly unprepared to face a person who was contemplating killing me. All my fantasies plus every *Charlie's Angels* rerun I'd watched as a kid had amounted to nothing.

My right eyelid went haywire. My bladder twitched and threatened to throw in the towel. I slowly raised my arms in surrender pose, trying out half a dozen responses in my head, afraid to utter any of them.

Ferdinand's hand was shaking and his eyes grew even wider.

"*Mierda, mierda,* MIERDA!" He puckered up his lips and spat on Roxana, a nasty gray loogie that landed on her cheek. He turned to me and I squeezed my eyes shut, bracing for either a wet missile or a metal one.

"*PUTA!*" he screamed. When nothing hit me, I opened my eyes in time to see him backing out of the apartment, still brandishing the gun. When he bumped into the door frame, he turned and disappeared down the stairs.

I stood frozen, my hands still in the air, irrelevantly mar-veling at my fluency in gutter Spanish. Fuck, shut up, shit, whore: I'd understood everything Ferdinand had said.

Roxana jumped up and slammed the door shut, bolted it with three different locks, and threw her arms around me. It felt like a gerbil was hugging me—a nearly weightless form practically hanging from my neck. I had never felt like more of an Amazon in my life. I brought my hands down and embraced her. Her frail body was shaking and I realized she was much thinner than I'd realized, far beyond envy-inducing French-woman thin.

"Roxana," I croaked, at a loss for where to make inroads. "Why was *he* . . . here?" I cast my eye over the ransacked, half-packed apartment, while another part of my brain wondered whether Roxana had planned to give thirty days' notice.

"I wus tryeen to get out, once James wus gone," she wailed into my neck. "I taut it wud be easier, but he said if I didn't keep it go-een he wode keel me. Tank got you came, Zepheer! He wus go-een to keel me!"

It. Keep it going. I didn't know whether I was supposed to know what she was talking about. I couldn't focus. I pulled Roxana's arms from me and pushed her gently onto her couch.

"Just hold on a second," I said. "Stop talking." She nodded vigorously and for a moment, I mourned the departure of the self-assured Gaul Gal. Apparently, I was in charge now, and I did my best to step up to the plate. "I need something to drink," I told her, heading for her kitchen. My knees still shook with adrenaline.

The kitchen was also in disarray, with plates and glasses stacked all over the counter, but what surprised me most was the kitchen itself. Bright Italian tiles lined the counter and backsplash, where before I knew there had been butcher block, just like in all the other apartments. The sink was smooth soapstone, and there were antique sconces on either side of the window. I ran the water until it grew icy cold, wondering at the copper swan's-neck faucet. Ask about the guy with the gun first, I reminded myself.

I brought two glasses of water out to the living room, my hands shaking. Roxana looked at me imploringly as I sat down beside her.

"I am so so sorry, Zepheer! I never meant to hurt you or your family. You hif all only ever been so kine to me." Her face turned bright red as she tried to hold back another flood of tears. "I dunt know what to do. I am so skerd. He said he wode keel me," she said, starting to sob again. "If I doan keep it go-een, he will keel me!" She was wailing now, her face in her hands.

It. It. My brain turned somersaults trying to catch up with her. Ferdinand was in love with Roxana, and James had shown him the pictures and now he wanted to keel her. A crime of passion. That still didn't explain why Ferdinand had been at the St. Regis. Or how James would know Ferdinand. Or much of anything, really.

Okay. I thought desperately as Roxana started gasping for air. Ferdinand was undercover FBI and he'd had to pull a gun on me to keep Roxana thinking he was . . . whoever he wanted her to believe he was. Roxana was doing something illegal on eBay and he was going to bust her, but he'd fallen in love with her. He was actually a buddy of Underhill's and Mulrooney's and was headed to the nearest bar to cry into a pint of beer with them and admit he'd strayed from his line of duty.

I was quickly going crazy right here on Roxana's Danish modern couch.

I gulped the rest of my water and my eye fell on a box stuffed with bolts of cloth. One of them looked very familiar. Very pink and satin and familiar.

Roxana was the madam of a brothel being run out of my very own beloved house. Mini-Dolly was for hire and James was the pimp. He had built the secret staircase so clients could come in through the alley—where they tossed their cigarette butts—and not through the front door. His own handcuff-and-condom-filled closet served as storage space, providing easy access to paraphernalia necessary for business. When he was arrested, the johns had begun entering through the front door—so to speak—but Roxana had decided she wanted out of the business. A lot of people were angry with that unilateral decision, including clients, like Senator Smith, and hookers who needed the money, like Mini-Dolly. Ferdinand was a member of the Pelarose family, which made money off of brothels, and he had come to threaten Roxana to keep it going or he would kill her. He wode keel her.

My glass slipped out of my hand and shattered on the floor. Beside me, I felt Roxana jump.

I leaned back on the couch and carefully placed my hands on my lap, stunned. I was *right*. I was aghast at the facts, the sordid truth, sure, but much more confounded that something in my real world was more exciting than anything I had ever been able to imagine. Or rather, something I'd imagined was turning out to be true. And I was smack in the middle of it.

Roxana watched me, red-eyed and rigid. I reached for the photos, which I'd dropped on the floor during my brief skirmish with death. I didn't want to move too quickly, afraid I'd shatter the fragile mosaic I'd pieced together in my head. I pulled the prints out of their envelopes.

"Are these . . . clients? With . . ." I was new to the terminology of the field. "With your women? Did James take these?"

Roxana glanced at the photos and nodded mutely, rubbing her gaunt cheeks. I was right! I was right! She knew what I was talking about!

I bit my lip. "For his own viewing pleasure or for blackmail ammunition against the"—I was going to say "johns" but it sounded absurdly late-night movie, even if it was accurate. "Against the men?"

She nodded again.

"Extortion," I said, as a new shot of adrenaline lurched along my limbs. Roxana looked at me with despair and I reminded myself that this was a doozy of a predicament for her, not just an exciting day for me. A day that had begun with humiliation in front of Hayden and an entire courtroom, and gone on to include false accusations by federal agents. My stomach turned over.

I was the only person who knew about the link between the Spanish mob and this brothel operating right over my head. If Underhill and Mulrooney hadn't asked me about the prostitutes after I gave them James's name and my address—if that hadn't made them slap cuffs on me this morning—then that must mean they didn't know about this. I was the only one who could place Ferdinand at both the St. Regis and in a den of iniquity, otherwise known as my home. The Pelarose family was into art fraud, murder, *and* prostitution. I pictured myself reviewing the job offers that would come from my hard—okay, lucky—work as a detective. I'd be asked to go undercover for the NYPD or the FBI, maybe even the CIA.

"We have to call the cops!" I jumped up and dug my fingers into my scalp, as if I could order my thoughts by pressing down hard.

"Non. Absoluement!" Roxana cried. "They'll keel me."

"No," I said, "not if you cooperate. You'll cut a deal and get protection." My dad was going to be so proud. I wondered if I could just xerox my law school applications and resubmit them.

"Zepheer, you dunt unnerstan! If I do zat, zay will keel James! I have no choice. I haf to keep it go-een." She tossed the photos on the floor and set her shoulders straight.

"He's in prison. They can't hurt him there," I said, but what I was thinking was: No, actually, you won't keep running a brothel out of my house.

She shook her head at me pityingly, which I found offensive given that I was exhibiting skills on par with a Pinkerton.

"In prison, hees the easiest target of all. Zey know egg-sackly war he ees." She stood up and started pulling knick-knacks out of a box.

"Roxana!" She stopped what she was doing. "Why the hell do you care what happens to James? The man enslaved you."

"Oh, Zepheer. Zepheer." She straightened up and looked at me pleadingly. "I luf heem. He ees zuh love of my life."

I looked at her dubiously. James with the saggy tool belt and the misbuttoned plaid shirts? The man who hoarded Marmite? The man who took photos of her having sex with other men?

But all I said was, "So was he British?"

"He's nut dead! Dunt refer to him in zee past."

"Sorry. Is he British or Brooklyn?"

"What do you mean?"

I raised my eyebrows at her. "Um, well, all these years, like, ten years . . ." I began. Was she putting me on? Was this some complicated double hoax I couldn't see through? I forged ahead, ". . . he's always spoken to me in a British accent. But when he was arrested, he was shouting in a New York accent. You know, baby, *Brooklyn*." I pursed my lips and affected the accent for the last sentence.

"James ees duh feef cousin of zee Duke of Curnwell," she said, offended. "I haf niver heard him speak in anysing uzzer zan a perfect English accent."

I hardly thought Roxana was a reliable judge of English accents.

"Okay, so you're in love with James," I said, stalling while I tried to digest this. Downstairs, I heard James's door slam shut, and Sandra's sharp voice made its way outside and down the stoop. I thought of the Italian tiles in Roxana's kitchen and guiltily wondered how much I could get for her place.

"Is he the one who upgraded your kitchen?" I asked her.

"Yes," she said, emptying another carton. "He liked me to have nice tings, and I wanted to run a classy beeznees."

More questions I didn't have time to ask right now sprang to mind.

"So," I said, tracing the pattern on her Turkish rug with my boot. "You can't go to the police because then Ferdinand and his family will kill James. And if you don't, then they'll make you continue this . . . line of work against your will, or, I assume, kill you." I tried not to sound like I was having too much fun.

"Who ees Ferdinand?" She furrowed her bony little brow.

The first job of a good investigator, I would write in my best-selling insider's account, is to learn real names instead of inventing them.

I coughed. "Sorry, the name of the man who just left?"

"Alonzo?"

I preferred Ferdinand.

"Alonzo, okay." I shivered, remembering his gun and the fear in his eyes. He had been just as surprised by our reunion as I was. Good Lord. He probably thought I was FBI. After all, I showed up everywhere he did. And the FBI thought I was with the mob because I showed up everywhere the Pelarose family did. Everyone had a reason to put me on their shit list, unless I cleared things up fast.

"Here's the thing, Roxana. I'm telling the police." When she started to wail in protest, I cut her off sharply. I liked her, but I wasn't going down for her. "I will help you. Protect you. My dad's going to help, too," I added, wondering whether he would or even could.

"Oh, Mr. Zuckerman! He has been so luffly, I cannot tell you how terrible I feel zat I had to do zis in hees building!"

"Had to?" I felt a shameful flicker of irritation. "Roxana, why *did* you do this?"

She looked at me, hurt. "Eets nut like I *wunted* to do eet. I had to." She sighed, and I waited. "I had a husband once."

"He died," I prompted.

"*Non.* He leff me. He took all zee money and he leff me. In a new country, wis no friends, no family, nussing. I really did try to do zuh eBay, but eet wus nut enough. I could not even make enough to fly home."

"Don't you have family who could have helped?"

"Zay tole me nut to marry heem." She shrugged. "Pride. In zee end, eet was nut worse keeping, I suppose."

"Were you running this"—don't say "whorehouse," Zephyr—"business the whole time you were living here?"

She nodded, not apologetically enough, I thought.

"I could not have afforded zees luffly place uzerwise."

I thought guiltily about the four grand I was so eager to separate from Sandra Oh. I was partly responsible for Roxana's predicament. Every high-charging landlord in New York was. We all had blood on our hands. Not blood exactly. Semen, maybe? I shuddered.

The intercom buzzed, startling both of us. My heart clenched. What if it was Ferdinand/Alonzo coming back to finish us off? I looked around for a phone to call 911. The door buzzed again. Roxana looked at me.

"Answer it," I instructed.

Rubbing her arms briskly as if she was cold, Roxana picked her way through the boxes.

"Yes?" she croaked into the speaker.

"I'm here for Yvette," said a gruff voice.

Roxana looked at me again and spread her hands, palms up. I shook my head. She put her finger on the lever to speak.

"I . . . I'm very surry. We are out of girls right now." She flicked the lever up to listen. I acted casual, like I was used to listening to the discussions between a madam and her clients.

"Fuck." Pause. "You free, Roxana? I'll pay extra."

It was an effort to keep my eyes from popping out of my head.

"Surry. Eet's nut a goot time. Tomorrow, meh-bee." I shot her a look.

"Fuck," the voice said again. I darted over to the window in time to see the top of a balding head bouncing down the stoop. At the bottom, he looked right, then turned left. Where the hell was he going now? How many buildings on this block were pandering to this prick? I felt a surge of anger toward Roxana.

"Jesus," I muttered. "It's one in the afternoon. Don't these people have jobs?"

Roxana stood in the middle of the living room, staring at her boxes. If she stayed, she was going to have to find another source of income. If she left, where would she go?

"Roxana," I said suddenly, "I want to see the rest of the apartment." It wasn't a question. She nodded silently and gestured for me to follow her.

The layout was the same as James's, up to the bedroom. At the end of the hallway, there were two doors where downstairs there was only one. Roxana slid her palm into her jeans pocket and fished out two keys. The two locked rooms Gregory hadn't been able to spray.

She pushed the first open, flipped on a light, and stepped back.

Oh, for a sweet pink staircase.

Inside, the tiny room was filled almost to the walls by what looked like a jungle gym. There was a small plastic swing, but where there would have been gymnastic bars were instead handcuffs dangling from chains. Leather straps and buckles hung from a third bar, and a side table—a nice Danish piece, I noticed, that matched the living room sofa—held whips and spiky instruments that looked like meat tenderizers. The walls were painted black, and a red light cast a hellish hue over the whole mess.

"So there's quite a demand for bondage?" I said weakly.

Without answering, Roxana opened the door to the other room and I braced myself. But when I peered inside, I saw only a modest bedroom, tastefully decorated in pale greens and yellows. It was half its original size, thanks to James's skillful handiwork.

"Is this your room?" I asked, spotting the closet door that led to the staircase.

She nodded. "And for customers."

"You don't have a bedroom that's just your own?" I asked, alarmed. The idea was too depressing.

Roxana shook her head. I stared across the room at the closet door, as if it were alive and taunting me. I pounced on it and flung it open. There were the silky negligees and the feathery mules. I pushed them aside to confirm that I hadn't imagined the secret doorway. There it was, looking worn and exposed, drained of mystery. My eyes lingered for a moment on the carpeted floor and I allowed myself a brief shudder of pleasure at a memory that I was now prepared to shelve forever. I slammed the door shut.

I turned and headed back down the hall, but stopped where there should have been a coat closet. Instead, there was a small alcove with a cushioned bench and a coffeemaker. I turned to Roxana, my eyebrows raised.

"Security," she said tiredly. "Guards. To protect zuh girls."

My jaw flapped in the breeze.

"Armed guards? With guns?"

She nodded, and I decided I'd seen enough. The entire day had been one big reality bender, and all I wanted was to get back to the safety of my own apartment, which seemed a hemisphere away.

"Zepheer." Roxana put her hand on my arm. "I'm skerd."

EIGHTEEN

D O YOU KNOW HOW MANY FRIGGING TIMES I'VE DROPPED everything and come running?" Mercedes hissed at me over the phone a few hours later. "Hayden stands you up, you freak out, I'm there. Hayden tells you he wants to go to Paris with you, your head disappears up your ass, I'm there. For the first time in my life, I need to talk to you about a relationship and you avoid me. You suck, Zephyr. You really suck."

"I know, Merce, I know," I wailed from my doorway as two more men in thin, nylon FBI jackets wrestled another box of James's oil-soaked, kitty litter–encrusted stuff up from the basement, a box the Sterling Girls and I had painstakingly filled and stored just six days before. I watched as they dropped it next to other boxes already stacked on a tarp in his living room.

"I can't believe you're so small that you'd be this jealous of me."

"Mercedes!" I yelled into the phone. "I'm dying to hear about you and Dover. *Dying*," I said truthfully. "There's nothing

I want more. But you have no idea what's been going on over here today. I just can't come over."

"If it involves Hayden, I'm never speaking to you again. That man makes you an assho—"

"It has nothing to do with Hayden," I assured her.

"You got the contents of the bedroom?" Agent Mulrooney shouted down the stairs at two men in NYPD jackets. "We needa label those!"

"We know, we know," one of the detectives crabbed. If this little petri dish was any indication, interagency rapport had not vastly improved since 9/11.

"Excuse me?" Mercedes said.

I took a deep breath. "You remember the staircase?"

"The pink one or the regular one?"

"Pink. The old super built it so that johns could get upstairs to visit prostitutes. Roxana's a madam and the whole operation is run by the nice folks whose party Tag and I crashed at the St. Regis three weeks ago. I can't come to Lucy's tonight and hear about Dover because I need to cooperate with the FBI and the NYPD and get them to protect me from the Spanish mob."

Silence.

"Spain has mafia?" she finally said.

"Turns out."

More silence.

"Do you need me to come over?"

I exhaled with relief. "No. Look, when we finish up here—" Mulrooney overheard me and laughed. "If we ever finish up here," I said with determination, "I will make a beeline to Lucy's. I swear."

"Zeph?"

"Hmm?" I said, grimacing as another duo dinged the wall with a box of flatware.

"I'll be right over."

I wandered through James's apartment, surveying the hive of activity. In the bedroom, agents were setting up a makeshift surveillance command center, showing Roxana how to work her wire and instructing her on what to say when a member from the Pelarose family next paid a call. She nodded wearily and sipped silently at a chalky orange protein drink my mother had foisted upon her.

Near the closet door, a young female agent was going through a box of handcuffs, tagging and recording everything. I recognized the purple pair Tag had clipped on Mercedes the week before.

"This guy would have given Pleasure Chest a run for their money!" I joked lamely, referring to the novelty shop down Seventh Avenue.

The agent looked at me over her glasses and said nothing.

Inside the staircase, agents were traipsing up and down the pink steps, swabbing, studying, photographing. My heart sank as I watched them. When was the next time I'd have such a weird and sordid secret? When was the next time I'd have a man to share it with?

I headed back to my apartment and collapsed on the couch, next to my parents, who had brought their sherry and whitefish downstairs to enjoy courtside seats. Technically, though, my dad was on the clock.

"So this is what it's like to work from home!" he chortled, running his eye over a wiretap request that a rookie prosecutor had put in front of him. He clapped his hand over the nape of my neck and shook me proudly.

"Da-a-a-d," I said, feeling like an over-loved puppy.

"I'm so impressed," he said for the tenth time.

"Da-a-a-d," I said again, hoping he'd continue.

"Not only did my daughter here have the courage to break

up an assault—" he said to the young attorney, who nodded dutifully.

"Dad, it wasn't an assault," I protested, wondering, not for the first time, how his fondness for hyperbole hadn't hampered his career.

"Did you or did you not have a gun pointed at you?"

My mother shuddered and downed her sherry.

"I did," I admitted.

"Not only," my father continued, "did she have the courage to break up an assault, but she, *she*"—another ragdoll shake of my neck—"she made the connection between the Pelarose family and the prostitution ring."

The A.U.S.A. nodded again, murmured respectfully, then darted out the door and across the hall clutching her paperwork.

My mother poured herself more sherry. "In whose business plan," she demanded, "does a kickback scheme serve as a *front* for a money-laundering operation?"

"Bella, honey, that wasn't their plan. The oil company itself was the money-laundering operation, but then James decided to steal from that, and it looked to the investigators like it was just kickbacks in an otherwise legit business. They didn't even realize until our daughter"—a proud hair tousling—"figured it out, that the entire oil company was a mob front."

In fact, I hadn't gotten quite that far in my detective work, but it couldn't hurt to let the details slide for now. I was glowing under the floodlight of my father's praise.

My mother shook her head. "I've seen lemonade stands run better. Ollie, are there any women in the mob? Because things would be a lot smoother if they had some female capos. Capas?" She munched thoughtfully on a cracker. "I don't suppose the mafia would pay for MWP to offer their wives—or sisters or mamas or whoever—some training seminars, do you?"

My father took away my mother's sherry glass.

"I know!" my mother shouted. "I know how to help Roxana! I'm going to hire her!"

"Honey?" said my father, who was normally my mother's biggest fan.

"Can you imagine the revenue she could generate for us? Name one other financial consulting business that can offer a seminar by a former madam!"

We couldn't.

"Ha!" my mother said, as if she'd won an argument.

"Mr. Zuckerman?" An agent popped his head in. "We still need your signature on the tap request before we bring it downtown. Could you come across the hall?"

My dad slapped my thigh and stood up. "Come on, Zephy. Let's go do this together." It was Take Your Daughter to Work Night here on Twelfth Street.

As we started across the hall, some new arrivals in NYPD jackets headed through the front door, chattering loudly, and made their way up the stairs. I glanced down at them, then did a double take. I'd only known it for two weeks, but I'd have recognized that soft, chestnut hair and those slightly sticking-out ears anywhere.

Gregory felt my gaze and looked up, pausing mid-sentence.

"Go on inside," he told the guy he'd been talking to. "Tell Mulrooney I'll be right up."

Excuse me? I tried to say it aloud, but my lips wouldn't form the words.

Is that Ridofem's new uniform? I wanted to say. Again, nothing came out.

Oh, Gregory, if you didn't waste your time rigging very complicated pranks such as this one—because this had to be a joke—we might actually have a chance . . .

"Hey!" my dad said. "It's the exterminator! The washer-dryer fix-it man extraordinaire."

"Dad."

"What are you doing here?" my father continued easily, as if the world wasn't standing on its head. Gregory looked at me with genuine apology. I'd never seen him look humble, and it was actually quite attractive. Too bad I was going to have to kill him.

My father, never one to be hindered by social convention, took Gregory by the shoulders and turned him around to get a better look at the stenciled letters announcing him as one of New York's finest. Either that, or he'd been cold and one of New York's finest had generously offered this random exterminator his jacket.

"I knew it! Zephy, I *told* your mother he didn't look like an exterminator."

"Mr. Zuckerman?" an agent said gently, entreating my father to follow him.

"Right, sure. But I knew it. I knew it," he muttered, disappearing into James's apartment. "I have a very finely attuned sense of character . . ."

Gregory and I stood alone on the landing.

"Zephyr, I'm sorry. I'm so sorry I couldn't tell you the truth."

I put my hand on the banister, feeling my face do acrobatics as it tried to land on an appropriate expression.

"That you're an undercover cop?" It sounded absurd. It was the kind of thought that was better off staying in my imagination.

"Yes."

"Seriously?"

"Yes."

I flipped through the last two weeks, trying to see everything through this lens, but all I saw were sunspots.

"So how do you know about Harvey Blane?" I finally sputtered. Gregory pressed his lips together, dimples appearing in both cheeks.

"Don't laugh at me!" I said threateningly.

"I'm sorry, it's just—that's what you want to know first?"

"Are you really in a position right now to question my questions?" If I couldn't kill him, maybe I could at least kick him in the knees.

"I really was a grad student studying Shakespeare at NYU," he said soothingly. "I really did have a fight with Professor Blane. I really did begin a thesis about Christopher Marlowe theorists—"

"What?"

"People who think Kit Marlowe actually wrote Shakespeare's plays."

"And?"

"And it turned out, a couple of hundred pages later, I thought all of them were completely off their respective rockers. And I got really depressed, and I was on the subway, and there was a recruitment ad for the police department."

"The subway ad? You called one of those subway ads?" I'd always fantasized about answering that ad, of taking the exam, of being the one person who could beat Hayden to a crime scene.

"Yep."

"Yep? And then you became a cop? That's it?"

"Yep."

"I need more, Gregory," I said, shaking my head, but unable to resist a surge of joy at merely being this close to him again.

"Well, as you and your friend and your mother and your father have all repeatedly pointed out, I don't look like much of anything besides a Jewish academic. I don't look like an exterminator and—"

"And you don't look like an undercover cop," I concluded, taking a deep breath. Then I pulled back and whacked him on his shoulder as hard as I could.

"Ow!" he said, glaring at me. "What the hell was that for?"

"What *wasn't* it for, you . . ." I felt tears spring to my eyes. "You made me feel like shit this whole time for not believing you were an exterminator. You left the second that schmuck on the skateboard made random accusations. And I don't even know why you're here at all—this is a federal case. And . . ." I was crying now, and my nose was running, and I didn't care. I felt like I was being given another opportunity to get Gregory, to get *to* him, but I had no idea how to pick my way across this new minefield.

Mulrooney appeared at James's door. "Hey, schoolboy! You finally got here. Man, you gotta come over to the Feds. We got cars that go over thirty! I keep tellin' him, he gotta come over to the Feds," Mulrooney said to me as if their camaraderie didn't look like an alien do-si-do from where I stood. "When the guvament goes on strike, you getta six-week vacation!"

Gregory rolled his eyes.

"Seriously, Samson, you gotta come see this stairway. It's fuckin' hilarious."

Gregory had the good grace to blush. He cleared his throat.

"I've seen it. Dude, I'll be there in a minute."

Mulrooney headed back in, chuckling to himself. "Six fuckin' weeks. Man, that was all right."

" 'Dude'?" I said. He shrugged. "You're such a man of the people."

"Okay, take it easy."

"So your name is actually Gregory Samson?"

"Yes. Have dinner with me."

"We tried that once. It didn't work," I said, wanting him to insist.

"Then lunch. A picnic on the Charles Street Pier. To-morrow. I'll answer every one of your questions. Every single one." He took my hand and threaded his fingers through mine. I blushed at the intimacy and looked around quickly—my mother was still just a few feet away, inside my apartment.

"Fine, but not a picnic." A few days ago, I might have ac-quiesced to this romantic overture, but if all secrets were com-ing out, big and small, I wasn't going to pretend anymore. "I hate picnics," I told him defiantly.

"That's un-American."

"I hate sitting cross-legged—it makes my back hurt," I told him. "No one brings a sharp enough knife and the tomatoes get all drippy. You wind up carting dirty dishes home, and every-thing stinks." I felt ridiculous.

"You've thought a lot about this." He burst out laughing and I almost protested, but then he drew me to him. "We're go-ing to start again, Zephyr."

He planted a quick, soft kiss on my lips and turned to go to work.

FINALLY, AT ONE IN THE MORNING, EVERYONE EXCEPT THE two men and one woman camping out in James's apartment manning the surveillance operation had cleared out. The re-maining agents were a quiet bunch, subsisting on bags of Chex mix and my mother's energy drinks, which they were imbibing with gusto.

I lay in bed, exhausted but wired. I was as excited about my second chance with Gregory as I was about the fact that Operation Barcelona was going down in my home. Watching Gregory at work that night, as he conferred with colleagues and spoke gently with Roxana—both of us catching each other's eyes and sharing knowing glances in the direction of the staircase—I thought I would combust from sheer longing. I couldn't stand that he was insisting on having a proper date before we could jump each other again.

I got out of bed after a third failed attempt at sleep and padded into the kitchen, where I lit the stove under the kettle and sank down on the step stool. I wondered how Roxana was doing upstairs. She wasn't out of the woods yet, not by a long shot. The successful prosecution of the Pelarose family for prostitution—and her own evasion of jail time—depended entirely on her. She had to pretend to Ferdinand/Alonzo that she had changed her mind, that she wanted to keep working for his family, and get him to say incriminating things either on the phone or in person. The FBI also wanted her to catch Senator Smith—who turned out to be a school district superintendent in Queens—in the act of handing over money. Thanks to James's pre-existing photo and video setup inside Roxana's apartment, surveillance would be a technological piece of cake.

I had felt sorry for Roxana, watching her trudge upstairs that evening as nothing more than a puppet in the hands of various men. She was a long way from starting over again, a dream she'd thought was within reach when she'd woken up that morning. Now it looked like the FBI and the police would be hanging around for weeks. I tried not to think about what this meant for my cash flow.

The kettle boiled and I took my tea into the living room, curling up in the dark to watch night owls make their way up and down the block. I cringed when a boisterous group passed by, knowing Mrs. Hannaham would renew her request for triple-pane windows the following morning.

Mrs. Hannaham had, in her usual way, made everything worse that evening.

"I knew it," she kept crowing gleefully to the various law

enforcement officials who had questioned her as a witness. For the occasion, she'd put on her dead husband's white, ballooning collared shirt; her white sequined pants; and ankle-high white leather boots that I'd never seen before. The effect was that of the Michelin Man if he had sat on Prince and one of the Bangles two decades earlier.

"I told the Zuckermans that there were unseemly people traipsing in and out of that woman's apartment at all hours. I *told* them. And I told James, though, of course, now I see why he didn't do anything about all those awful people. He was one of them." She glared at Roxana, sitting across the room.

Roxana roused herself from her defeated stupor long enough to erupt in a string of beautiful French curses, bestowing upon Mrs. Hannaham a long-overdue tongue-lashing. The cops made a dilatory show of chastising Roxana, clearly enjoying the performance.

My breath caught as someone started up the stoop in the dark, but it was only Cliff, lugging his bass home from a late-night gig. He'd missed the whole thing.

I squinted at him suspiciously through the window as he fished for his keys. What did we really know about him? I was no longer certain there wasn't a dead body crammed into that case. The "ponytailed jazz musician working late nights" bit *had* to be a cover. After all, how did he afford the rent here?

I sighed and padded back to the kitchen, aimlessly opening and closing cupboards. I opened the fridge and then the freezer, thinking that if I was going to be up all night, I might have time to at least freeze some juice in ice cube trays.

But in the freezer were the ice packs I'd found inside James's window seat. I had forgotten about his mysterious liquids. I slammed the door closed, finally feeling tired, but certain now that I was never going to fall asleep.

I opened my apartment door and peered across the hall. Two of the agents were dozing and the third, the one who'd been sorting handcuffs earlier, was reading a newspaper.

"Excuse me," I said. She looked up, unsurprised to find me there in my T-shirt and boxers. "Am I, uh, allowed to talk to her?" I pointed upstairs.

The agent shrugged. "As long as it's not about the case, sure." She went back to reading her paper.

I hesitated. Really, an FBI agent should be more explicit. I tiptoed up the stairs and knocked lightly on the door.

"What? What is it?" came Roxana's panicked voice. She must have been in her living room, wide awake.

"It's okay, Roxana, it's just me."

She opened the door. "I con't zleep" she said, her gravelly voice rougher than usual. "I con't zleep at all."

"I have a question."

She waved her hand at me as if to say she'd had enough questions for a lifetime and slumped back to the couch.

"Roxana, do you know anything about some liquid James was keeping refrigerated in his window seat downstairs?"

"Hees beer?"

"No, not in the refrigerator. Refrigerated. In the window seat. It was in test tubes."

"Ooooh," she groaned. "Zay found dat?"

"No, I found it," I said, alarmed. "I forgot to tell anyone today."

"Oh, Zepheer." I waited. She passed her thumb and forefinger along her forehead in a series of pinches. "I dun't know why he wunted it. I deedn't ask."

"Just tell me," I said, ready for the worst.

"James made us geev him zee used condoms. He wus doing an experiment."

I wasn't ready for the worst.

"With the condoms?" I asked, feeling queasy.

"Wees duh sperm. He wunted to be a biologeest when he was a leetle boy. Hees fahder unly laughed at heem." She shook her head sadly.

I stared at her. Was I supposed to give a rat's ass about James's stifled dreams when he had amassed a veritable Baskin Robbins of semen in my house?

"And you don't know why?" I prodded.

She shook her head, sniffling. My eyes had focused now in her dark apartment, and I spotted an empty bottle of vodka on the floor next to the couch.

"Okay, then, Roxana. You get some sleep." She nodded morosely.

I made my way downstairs again, pausing only for a second in front of the agent. She glanced at me and I waved.

I had probably just gleaned some very important news about something that was almost definitely evidence. It was crucial that law enforcement be alerted immediately.

I went back inside my apartment and picked up the phone. Luckily, I now had the home number of my very own law enforcement official.

FORTY-FIVE MINUTES LATER, AT TWO IN THE MORNING, GREGORY arrived. He opened my door, waved bashfully at the agents across the hall, muttering something about new information, and then slipped inside my apartment, where I was waiting for him in the dark living room.

"Where are you?" he whispered.

"Here," I rasped from the couch. I was clutching a throw pillow, my nerves on edge from a deadly combination of sleep deprivation and the singular strain of middle-of-the-night lust.

He felt his way over and sat down on my feet.

"Sorry," I said, starting to pull them out from under him.

"It's fine. Leave them," he said, adjusting himself so that my feet were in his lap, pressing against his crotch, which was already hard. I felt my chest cave in as the oxygen left.

"Do I really need to tell you right now about this creepy new evidence?" I panted, raising myself up on my elbows. I could only make out his silhouette in the light from the street lamp.

"No," he said gruffly, pressing my feet onto him harder. "I'm just glad there was creepy new evidence you needed to tell me about tonight."

Gregory got up on his knees, pushed my elbows down and stretched out on top of me. I moaned and closed my eyes.

"Did you lock the door?"

"Uh-huh," he said, his breath hot in my ear. He ran his lips along the length of my neck, then nudged the collar of my T-shirt aside and lightly bit my shoulder.

"Zephyr?"

"I've got condoms," I assured him. "Plenty of them. And *not* from James's stash," I clarified.

"Did you sleep with that guy who was here the other day? The barefoot one with the beer?"

I froze.

"I don't think you have a right to ask me that," I said softly. "Not yet."

"I know. I know I don't," he said quickly.

"You're still thinking about what LinguaFrank said about me," I said sharply. We were face-to-face, his hands pinning mine down, our breath mixing into one warm cloud.

"Zephyr," he pleaded. "Wait, who's Ling—the skateboard? No. I mean, yeah, at the time I was trying to figure out whether you were one of Roxana's prostitutes—"

"What!" I freed my hands and heaved him off me. *"What?"*

"Oh, shit." He flopped back on the couch. "I don't know why I said that. I mean, obviously, I know *now* you're not. I only asked about that other guy because—"

"Wait," I said coldly, "you thought I was a *prostitute*?" As I said it, I realized he hadn't been the only one. I suddenly remembered Senator Smith eyeing my friends and me on the landing the night we'd gone to Soho House, as if he was sizing up the juiciest lobsters in the tank.

"No. I really didn't. Not at all." Gregory put his head in his hands. "But when that guy said it, suddenly I wondered if I had lost all judgment. I mean, here I was, investigating what I suspected was a whorehouse, but I was also falling in love with you, and I got scared that I was falling for a subject. I shouldn't even be involved with you *now*."

"You're in love with me?" I asked.

"But the only reason I asked about the other guy," he continued, his voice straining with the effort to persuade me, "is because I just want to know where we're starting from. I want to know that neither of us is tangled up in something else." He paused. "Yes, I'm in love with you."

"I didn't sleep with him," I said, happy for the first time since I'd laid eyes on Hayden that this was true. "And I'm not a hooker," I confirmed, letting a snort of laughter escape.

He reached for me again, letting his palms cup my breasts, feeling their weight in his hands. He squeezed gently.

"I'm really glad," he whispered hoarsely. "About both."

NINETEEN

THE SOUND OF THUNDER ROUSED ME FROM A DEEP SLEEP THE next morning. My arm automatically shot out to answer the phone.

"Mrs. Hannaham?" I said blearily, deciding to change my phone number.

Thunder again, and pounding. I pulled the phone from my cheek and looked at it, slow to understand that no one was on the other end.

"They got him." Gregory was at the foot of my bed, hastily pulling on his pants.

Oh, right. Gregory. I smiled lazily. "They got Hayden?" I said, still half-asleep. I clamped my hand over my mouth. Jesus, Zephyr, wake up.

"Who? No, they got Alonzo Pelarose. He's in custody. Across the hall. Came back at four-thirty this morning to try to kill Roxana. Stupid people make our job a lot easier." The thunder was the pounding of law enforcement feet up and down the stairs.

"Oh my God!" I was awake. No one had expected action this quickly. "Is she okay?"

"She's fine. Hungover and rattled, but fine. How are you?" Gregory said, his voice suddenly soft. He sat down on the side of the bed and stroked my face.

"I'm great," I purred, realizing I wasn't even worried about morning breath around him.

"Great," he said, jumping up, pillow talk concluded. "I'm sorry, Zeph, but I have to . . ." He nodded his head toward the door.

I was forever destined to be ditched by men for crime scenes.

"Kind of convenient," he said sheepishly. "I didn't know how I was going to explain myself to the guys this morning. This way, I was only checking on you just now."

I tried to smile, but my heart was already tightening at the thought of Gregory, the undercover detective, trying to make conversation with Zephyr, the super of her mommy and daddy's building. For him, I thought, I'd go back to medical school. Anything to keep him interested.

He threw on his shirt and ran his hands through his hair. "Instead of that picnic . . ."

He was already losing interest. I pulled the comforter higher over my chest.

". . . what do you say we go on a field trip to Rikers this afternoon and ask James about his science project?" Just a few hours earlier, we'd sprawled naked on my living room rug, punchy with exhaustion, giggling over the possible purposes of James's test tubes.

"Really?" I said eagerly. Prison! Even my dad had never taken me to a prison. This was a sad, somber thing, I reminded myself. I toned down my voice. "That would be great."

Gregory came to my side again and put his hand over mine.

"Is there anything that doesn't excite you? It's amazing to watch your face."

Well, now. This was news. I tried to smile in an excited way. He frowned.

"Are you okay?"

I cleared my throat. "Go. Do your thing. Let me know when you want to leave. I'll be here."

Two hours later, Gregory and I were zipping along the BQE toward Rikers Island in an undercover police car posing as a gypsy cab, complete with rosary and E-ZPass. I had an oily box of Bleecker Street pizza in my lap. It wasn't wine and candlelight, but so far, it was the best date I'd ever been on. Gregory glanced over at me and smiled.

"What?"

"Your eyes are super green this morning."

I snorted and nearly choked on my pizza.

"Is that funny?"

"Let's just say there's never been a consensus on the color of my eyes."

"Are you kidding? Look at them, they're green. Like emeralds. Like algae. Look!" he insisted, pulling down the sun visor so I could look at myself in the mirror. Maybe it was just the blob of grease glistening on my cheek that made my eyes brighter than usual, but they really did look pretty green. I was so used to having "ish" eyes, I wasn't sure what to do with this definitive, incontrovertible evidence: I'm Zephyr. I have green eyes. I helped snare a murderous mafioso. I bit my lip to keep from grinning at myself, and flipped the visor back up.

"Ask me things," Gregory said, his mouth partly open as he tried to cool off a bite of hot cheese.

"Okay." I wiped the grease off my face. "Was there actually any poison in your exterminator canister?"

He glanced over at me as if he was going to give me a hard time, then changed his mind.

"Yes. I didn't think it would be nice to let your building get overrun with roaches just because we'd arrested your super."

"Are you qualified to spray poison?" I said, sheepishly aware that I was once again trying to prove to him that I was good at my job.

"Seriously? These are your questions?"

"I have a responsibility to my tenants," I said primly.

Gregory blew out his cheeks impatiently.

"Here's what happened," he said, pressing hard on the horn as a cabbie cut him off. "I was working with the rackets bureau in the DA's office, looking at oil companies all over the city. The company James was dealing with—the one you guys were buying oil from—got red-flagged, and then I got very interested in James and started digging deeper. There was stuff in his taps—wiretaps—that was completely baffling. Like, I thought there were a lot more people involved, but it turned out—"

"That sometimes he's British and sometimes he's Brooklyn!" I said excitedly. "Did he use the Brooklyn voice? I'd never heard it till the night he was arrested!"

"A lot of Brooklyn," Gregory said, smiling, and I hoped that this was one of those occasions where my enthusiasm was attractive. "So, yeah, I thought it was multiple people, and that kept me guessing for a while. But I didn't have a clue until I met you and saw the staircase and those two locked rooms in Roxana's apartment that Roxana and her girls were in the picture. No idea." He shook his head, mildly disgusted with himself.

"So why didn't you wait to arrest him? Until you could find out more?"

Gregory glanced over at me approvingly. "I wanted to wait, but sometimes there are assholes who—" He took a deep breath through his nose and waved away his incipient tirade. "My boss and I disagreed and he went ahead with the arrest. Prematurely, very prematurely."

He reached over and put his hand on my thigh. So warm. Did he always radiate this kind of delicious heat? I'd save in heating bills this winter, I thought stupidly.

"Any other questions?"

I hesitated. Don't blow it, Zephyr. Don't move backward when you can move forward. But the devil homunculus was restless.

"Why did you keep making me feel so bad about saying you didn't look like an exterminator? You weren't one. Aren't one."

He took his hand back and I felt like I'd been abandoned.

"Because I thought maybe you were a snob." He squinted through the windshield.

I cringed. "But all I was saying was that you didn't *look* like one, not that you couldn't *be* one or that I wouldn't date one," I insisted, certain now that this was the absolute truth. Frustrated, I tossed my pizza crust back into the box. How much proof would he need?

"I believe you," he said after a moment. "I'm sorry. It was an unfair position to put you in." He moved his hand to my leg again and squeezed, silently asking me to forgive him for being such a complicated pain in the ass.

A plane loomed low over the highway, coming in for a landing at LaGuardia. I studied its metal underbelly and realized that if it were to crash into us at that moment, I was glad I'd be going down beside Gregory. I pushed away the thought. He was a complicated pain in the ass and I was a morbid psycho. It was looking like we might be perfect for each other.

I looked over at him, to find him looking back at me expectantly. He had a blob of tomato sauce on his cheek. I leaned over and gently licked it off.

"So you really never noticed anything unusual going on upstairs?" he said happily, gunning past a dyspeptic diesel truck.

"You don't ever have to worry about speeding tickets, do you?" I said with awe, as impressed as if he'd invented the radar gun.

"Nope." He grinned at me. "Are you a lead foot?"

I shrugged. Points on a license was the stuff of fourth or fifth dates.

"I try not to be nosy," I lied, in answer to his first question.

"Nosy? There was an entire stairwell on your property that escaped your attention!"

"Hey, listen," I said sharply, "not all of us are cut out to be undercover cops. I didn't notice it." I glared at him, waiting for the next time he glanced away from the wheel. But he only smiled. Now that he could be himself around me, he was unflappable. It was both completely annoying and a huge relief.

"Well, I think you'd be a great detective."

"Ha." I slumped back in the seat. I felt vulnerable, remembering our heart-to-heart on the stoop. He knew exactly where I stood, career-wise.

"I'm serious. You need a pretty rich imagination to piece together something like the Roxana–Pelarose connection. I was working on James for months and I never got that close. That's one aspect of detective work—trying to imagine all the permutations of how the different pieces fit together. Some truth is more outrageous than what most people can imagine."

I still wasn't sure whether he was putting me on.

"And I think," he continued, turning the car onto a low causeway, "that our ability to distinguish between truth, fiction, and mental illness is about to be tested. Welcome to the isle of Rikers."

*   *   *

ZEPHYR, LOVE! DARLING! AREN'T YOU SPLENDID TO COME PAY
your uncle James a visit!"

Three weeks in prison had rendered James sallow and
bruised. His shoulders were hunched and his beard was an
overgrown tangle, but you would have thought we were having
high tea at the Savoy. Instead, we were sitting at a cafeteria-
style table in a gray-tiled cavern surrounded by armed guards.
James rubbed his unshackled wrists and looked genuinely delighted to see me.

James was considered a low security risk, but apparently, I
was a high one. Despite Gregory's badge, I had been put
through the ringer by a wall of a woman manning the X-ray
scanner. In another life, Corrections Officer Dredgeholz must
have worked Checkpoint Charlie. She clearly pined for the fine,
orderly days she had enjoyed in the eastern sector. She patted
me down three times, ran her hand scanner over my beeping
jeans zipper three times, and made me take off my shoes and
my fleece vest (picked with great care to convey a sexy, athletic
look to Gregory). She ordered me to empty my backpack and
pawed through my things with the delicacy of a grizzly bear in
a campground.

It was one thing to sleep with someone, but an entirely
other rite of intimacy to have the contents of your backpack
emptied out in front of him. I blushed hotly as Dredgeholz ex-
amined a crumpled but clean panty liner, a handful of ATM
receipts broadcasting my triple-digit bank balance, a linty
ChapStick with no cap, another linty ChapStick (mentholated)
with no cap, a mildewed fold-up umbrella, a copy of 287 West
12th's bylaws, which I'd been meaning to read, and a coffee-
stained *Times* article about cervical cancer my mother had

clipped, with "You get your paps every year, right???" scrawled across it in red ink.

Gregory just crossed his arms and frowned at the proceedings. He may have been Gregory the detective now, but he still had the social graces of Gregory in the rat/roach jumpsuit. A decent guy would have looked away. I took a deep breath and reminded myself to accept his imperfections.

Of course, I felt no need to refrain from staring goggle-eyed when he handed over his revolver for lockup. In high school, right after I'd broken up with Lance the musical-theater aficionado, I'd briefly dated a stutterer named Nelson. He attended Dowling, the school for bad boys who'd been kicked out of other schools for bad boys. Nelson had carried nunchucks concealed in his lacrosse bag, but that was the closest I'd gotten to dating an armed man.

"Did you have that in my apartment last night?" I demanded as he stood at a counter to sign a custody form.

Gregory nodded.

"Where? Just lying around?"

"Of course not. I brought a lockbox with me." Oh, for the days when condoms were enough preparation for a date.

"Do you always carry a gun?"

"Usually. Not always, but usually. Is that going to be a problem?" He looked at me worriedly. It was a bit of a problem, but I was momentarily blindsided by his casual allusion to our future together.

"Where was the lockbox?"

"Under the bed."

Why, *why* was I continually attracted to men who left unsavory souvenirs beneath my bed? Was a gun, a locked-up gun, better than empty beer bottles? Yes, I decided there in front of the metal grille. Yes, it was.

"Who's the handsome chap you've brought with you, Zephyr love?" James continued now.

"Mr. Windsor, don't you remember me?"

James smiled at Gregory brightly, blankly.

"I was the new exterminator from Ridofem? We met a few weeks ago?"

Nothing.

Gregory glanced at me. Was this all an act or was James a very sick man?

"Mr. Windsor," he tried again, leaning forward, "do you know why you're here?"

James waved his arms forward. "Oh, a small misunderstanding between gentlemen. Straightened out in a jiff, no doubt, no doubt."

"James," I said, my concern growing. "Do you or do you not know someone named Alonzo Pelarose?" I looked hard into his eyes, but there wasn't so much as a fleeting glimmer of recognition.

"Beautiful name, beautiful name. Another beau of yours, sweet Zephyr? You know what 'Zephyr' means?" he asked Gregory. "The west wind. A gentle, warming breeze. And she is, isn't she?" He put his hand over mine affectionately.

"HANDS OFF!" three guards roared in unison, storming our table. My heart pounded as I imagined the ensuing riot. Smeared feces, flooded toilets, projectile chairs, murdered guards, trampled prisoners. I'd be despised from the Battery to the Bronx, and most of all by the Sterling Girls, who would be pissed to hear about everything that had happened to me in the last twenty-four hours from the media instead of from me.

The guards walked away and hushed conversations resumed all around us.

"James," I pleaded, "what about Roxana? Roxana Boureau? Does she mean anything to you?"

"A whore." Except it came out as "Uh hoah." Brooklyn was now in the house.

Gregory and I sat up straighter.

"Fuckin' bitch. Fuckin' fuckin' bitch did this shit to me!" James's entire face squared off and turned bright red. His eyes grew hard and he didn't seem to see us in front of him.

"What did she do?" Gregory said quietly, trying to hold on to this James while we had him.

James grunted. "Bitch moves in, tells me she's gotta brother who's gotta oil company can gimme a discount. I think, that's great, I could save the Zuckermans some dough. They're nice people, that family, you know? I try to do right by 'em. They been good to me."

I nodded, speechless.

"Shit and the next thing you know, her fuckin' 'brother'—who ain't her fuckin' brother, by the way—has me takin' delivery on envelopes fulla cash, and before I know what the fuck is goin' on, he tells me I been holdin' drug money and if I don't build this fuckin' staircase and take pictures of the shit goin' on upstairs, he's gonna set me up to take the fall for this drug money. He's got fingerprints, photos, conversations, all that shit. Shit," he concluded, hunching over and drumming on the table with his palms.

"James," Gregory continued in the same placating voice, "what were the test tubes for? Roxana said you made her turn over the condoms to her. Were the tubes full of semen?"

But the winds of James's mind shifted and he sat up straight again, smacking the table, as jovial and carefree as any inebriated member of the mother country's leather-chair class.

"I do aim to look out for those less fortunate than I," he boasted. "It's a brilliant plan. Absoluuuutely brilliant."

"A plan?" Gregory asked.

"A sperm bank for the poor."

I covered my mouth with my hand. Gregory coughed.

"A sperm bank for the poor?"

"You know, there's all this infertility in the world." James gestured expansively.

"There is?"

"*You* know, darling, one always reads about these women who are forty and want a baby and can't have one. Well, what about the poor welfare mothers who want a baby and can't have one? I decided," he leaned forward, his eyes dancing, "to create a sperm bank for poor women, so that something good would come out of this whole nasty mess."

Gregory jumped at British James's slip.

"Whole nasty mess. You acknowledge you had dealings with Alonzo Pelarose and Roxana Boureau?"

James's eyes clouded over again.

"Fuck, yeah. At first I thought, shit, if they're draggin' me down, I'll go all the way down, since there's no turning back unless I wanna wind up dead. I'll sell sperm samples to dickheads accused of rape, give 'em some other shithead's DNA, to get themselves off the hook. They're all scumbags anyway. I figured that would sell for a whole lot and then I could just move to Tahiti or wherever the fuck, and get away from the whole goddamn Pelarose family. But then, you know, shit, there wasn't any way to, you know, get the sperm onto raped women and shit. So . . ."

I let forth an awful, choking sound. Gregory clasped his hands together and bounced them against his chin. In a quiet and twisted way, I felt close to him—our first adventure together, side by side.

"But Roxana," I tried again. "She loves you. She was going to keep running the . . . the business so they wouldn't hurt you in here. Was she lying to protect herself or are you two really in love?"

"Ah, Zephyr," James said, smiling into what distance there was inside a prison common room. "I did once love a woman named Roxana. And she really did love me. But she broke my heart and now . . ." James turned to look straight at me and, for a brief moment, there was clarity in those blue eyes. "Now, I am alone." He sniffed melodramatically. "I'm awfully tired, love. I think I need a bit of a kip just now." He raised his arms and summoned the guard as if he were his footman. He stood and put his wrists behind his back.

"Don't you worry about your uncle James, Zephyr dear. I've a call in to Her Majesty. No worries, no worries . . ."

TWENTY

Hᴏᴛ, ꜱᴛᴀɢɴᴀɴᴛ ᴀɪʀ ʟᴇꜰᴛ ᴛʜᴇ ʟᴀɴᴛᴇʀɴꜱ ᴏɴ ꜱᴏʜᴏ ʜᴏᴜꜱᴇ'ꜱ rooftop hanging limp and motionless from their bamboo rafters. Candles did not glide around the pool on their lily pads like flickering water sprites, but instead bumped around lifelessly in one corner, near a drain. My silky but not silk dress, whose retro browns and greens had compelled my mother to reminisce about *her* mother's plastic-covered couch, was not flowing around my legs, but clinging stickily to them instead. Every few minutes, I had to extricate the fabric from where it bunched up in my crotch.

I'd never been happier in my life.

"But did you really believe he would have done that presentation in a jester hat?" Tag asked Abigail, pressing her sweating mojito glass against her forehead.

"Tag," Abigail murmured, her dark eyes growing wide as she watched Dover Carter and my brother trade slaps on the back by the far side of the pool, "I don't think you're allowed to criticize a movie at the party for it."

Abigail had taken the red-eye the night before, having dug up a conference on Aramaic texts that, she convinced the university, was essential for her to attend. Conveniently, the conference coincided with my brother's film premiere party.

"Critique, not criticize. I'm critiquing, and this is exactly where I should be doing it. Everything we talk about tonight should be *Boardroom*. Good, bad, *Boardroom*!" Tag had returned from Spain a week after Alonzo Pelarose had been arrested and remanded without bail and, to my continuing delight, she was still upset that she'd missed all the excitement. Jealous that I'd had an honest-to-God whorehouse upstairs from me, an FBI/NYPD command center across the hall, and had scored an undercover cop for a boyfriend, to boot.

"Tell me again about the photos," she insisted, adjusting her repurposed wedding dress over her thigh so that it covered the fresh gash she'd sustained in an Andalusian fishing village.

"Oh, enough." Mercedes gestured for Tag to move over, then squeezed in next to her on the lounge chair. "Zeph actually had something happen to her that was more interesting than something that happened to you. Get over it." She shot her arm out and grabbed a drink the bartenders were calling a French 69 off a passing tray. "How does it feel to be at a party you're actually invited to?"

Tag shrugged and I kicked her from the lounge chair I was sharing with Abigail.

"Come on, admit it. It's pretty relaxing not being hunted by angry royalty."

"If you had just *called* me, I would happily have hopped on the next flight to talk to the investigators," Tag persisted.

Abigail was still staring at Gideon and Dover, who were now deep in conversation. "So, what, is Dover Carter going to star in Gid's next movie or something?" she asked Mercedes incredulously.

Mercedes shrugged, exuding an air of wifely propriety. "Depends what Gideon's offering."

I gave a disgusted grunt. Until two hours ago, my brother, newly minted winner of the audience award at the Tribeca Film Festival, had been pretending indifference to my connection to Hollywood's top earner. It was now apparent that Gideon was as susceptible to Dover's sincerity as the rest of us.

I was still unmoored after spending three weeks watching my slacker brother be treated like a respectable adult. I loved him—I really did—and I was happy for him—I really was—but his transformation in the eyes of others was a mystery to me. I had trouble picturing my brother on a set, being organized, telling other people what to do, and, most troubling, picturing people actually doing what he told them.

On the other hand, in just a few months, if all went well, I'd have less reason to be jealous of him.

"So where's Gregory, the Jewish cop?" Abigail asked. "Not yet in my two months on JDate have I ever . . ." She shook her head. "Did I tell you about the guy I dated last week, the one who borrowed his mother's car?"

"Just because a guy can't afford his own car . . ." I chastised her.

"Oh, I don't care that he borrowed her car. I care that her car still has a 'Baby on Board' sticker. Hey," she added suddenly, pulling her iPhone out of the freebie tote bag she'd received at her conference that morning. (None of the SGs had been able to persuade her that a canvas bag bearing a language society logo was not a party-appropriate accessory.) "Did I ever show you what Darren Schwartz texted me after you guys turned your guns on him?" She tapped the screen and handed the phone to Mercedes, who passed it to me and pressed her palms to her eyes.

"Ab, can I get the # of your skinny blond shiksa? Hot. xtra hot."

Mercedes handed Abigail her glass. "Drink. Just keep drinking."

"So where *is* the Jewish cop, Zephyr?" Tag asked me.

I hesitated. "He'll be here any minute. He got held up with work."

"It's Saturday," Mercedes said suspiciously.

"It's . . . he . . . he wanted to be there when they picked up some of the other Pelarose family members," I admitted.

"So he's at a crime scene," Tag said sharply.

"It's not the same as Hayden," I protested.

"How is it not the same?" Mercedes shot back, her dreds popping accusingly around her face.

"Because . . ." I groped for a way to make them understand. And then I saw the mop of brown hair looming above the crowd, the angular, beautiful face looking around expectantly—looking for me. "Because he's here."

I started to wave to him, and then froze.

"And so is Hayden." I hid my face in Abigail's neck.

Mercedes and Tag jerked around so fast they knocked heads, but didn't utter so much as a whimper. Abigail landed an elbow in my ribs as she whipped her feet to the ground.

"Where? *Where?*"

"Is it the guy with the unbuttoned shirt or the one with the goatee?"

"Did you *invite* him, you moron?"

I rubbed my side and scowled at them.

"The redhead at eight o'clock. Of course I didn't *invite* him," I snapped, feeling my pulse pick up speed.

They swiveled their heads in unison.

"Oh my God," said Abigail.

"Wow," Mercedes agreed.

Tag nodded, pursing her lips in concession. "Hot. Very hot. I see why you went apeshit."

I gaped at them. "Are you kidding me? This is not what I need," I hissed as Gregory approached.

"Hi," he said, nervously eyeing the tangle of eight legs in two chairs. He had admitted to me a few nights earlier that the whole Sterling Girl concept made him extremely nervous.

"Hey." I aligned my head so that Gregory's body blocked me from Hayden's line of vision. I tilted my face up for a kiss, while surreptitiously kicking Tag and Mercedes so they'd turn back to us. "I'm so glad you're here," I said, trying to sound like I meant it. I did mean it in general. I just wish he hadn't been in that particular square foot of Soho House's roof at that particular moment.

"I just saw Lucy and her boyfriend. She's looking for you," he said, unaware of the bomb he was exploding.

"Hi, I'm Abigail. Boyfriend?" Abigail said, flashing her palm in a shorthand wave. Tag and Mercedes finally turned around to study Gregory, who took a step back.

"Nice to meet you. I . . . I don't know. Not her boyfriend?" he said, looking to me for help.

"Did Lucy use the word 'boyfriend' when she introduced him, or are you using the word 'boyfriend'?" I asked soothingly.

"I can't remember," he said, looking distressed.

Ever since Lucy had met Leonard at Three Lives bookstore the Sunday after I'd caught him in possession of her defaced ten-dollar bill, she'd dropped the idea of a death party. We took this as a sign that things were going well, but we didn't know Leonard had graduated to Boyfriend. There were many qualifications for this appellation, according to Lucy, including each person having memorized the other one's phone number, seeing each other two to three nights a week for a minimum of four weeks, and knowing middle names.

"Hey, it's the exterminator," Hayden drawled, appearing next to us.

I held my breath.

"She's mine, by God, and if I so much as see your monstrous visage east of Passaic, so help me, I'll slay thee!" Cling, clang, thwoop! Swords flying, chests heaving, bodices ripping!

Gregory crossed his arms and nodded curtly at Hayden. I let out my breath, just the teensiest bit disappointed.

"What are you doing here?" I asked Hayden, acutely aware of Gregory's eyes shooting daggers at me.

He flashed his press pass and shrugged. "It's like a universal ticket to anything. We were at the festival."

My goose bumps would never ever *ever* be immune to Hayden's voice.

"We?" I asked, and regretted it instantly. Gregory took a step away from me.

Tag shook her head and Mercedes put her hand over her eyes. Abigail snorted.

"I'm Nanda." A tiny, slender Indian woman with perfect skin and a diamond in her nose came charging at us, and proffered a handshake twice her size. She studied each of us quickly, trying to mask suspicion with false enthusiasm. "Friends of yours, honey?" she asked, and as she got around to greeting me, I noticed the wedding ring on her left hand. I heard my friends suck in their breath in unison.

I dug my nails into Abigail's knee.

"Are you Hayden's wife?" Mercedes asked breezily as I felt my legs go hollow.

Nanda nodded, and squinted at me, squeezing my hand harder. I tried to look innocent. Hayden just tilted his glass to his lips. I glanced over at Gregory, who watched me balefully.

"Glad you came," I said in what I hoped was an even voice. "We're all really proud of my brother," I said, childishly asserting my legitimacy at the party.

I extracted my hand and met her piercing gaze. I suddenly felt sorry for her. Hayden's wife. What an awful thing to be.

"Mazel tov," Abigail said dryly. "When's the honeymoon?"

Nanda looked confused and even Hayden started to contort his lips into odd shapes.

"Our honeymoon?" Nanda said. "We went to Hawaii. Last summer. Are you looking for a place to go?"

A year. They'd already been married for a year. That meant they'd tied the knot less than a year after he and I met. That meant that a month ago I'd nearly had sex with a married man. I squeezed my eyes shut, trying to purge the memory.

"Zephy! Taggy! Mercy! Abby!" crowed Lucy, pulling my jury-duty catch behind her.

"Oh, no," Tag muttered into her glass. "She's at Defcon Five."

Lucy threw her arms around all of us in turn. "This is Leonard! Aren't you excited to finally meet him? Leonard, these are my best friends in the whole world!"

Leonard nodded sheepishly in greeting and flicked at his ear.

"I was just telling Leonard how the last time I was here, a fortune-teller told me I was going to die, and how that made me carpe diem and now I have her to thank for finding him! Hey, and it turns out his dad and my dad are buried in the same cemetery in Westchester, can you believe it?" She grinned at Leonard proudly.

I started to protest that Renee Ricardo had not been the one slinking around an ice-cold jury-pool room playing currency Cupid, but changed my mind.

"And Zephyr can thank her for Gregory," Lucy added gen-

erously. "She told her you two would be spending your lives together."

"You asked a fortune-teller about me?" Gregory asked, his
dimples appearing. "What else did she tell you? Bet she didn't
know you'd apply for a P.I. license," he said, laughing.

Silence.

I hadn't planned on telling anyone until I was sure I was
going through with this new idea, not even the college class-
mates I'd be facing tomorrow morning at my reunion. To
them, I'd still be a super. I hadn't planned on telling anyone
until after I had landed a junior investigator's position with the
Department of Investigation, and perhaps not even until I'd
completed my three years' training, passed the state exam, and
actually had my New York State private investigator's license
in hand. If I could have managed it, I would have kept the
news from my parents until they were senile and unable to
process the fact that their daughter might have occasional
need of a bulletproof vest.

"Uh," Gregory said, looking horrified. "Sorry."

"Zephyr?" Tag said, her eyes wide. Mercedes, Abigail, and
Lucy gaped at me.

"Cool," Leonard said.

"Lucy," I blurted. "This is Hayden."

That did the trick.

Whatever fragile web of diplomacy the rest of us had managed to achieve in the preceding minutes was instantly shattered by Lucy. Her lips formed an O and her eyes went just as
round.

"*Hayden?* As in *Hayden* Hayden?" She whipped around to
confirm this with the rest of us.

"And his wife," Mercedes added cheerfully, tugging her
strapless sheath dress higher. "Nanda."

"Okay," Gregory said suddenly. "Zeph, I'm gonna go get a drink. Coming?" He studied me.

I looked over at Hayden, who was grinning the same cocky grin he'd reeled me in with at the Odeon two years earlier. Close a door, Zephyr, I thought. Close it and see what it feels like. My friends were watching me. Nanda was watching me. Even Leonard was watching me.

I turned and followed Gregory, peeling my dress off my sweaty legs as I went. He led me through the crowd, but stopped short of the bar. He put his hands on my waist. I traced his jaw with one finger and looked into his brown eyes. This was a man who would drive me up a wall and teach me about myself and let me be myself and make me laugh and turn me on and never hurt me. This was a man I already loved.

"All done?" he asked.

I nodded. "All done."

"Good. What are we drinking?"

What did the super of 287 West 12th Street drink? What did a medical school dropout drink? What did a law school non-enroller drink? What did the sister of the next Coen brother drink? What did a future ace detective drink? What did someone who'd finally unhitched a wagonful of horseshit, romantically speaking, drink? What did someone on the rooftop of Soho House having a first-world moment drink?

"Lemonade," I said, going up on tiptoe to plant a kiss on his soft, full lips. "I'm drinking lemonade."

ACKNOWLEDGMENTS

A person can feel pretty foolish sitting alone in front of her computer writing a story that no one asked her to write. For vaporizing the alone part, I thank the generous, tolerant staffs at 'SNice, Grounded, and Così in New York City, and at the Tuscan Café and Caffè à la Mode in Warwick, N.Y. You do so much more than sell coffee—you nurture creative communities. For diminishing the foolish part, I yell to the world my love and admiration for Deborah Siegel: copilot, confidante, colleague. Laptop à laptop, we forge ahead. Also making writing a team sport is Heather Hewett, whose intelligence, wit, and perseverance in scheduling writing retreats have sustained me for years.

I thank all my friends for letting me steal from their lives and their stories. In particular, Rebekah Gross for medical details and a singularly dry outlook on life that is often just what the doctor ordered; Amanda Robinson for letting me benefit from her erudition and early encouragement; Shannon and Ben Agin for jaw-dropping generosity, including giving us and our rambunctious toddler months of shelter; Elisha Cooper and Michael Lee for buoying me in their inimitable ways whenever I hit the rocky shores of self-doubt; and Elizabeth Gilbert, for telling me to be a mule when I most needed to hear it, for keeping old promises like nobody's business, and for inspiring me with her generosity lo those many years ago. For taking dozens of precious hours away from their families to read drafts and give keen, detailed, invaluable comments, I am deeply indebted to Shannon Agin (again), to Alix McLean, and to Alex Sapirstein.

Alix McLean, Kathy Sillman, Nicole Krieger, Sarah Kirshbaum Levy, and Sarah Trillin—this stable of dependable, caring truthtellers are my beloved inspiration for Zephyr's Sterling Girls. I am kept sane by their unwavering candor, irreverence, and steady flow of hand-me-downs.

Kate Miciak, Kerri Buckley, Molly Boyle, and the entire team at Bantam Dell—including the second-to-none Pam Feinstein—devoted a kind of editorial attention to this book that I thought had gone the way of the typewriter. They manage to be eagle-eyed while maintaining the lightest of touches. Most astoundingly, their commitment to Zephyr matches my own, a gift for which I can never thank them enough. I am grateful on a nearly daily basis to have Tracy Brown as my agent. His decades of editorial experience, his gentle demeanor, and his genuine love of the book business make him nothing less than a fairy godfather.

As for my astounding family, I thank my daughter, Talia, after whose birth, for better and worse, I became an efficiency expert who never again knew an idle moment. Her wild embrace of life fills gaps I didn't know existed in mine: somehow, mysteriously, she has made me a better writer. Of course, so have her babysitters—Ofelia Ariza and Catie Quinn—without whom I couldn't have finished this book. My in-laws, Paula, Jerome, and Jennie Spector, continue to floor me with their generosity—they feed us, they move our furniture, they take our kids for entire weekends; I hope I am half as helpful to others as they are to me.

I hope to write many more books in the future if only to keep singing the praises of my parents, Rena and Richard, in the acknowledgments. I stole the most dialogue, the most stories, and the most observations about human nature from my mother, from whom I learned to love and delight in absurdity.

And the memory of my father's fierce, often blinding pride in me continues to fuel each of my waking moments.

Always, always my boundless gratitude to my steadfast mate, Sacha Spector, who takes my writing seriously (or at least graciously keeps his doubts well hidden) and whose own creativity is as varied and inspiring as any I have ever witnessed in a mere mortal. It's a privilege and a thrill to share my life with him.

Finally, I thank New York City, my muse, for being a bottomless well of material, for having a spirit unmatched by any other city (though how would I really know, since I rarely leave it?), for being a hometown that I love deeply, despite, and often because of, its many flaws.

ABOUT THE AUTHOR

DAPHNE UVILLER was superintendent of her family's building in the West Village for ten long years. She is a former books/poetry editor for *Time Out New York*, is the co-editor of the anthology *Only Child*, and has written for the *New York Times*, *Washington Post*, *Newsday*, *New York*, *Allure*, and *Self*. A third-generation Greenwich Village resident, she now lives in her childhood apartment with her husband and two children.